THE MEANS THAT MAKE US STRANGERS

THE MEANS THAT MAKE US STRANGERS

A NOVEL BY

Christine Kindberg

Bellflower Press, Wheaton, IL

To my grandma,
Pat McCubbin,
who's always told me
I'll never lack for stories to tell.

And to my parents,
Eric and Mary Lynn Kindberg,
who've supported me in every way imaginable.

Macduff	*See who comes here.*
Malcolm	*My countryman; but yet I know him not.*
Macduff	*My ever gentle cousin, welcome hither.*
Malcolm	*I know him now. Good God betimes remove*
	The means that makes us strangers.

(MACBETH, ACT IV, SCENE 3)

CHAPTER 1

A TANGLE OF ARMS reaching toward the fig tree. Among the thicket of deep-black arms stretching toward the fruit, two arms stood out, pale as a full moon.

I remember thinking how different those arms looked, while waiting for fruit to drop as Maicaah shook the branch. A fig hit the white hands and fell to the ground, and it was with shock that I felt the pain in *my* hands.

The others scrambled to get the figs that had landed in the grass. I stayed standing, turning my hands over and over in the sunlight that filtered through the leaves.

When Kinci stood up, I pulled her wrist until her arm was elbow-to-elbow with mine. Our arms were the same length, and we both had beaded cuffs of yellow, purple, green, and red beads in the same zig-zag pattern. Underneath and around her bracelet, the skin of her arm was as dark as a burnt clay pot, with pink scar spots where she'd scratched at bug bites. My arm was the color of dried grass, even paler in the crease of my elbow, against the contrast of the dirt that gathered there.

"I'm white," I said.

"Of course you're white," said Ibsituu, picking fig skin from between her teeth. "What did you think you were, green?"

"No, I mean, I look different. See?" I put my arm next to Kinci's again to show her.

"So?" said Bikeltu. "Tlahoun has big ears. Ibsituu is short."

Kinci laughed around her bite of fig. "Ibsituu is short because she's younger. Adelaide's whole family is different."

I wanted her to take it back, to tell me that I looked just like her and the rest of them.

"It's because you're *firanji*," said Maicaah. "Maybe where your family is from everyone is white." He handed me a section of his fig. The pulp was tart and sticky, pink and not quite ripe. It stung the corners of my lips and the top of my tongue. I chewed quickly, swallowing large pieces of pulp and seeds, eager to get out my objection.

"But. . . the foreigners at the market don't look like this."

"The foreigners at the market are Tigray or Amhara. Or Italian—they're light brown. But you're more very light yellow."

Bikeltu knelt in the grass to look for other figs. "Grandfather says God made all Oromo out of dirt. Maybe your people were made from something different."

"Like what?"

"Like water," suggested Ibsituu.

"Water isn't white. That's silly," said Kinci.

"Is not! Water can too be white!"

Bikeltu looked doubtful. "Water is only white when bumping up against a rock and going fast, and God would have to move pretty quickly to make people out of that."

"I don't think God made your people out of water. It has too many colors." Maicaah pointed at the stream that meandered a few yards away from the fig tree's shade. Parts of the stream looked greenish, reflecting the grass growing on the banks. Parts were brown with silt. Parts were so clear you could see the pebbles and the minnows underwater. Sunlight glinted off the planes of the water, moving continually.

"If your people were made out of the river, I think you would change colors depending on what was around you," Kinci decided.

"Maybe your people were made out of clouds," said Bikeltu.

"My skin isn't that white!"

"Pretty close. . ."

"If her people were made out of clouds, wouldn't they float? Or live in the sky?"

"Where did your parents live before they came here?" asked Kinci.

I didn't like all this talk about "my people," as if I didn't belong in the village. I tossed the rest of the fig toward the stream and wiped my hands on the folds of my skirt. "Sometimes they talk about a place called Carolina."

"What's it like?"

I had no idea how to answer. I was born there, but I didn't remember anything about it. I was relieved when Tlahoun and Ibsituu spotted an ostrich drinking upstream and ran away to chase it. The rest of us ran after them, urging them on and laughing. We never caught an ostrich, despite the number of times we tried. We sometimes got close, but never close enough to touch, not even the dirty-white tail feathers.

I was two when my parents moved to Ethiopia so my father could do his anthropological research among the Borana Oromo people of Ethiopia. I was sixteen when we left, in September of 1964.

My father told us we were moving two weeks before we left. He told us as we were finishing dinner, as my mother gathered up the plates from the table. He said he needed to report back to the universities that had provided his funding. He said it would be good for us, too—for me and Mary and Cassie to go back home.

He said they had just sent word about the tickets. He told us as if it was good news, with the same tone of voice he would have used to tell us about a neighbor who bought a cow for a good price at market and it turned out to be pregnant. My mother piled the dishes carefully and did not look up.

"What do you mean, 'back home'?" I said. "This is our home. This is the only place Marmee and I remember. Cassie was even born here."

"Of course the United States is your home," he said. "We always knew we'd be going back sometime." He'd already taken the lamp back to his typewriter and was reading over what he'd written before dinner.

"I don't want to go."

He laughed. "You can't stay here by yourself, Adelaide. If your mother and I go, you have to come with us."

"Most of my friends are married—I'm fully grown!"

"Adelaide, in American culture, you're a child until you turn eighteen. We've talked about that." He leaned back from his table and took a breath, as if he was going to start one of his lectures on the sociological construct of families in North American versus Oromo culture.

I walked out of the house. I wasn't a kid, no matter what he said. Of the girls I'd grown up with, I was the only one still stuck under my parents' roof, having to follow their rules and decisions. Now they were going to make me leave with them and move to an entirely different country.

No one followed me outside to make me come back in. My father hated shouting, and I was in a mood to shout—at him or at anyone who stopped me. I left the dinner cleanup for my mother and Marmee and went to Kinci's.

My father didn't say anything more about it, and he left for a conference two days later. My mother never brought it up, but a few days before my father was due back, she pulled the suitcases out from under the sleeping cots and told us to start packing.

※

We packed everything—clothes, books, baskets, cooking utensils—in five suitcases and a big green trunk my parents had brought with us when we first arrived.

Marmee and I started with the spare linen, the sheets and pillowcases and tablecloths that always made other people in the village stare at our excess. We packed the school books we weren't using: Marmee checked to make sure our mother wasn't looking, then slipped her Latin textbook into the bottom of the heaviest suitcase. We folded our spare clothes, carefully running our hands over the drape of the long skirts, the printed patterns of headscarves, the knots of the beaded jewelry we only used on special occasions. We left my father's books on his shelf so he could pack them himself exactly the way he wanted.

Later, I would wish I could have packed my favorite tree, the wide expanse of the fields, the smell of coffee roasting over the fire, the sunset. Later I would wish I could have found a way to stay there in the village, where I belonged.

Mother told us to fill the suitcases while she cooked. All the other mothers in the village made their daughters help them with every step, but Mother preferred to cook over the open fire herself; she said the flames and ash made her nervous for our safety, even after all these years.

Cassie sat on one of the goat-skin cots reading, mouthing the sounds of letters like I'd taught her. The sunlight pouring through the open doorway didn't really reach her in that corner, and she had to angle the page to catch the chinks of light that came through the bound sticks that formed our walls. The thatch roof always made it dark and cool inside, which was nice for almost everything, except for reading.

Cassie's friends came and crowded around the doorway, blocking most of the light. They greeted my mother politely, as was expected of them, but after that they never lapsed into friendliness the way they teased the village mothers. They simply stood, balancing with one foot on the calf of the other leg, imitating hunters, staring at the things strewn about the room and the open suitcases that covered the dirt floor.

"Adelie, Marmee, why are you still inside? We're going to see the goatherds. Do you want to come?"

Mother told us we couldn't, and eventually our friends went away, taking Cassie with them.

When we packed everything else we could think of, Marmee and I started taking down the herbs and spices hanging from the roof beams. We wrapped them carefully in spare strips of cotton: fenugreek, basil, turmeric, ginger, cumin seeds, cardamom pods, red peppers—and then we tucked them between layers of clothes in the suitcase. Our mother looked over and frowned.

"Don't pack those," she said, as if we should have known.

She leaned over the nearest suitcase and pulled out the head scarves, the long skirts, the beaded necklaces and bracelets and head ornaments.

"You won't need these in Carolina," she said. She left them in a heap and returned to the fire pit. Marmee and I looked at each other.

Marmee whispered, "What does she mean we won't. . ."

I asked aloud, "What do you mean we won't need these? They're the only clothes we have."

Mother barely looked up from the cooking. "Your father is bringing some American clothes back with him after this conference." Her voice was the same even tone as always, like the walk of a mule, unwavering, unemotional. Her eyes were half open, the way they had been almost every day for the last six months, since the baby came too early.

"What does American clothing look like?" Marmee whispered again.

I shrugged. The only American clothing I knew were the

things our dad wore to conferences and the old baby clothes our parents had kept in the trunk. When Mother stepped outside, I repacked the head scarves, the skirts, and the beaded jewelry. I covered them up with a large maroon sheet and shut the suitcase. We left the rest of the herbs hanging in their place.

Marmee and I carefully packed the baby things when my mother was outside. They were still folded, neatly, in the basket next to my parents' bed, where my mother had put them when she was preparing things between contractions. When he was born blue, too still and soundless, we buried him in the local way: a shawl for a shroud, a grave covered by rocks. He never needed the basket or the clothes. Now none of us wanted to touch the things.

Marmee put the baby basket and everything inside it at the bottom of one of the suitcases, but the suitcase wouldn't close on top of it. As quickly as I could, handling them as little as I could, I unpacked all the white, lacy clothes, the soft bibs, the ancient-stained but clean-smelling diaper cloths, the plastic-headed diaper pins, and I hid them all under other, unsuspicious things. The clothes had belonged to me and Marmee and Cassie, but they were *his* now. We put the basket under our bed, to deal with it later.

Somehow we didn't do a good enough job hiding the baby things. Two days before we left, in a torrent of last-minute activity, my mother suddenly stilled where she was kneeling, her fingers caught in the pastel green cable knit of a baby blanket. She stood up and went outside, and we didn't see her for half an hour. I couldn't tell where she'd gone.

"Is *haadha* all right?" asked Cassie, using the word for *mother* that all of our friends used. Our parents made us speak English in our house, but we let Oromiffa words creep in when we were talking to each other, when we didn't want to have to stop and think of the English equivalent.

"Wrap that sheet tighter around the pot, Cassie," I said, and I stuffed the baby blanket down between two of our dad's old sweaters. I watched the doorway until Mother returned.

In the afternoon, I heard the ibis call just outside the window.

"I have to go use the bushes, Mama. I'll be gone for a bit." I didn't look at my sisters—I wasn't sure if they recognized Maicaah's signal—and I didn't wait for my mother's answer.

I ran toward the cape chestnut tree and answered his call with one slightly lower-pitched. He dropped a nut on my head, and I cursed at him, smiling. I looked around to make sure no one would see me climbing the tree.

"You know you aren't supposed to climb like that," he said. "Only boys climb that way."

"It's the easiest way to climb! And are you saying I'm not a girl?" I smiled, chin down, the look that usually made him look at my mouth. I loved it when he looked at me that way.

"You are definitely not a village girl." He looked away instead of at me. Sunlight and leaf shadows dappled his narrow head with its loose curls.

I let him be in his mood. I settled myself more comfortably on the tree branch, the lower of the two at this perch. I pulled a leaf off the tree and dropped it; it caught the wind and twirled to the ground slowly.

"Maybe I could come visit you," he said. "Next year I'll be old enough to work in the city. I can earn enough for the trip, and I can visit you." His eyebrows were so much thicker than they had been when we were younger, but his eyes had the intense, dark pressure that they always did when he was serious.

"I think it costs a lot of money."

"That's all right. I'll save up my money. I won't eat, if I have to."

"You have to eat," I told him. "If you don't eat, you'll get even skinnier and then your mother will really hate me."

His eyelashes looked so long when he blinked. He smiled, the dark shadow of hair moving on his upper lip. "My mother doesn't hate you. She would like you better if you were staying." He had a different explanation every time I brought up his mother.

"Maybe," I said. "We'll see when I return."

"When will that be, Adelie?" He reached forward, and I thought for a second that his fingers would touch my face, but he pulled on one of my braids instead.

"I won't be gone long; you'll see. When I turn eighteen, I won't be a child anymore and I can leave them to come back here."

"You had better," he said. He let go of my hair and leaned back. "I still wish I could go with you. You could hide me in one of those big suitcases."

I imagined him with his knees tucked under his chin, legs pressed against his chest, trying to fit his tall frame inside a suitcase. He used to fold himself up like that when we were children. Once we were hiding from Kinci, and he skinned his knee while rushing to get into the hiding spot between his parents' house and the tree that grew so close to its walls. The deep scrape had bled all over both of us, and he had started crying.

The scar, still on his knee, was eye level in front of me. The skin was faded, pink, puckered just below the sharp angles of his knee. I reached out a finger and touched it lightly.

"Do you remember when you got this?" I asked.

He said nothing, and I looked up at him. His eyes were so serious again, and I couldn't look away. I wasn't sure what was going to happen, but it felt important, like whatever came next would change the world.

Slowly, he put the tips of his fingers over mine. It was very gentle pressure; my fingers pressed lightly into the top of his shinbone.

"Promise. . . promise me you will come back," he said. "And that things will be the same."

"What things?"

I knew what he meant. I wanted to hear him say it, to acknowledge the agreement we made in joking seriousness when we started using the ibis call, after I was too old to be spending time alone with a boy. A fly landed in the place where his shoulder met his collar bone, and a second passed before he swatted it away with his free hand. I leaned forward, my weight shifting on the tree branch.

Then I heard my mother calling from the riverbank. "Adelaide!"

If it had been one of my sisters calling, I would have ignored her. I would have stayed in the tree with Maicaah until he said what I wanted to hear.

My mother called again, searching, the tinge of worry already creeping into the vowels of my name. The semblance of our small, private world up in the tree faded.

"I have to go," I told him.

"Don't go, Adelie," he said.

"*Adelaide!*"

"I will come back. Soon."

"Promise you won't stay in that foreign land with your people?"

"They're not my people."

"Promise?" He pressed a little harder against my fingers, still against his knee. The paleness of my fingers was almost camouflaged between the dark skin of his hand and his knee.

"I promise. The village is my home."

"*Adelaide!*" I began to pull away. I checked to make sure no one would see me emerging from the foliage.

"Adelie. Don't go," he whispered. It stole my breath.

"I promised you: I'll be back." The first tear rolled out of my eye just before I pulled my hand free and jumped out of the tree. I landed hard on my feet. "Coming!" I said in English, loud enough so I hoped my mother heard. I brushed the wetness off my face and made sure there were no leaves clinging to my skirt or scarf before I walked back to the house.

I didn't look back at the tree. I couldn't.

※

I went to Kinci's mother's house after dinner, just before dark. It was a time when only immediate family visited each other, not a time for polite company. It was the time when Kinci's mother always told me to come so she could braid my hair.

I sat as I had so many times, on the soft floor with her rounded knees at my ears. She undid the old braids and started anew; Kinci kneeled on the floor next to me, helping her. They kept tilting my head one way or the other as they braided, and my neck was a familiar kind of stiff from trying to hold still. My hair was so different from the other girls', so slippery in comparison, but Kinci's mother was willing to do it. Haadha Meti had braided my hair my whole life, ever since we arrived in the village. She took pity on me and my two-year-old tangles while my own mother fussed night and day over the implacable baby that my sister Mary had been. Kinci and I got our first braids on the same day, matching rows of neat, parallel braids ending in twists. Haadha Meti said she had to try putting all sorts of fats and oils and pastes in my hair before she could get the twists to stay properly.

The fire flickered its shadows over the uneven wooden walls, and Kinci's mother told us stories like she always did. Kinci had to lean back frequently to give herself a break; her pregnant belly looked even bigger when she stretched.

"Almost done, Adelie," said Haadha Meti.

She had taken extra care this time, parting my hair precisely and weaving small, careful braids. I could feel her twisting the ends so they stayed put. "Are you giving me an updo, Haadha Meti? It feels very elegant."

"There," she said. Both she and Kinci stepped back to look at me. I stood up, feeling self-conscious at their staring. I ran my fingers over the thin lines that crossed my scalp.

"Beautiful," said Kinci. She tweaked the ends of a few braids to lay straighter.

Haadha Meti swatted Kinci's hands away. "You look much more grown up, Adelie. You can go forth into the world and represent our village well." She pulled my head down so she could kiss my forehead.

It felt like she was sending me off for a wedding. "I'll be back, Haadha Meti, I promise."

Her eyes looked like they didn't believe me. "May God grant that," is all she said.

Kinci and I walked in the dark to her house on the other side of the village. Her little brother escorted us, but he stayed several feet behind, kicking rocks. The night air smelled of rain; we pulled our long scarves closer around our shoulders. Kinci and I walked arm in arm, like we had the night before her wedding. She was eager to go home now, but she had been so nervous that day.

"How's the baby? Still kicking?"

"Not so bad right now," she said. "I think he calmed down listening to Haadha's stories."

"You still think it's a boy?"

She ran her hand down the side of her swollen belly. It was so strange—I knew her hands as well as I knew my own, but this Kinci was different from the little girl I'd grown up with. I could see it in her eyes and her face; every day she was changing into someone beyond me.

"I'm sure it's a boy. Solomon's family always has boys first. Also, my dream."

I nodded. Two months earlier, when we were alone doing chores, she told me she had dreamed about a baby boy who wouldn't stop crying. She told me how afraid she was to have this baby, afraid to go through childbirth, afraid to become a mother. She had become so terrified as she talked that her hands started to shake and she couldn't shuck any more corn. I hugged her until the crying stopped, but I hadn't known what to say. That was before I knew I had to leave.

"I'm sorry I'll miss the baby's birth," I said. "I'll have to bring back something special for him from Carolina. What should it be?"

Kinci laughed and thought for a minute. "One of those strange hats your dad sometimes wears." Everyone in the village thought my dad's blue Marines baseball cap was funny.

"All right," I told her. "I'll bring back a strange hat for this little one. He can wear it with pride all over the village." I hugged her good night around the mound of her belly.

All too soon my house was all packed, and it was time to go.

We walked from our house out into the sunlight—Dad first, then Mother, Cassie, and Marmee. I lingered. Each of us carried a suitcase, and we also had woven bags, the kind the women used for sowing, only ours now held books to read on the trip and fruit to eat and a change of underwear, just in case something happened to our luggage.

Everyone was to walk with us to Nekemte, and my family would catch a bus from there for the first leg of our trip. There wasn't a village custom for what to do when a family moved away. So, after much discussion, the village elders had decided to follow the custom for when a daughter leaves to marry someone from a village far away. I could tell my father was uncomfortable with that innovation, but I felt glad there was some protocol that could be adapted, even if it didn't really fit.

I had never before seen a house as empty as ours. The dirt floor looked smooth and interminable, like it had doubled in size; the crooked legs of our table looked like the bones of a skeleton, and the two cots were like dead animals against the walls. The thatch roof didn't have the usual odds and ends hanging down— no herbs drying, rustling. Even my dad's books were gone from his shelves. The house smelled of smoke and wool like normal, but the air was clear, for once. Without the haze I could plainly see the sooty thatch above the fire pit.

"What's happening to our house?" I asked suddenly from just inside the doorway. My parents turned back to look at me. Behind them, my mother's bright Carolina sunflowers leaned in their usual angle away from the wall of the house, but it looked as if they were reaching toward my mother, trying to cling to her before she left them.

Mother waved me forward impatiently. "We gave it to the village elders. Come on, Adelaide. We have to get there before noon or we might miss the bus."

I gripped the edge of the doorway as I stepped out of the house into the common space of the village. One of the men took the suitcase from me, and I finally walked forward, toward my family and the gathered villagers. I felt like I'd forgotten something, and I kept clutching my bag, my pockets, my beaded bracelet, to see if it was all there.

"What are you wearing?" Kinci asked when she joined us.

"Clothes like they wear in Carolina. Aren't they strange?"

My father had brought back three identical khaki skirts for Mother, Mary, and me, and a shorter dress for Cassie. My skirt landed at the middle of my calf, slightly shorter than I was used to. The fabric itself was thicker than the village dress, and I couldn't walk in it as easily. Our blouses were different colors but matching styles for the three of us—short sleeves, buttons, collars. My light blue blouse was puffy at the shoulders and tight under my armpits. Mary and I had fastened all the buttons, up to the highest one that pinched the skin at our throats, but then Mother told us we could undo one button—just one, she repeated. Mother carried our shoes in her woven bag. She said we didn't need to wear them until the bus picked us up from the market.

Kinci pulled at my skirt and fingered the sleeve on my blouse. "They look strange. But not bad, I guess. At least, I am pretty sure Maicaah doesn't think they look bad." Maicaah stood several feet away, staring. I couldn't quite understand his expression, so I laughed at him with Kinci.

A village elder made a speech about bonds that went beyond blood, then my father made a speech expressing gratitude for their generosity. Then the singing began. It felt like a holiday with all the singing, the way it had when we accompanied Ibsituu last year to her new husband's village, only now we were singing a mixture of songs from harvest, church, and festivals instead of just the traditional wedding songs. The elderly women marched my sisters and me up to the front of the crowd to join our mother. I pulled Kinci with us, but she held back.

"Aren't you coming?"

"I can't," she said in a low voice, as if she didn't want to be overheard.

"What? Why not? Everyone is coming. Only the oldest women are staying behind."

"And the young women who are heavy with children." Her arms rested on her middle. "My mother and Solomon agreed that I shouldn't walk to Nekemte today. I have to stay here."

I hadn't thought what it would be like to actually say good-bye to her. I didn't know what it would be like to walk to town without her, to not be able to tell her about it right afterward. It would be so long before I saw her again. How would I remember all the things I had to tell her? "My sister. . ." I said.

Kinci started to cry as well, wiping away tears with her pink palms. "Stop it. The baby doesn't like me crying."

We hugged, gripping each other tightly. The beads of her necklace pressed against my collar bone, and my stomach bumped against the bulk of her belly. I felt the baby kick, and I jumped back. We laughed together, looking down at her stomach.

"Come, Adelaide," my father called. The front of the procession was already beyond the farthest of the village houses, and there were only a few people left to make up the end of the crowd.

"Come back soon, Adelie," said Kinci.

I hugged her again, leaning into the sharp pain from her beads, then wiped away my eyes so I could see clearly and ran toward the front of the procession to join my family.

My mother didn't speak the whole walk to Nekemte. She stared straight ahead, as if there was nothing to see; she wore her old, odd straw hat that shaded her face with crisscrosses. My father walked hand in hand with the village elders, singing loudly with them and joining each new song as the previous one finished.

Mary, Cassie, and I followed, the three of us in a row, me in the middle. The road was fine dust under my feet, and the cotton-soft top layer rose in puffs with each step to cover our clothes and skin. I could feel the grit settling on my face and in my teeth. First Cassie took my hand, and then I grabbed Marmee's. I felt like Jethro's daughter in that story from the Bible.

We walked away from our thatch-roof home, away from the cluster of open-air ovens buried in the open space at the center of the village, away from the little stone-covered grave on the hill, away from the cape chestnut and the fig tree and the stream.

I could see Maicaah's oblong head in front of us, where he was walking a few steps behind the village elders. He was eating a pomegranate, periodically flicking bits of fruit skin into the shrubs. He didn't once look back at me. I hoped the elders wouldn't realize he wasn't singing.

The group's singing gradually became a murmur as we came to the edge of Nekemte. When we reached the square it faded away altogether, and we just stood there, self-conscious in front of the town dwellers. Everyone waited with us for the bus, a whole crowd of us, but no one knew what to do while we waited. It was a while before we saw the moving cloud of dust on the horizon—the bus that was approaching to take us away.

My mother took out of her bag lace-trimmed socks and stiff shoes and handed them to me. Then she pointed us to the well in the center of the square.

We waited our turn for the water. It was cool to the touch, and I first drank some and carefully splashed some over my face, wiping the drips off my chin with the bottom of my blouse. Then my sisters and I leaned into each other as we each balanced on one foot to wash the other one. I poured a little water on my right foot and rubbed away the muddy trickles with my sock, careful to use every drop under the watchful eyes of the Nekemte women. I could feel their triple scorn for us—because we were with the villagers, because we were so strangely white, and because we were using their water to clean something as innocent as dirt off our *feet*. The socks stuck to my damp skin when I tried to put them on, and the shoes made my feet feel clamped in.

Cassie splashed a handful of water on her clean foot and let the excess run off, not even trying to catch it and reuse it.

"Cassie, don't be wasteful," I scolded her in Oromiffa for the benefit of our spectators.

Marmee dried Cassie's foot quickly and tied the shoelaces for her. Our feet looked odd in shoes, with thin bows erect at odd angles. Mother had taught us the knots, but we had rarely used them.

"It is time," my father said to the villagers. The eldest of the elders gave a last speech and led us all in one last song. Then the women said goodbye to my father and mother and hugged my sisters and me. Some of the men were crying as well. Kinci's littlest sister clung to my legs until her father pried her away.

"Good bye, Adelie," said Maicaah from two feet away. His hands were on his hips, and he kept his distance, as if we were little more than strangers. I searched his face for some sign of our promise, but there was none.

"Good bye." My sight clouded with tears, and I turned to follow my father. Maicaah stopped me and put his arms around me for a quick hug. I barely registered the flat sinews and muscles of his arms and his chest before he pulled away again. I heard a few adults clear their throats around us.

"Come back soon," he whispered, a little hoarse.

"I will." I smiled at him, blinking at the blur that threatened my sight of his face. Then I turned and boarded the bus.

My sisters and I had never been on a bus before, and we had marveled at them along with the rest of the village kids as they snaked their way through the market town. Sometimes we had ridden with Dad on his motorcycle for short trips, but now the motorcycle was staying in the village, a bequest to the elders, to help with hospital visits.

I wasn't sure what to think of the long stretch of the bus aisle cluttered with bags and animals, people sitting one behind the other and staring at the back of the next person's head, the seats with stuffing and springs that clawed their way out of the leather covers. The windows were smudged and streaked inside and out. The seats we found were fenced in by cages of chickens in the aisle. My sisters and I shared a seat behind our parents.

We waved, and the villagers waved back: Tlahoun, Bikeltu, Haadha Meti, Kinci's father, other elders, Kinci's little sister and brother, Cassie's friends, Maicaah. The bus jolted forward, and we waved out the window until the villagers were out of sight and Nekemte faded into the horizon.

It was a few hours later, when Marmee was asleep against the window and Cassie was asleep against my shoulder, that I felt something in the pocket of my skirt. I pulled out several small, jewel-red lumps: pomegranate seeds. Five of them. I held them carefully in my palm with my fingers curled around them to make sure they didn't fall.

I had no idea when Maicaah had slipped them in my pocket. When he was giving me a hug? I hoped no one had seen.

They were so pretty, luminous really. And from Maicaah—the last thing I had from him. I remembered the feeling, so brief, of his hug. In front of everyone else, even his mother. It seemed a sacrilege to eat the seeds and make them disappear, to have no more physical trace of their small, gleaming beauty, no more trace of him, of the hug, of the large group in the square waiting to wave us away.

I carefully sucked the flesh off each seed, using my teeth to clean away the clinging fibers that I knew would rot soon, the fruit that wasn't meant to last. When I was done, the seed cores lay pale yellow in my hand, like tiny dried bones. I cupped my palm carefully around them and put them back in my pocket for safe-keeping. Every few minutes I checked my pocket and recounted the seeds to make sure none had fallen out. The chickens in the aisle watched me, jealous, but no one in my family noticed.

The bus took us to Addis Ababa, descending into the city around dinner time. It was already dark, but I could tell from the lights and the number of buildings that this was a city larger than I could imagine. It smelled of diesel exhaust and hot metal, like my dad's motorcycle but stronger. We were speckled with chicken poop and feathers. I still had dirt in my teeth and inside my nose. The tightness of my shoes was mirrored by a headache.

We stayed that night at the home of some missionaries, white like us. The next morning they took us to the airport.

I remember the signs at the airport in Addis had translations in five languages—English, Italian, Arabic, French, and Portuguese. There were men wearing elaborate turbans, suits and ties in brown and black, or colorful long tunics like I'd never seen before. There were fewer women, but they were in all sorts of styles too—most in dress suits with hats and gloves, some in long skirts, a few in what my mother explained were burqas, two in Chinese gowns, one woman in a sari. The stewardesses all wore matching light blue outfits with white gloves and blue hats. We spent the whole flight with our faces pressed against the airplane windows, mar-veling at the world passing by beneath us. The city of Addis and its mountains gave way to tiny-animal herds on dusty plains, then desert, and then we were in a landscape of clouds.

We flew to Rome and had to wait there two days before we could fly to London. We went on one sightseeing excursion in Rome. There were so many people, and the noise was deafening. We stayed the rest of the time in our room, playing cards. The suitcase with our American clothing hadn't arrived with us, so we washed our blouses and underwear in the bathroom sink. My skirt still had the speckled white outline of a stain from chicken poop. The pomegranate seeds were still safely tucked into the right-hand pocket.

At the airport in London, all the people looked as if they had been left out in the sun too long and been bleached of all their color. I couldn't stop staring.

"There are so many white people," I said to Marmee.

A woman standing five feet away frowned at us, and I realized that she could understand. English was no longer our family's secret language. Here everyone else spoke it too, and I felt exposed somehow, or betrayed.

"Everyone looks just like us," said Cassie. "We don't stand out here." It made me anxious too—as if, camouflaged, we would be lost in the crowd.

"Excuse me, love," said someone behind us, with a luggage cart. We turned to stare, confused about what the man needed. "Pardon me; I just need to get by." We moved out of his way and stood back against the wall. I felt like a stray animal, stuck in the path of an oncoming herd.

The next day we flew from London to New York and from New York to Atlanta. By the time we arrived in Atlanta, we'd been in five cities on three continents in the course of six days. My head was so overwhelmed with unfamiliar sounds, colors, smells, textures, that I couldn't take in anything more that was new. Cassie had broken out in a rash. Marmee's eyes had been glazed for days. My feet had raw spots where the stiff shoes had caused blisters and then rubbed them away, and my braids had gotten fuzzy from sleeping in strange places. My arm was red around the cuff of my bracelet beads; Dad said it was from swelling caused by airplane altitude. I'd gripped the seeds so often that my mother noticed and asked me what I had in my pocket. I didn't answer, and she didn't ask again.

When we arrived in Atlanta, I could only feel relief that the journey was almost over.

Two aunts, three uncles, and five cousins met us in Atlanta. I was struck by how white-pink they looked, how yellow their hair was. They greeted us effusively, in a clump, everyone close together, talking at us. I smiled as best as I could and held tightly to my sisters' arms.

They drove us, in a caravan of three cars, to my mother's home town: Greenville, South Carolina. I was in the middle of the front seat of my uncle's car, sandwiched between my father and my aunt, whose name I couldn't remember, while my uncle drove. The adults talked around me as if I wasn't there.

I leaned to the side just enough to reach into my pocket. I ran my fingertip over each seed, counting them again: feeling the small, smooth pits, the one pointy end, and the other more rounded side. They were so slight I was afraid they'd slip through the seam of the pocket and fall to the floorboard of my uncle's car and be lost forever. I gathered them into my fist and kept my hand wedged in my pocket.

Eventually I fell asleep on my father's shoulder, thinking of

Maicaah's head against the wide sky as we walked to the market town, singing as if it were a holiday.

I just had to hold on until I turned eighteen. And then I'd go back. I had promised I would.

CHAPTER 2

IT WAS NEAR THE END of September when we arrived in Greenville. The sunlight filtered through a tired-blue sky, the fields were shorn, the weather was cool, and the rumble of fabric mills reached us when everything else was still in the early mornings.

The school year had already started, but Dad announced that my sisters and I could have a little bit of time to settle in before we had to go to classes. So we hid for a week and a half at my grandmother's house, the house where Mother grew up, where Grandmother and Aunt Be had been living on their own.

"I'm so glad you're here," my grandmother told us repeatedly when we were spread around the table for dinner. "This table needs a crowd. It was so empty with only Beulah and me."

Aunt Be never said anything in response. Her smile was firmly closed, forced. When Aunt Be smiled or spoke, her skin folded along marked lines as if it was ironed into creases. She always wore an old cream-colored apron cinched around her waist, so tight it caused bubbles of flesh above and beneath the bow.

Grandmother was thin and tiny. She had raised my mother and her siblings—five girls and two boys—on the farm my grandfather worked. Though none of their neighbors had one, my grandmother had her husband build a summer kitchen in the yard so that the whole house wouldn't boil when they put up the produce in the summer.

"Bugs were always getting in the jars," said Aunt Be.

"Only if you weren't careful," said Grandmother.

Uncle Henry ran the farm now, with occasional help from Uncle Robert or one of my aunts' husbands. Grandmother still scrubbed the floors daily.

The first few days we stayed mostly inside the house, roaming the hallways. The house seemed palatial: there were five bedrooms, a parlor, a dining room, a den, a bathroom with two sinks and a huge tub, and the indoor kitchen, plus a damp-smelling concrete cellar and a musty attic with a dormer window high up in the wall. The hallways were worn in a path to the kitchen, and the front porch sagged a little toward the steps. The windows' thick glass rattled when you opened them. Some were impossible to push up; other windows slammed down unless they were propped open with a stick.

I missed our village house. I missed the one room where you could see everyone at once; I missed the give of the goat-skin cot where I could fall asleep watching the fire embers winking and glowing. I missed the popping of coffee beans roasting over the fire. I missed the tang of enjera and the spiciness of Haadha Meti's peppers. Bottled cow's milk tasted so bland compared to our fresh goat's milk. I fumbled with fork and knife, wishing I could go back to eating with my fingers.

I had to take the braids out of my hair two days after we arrived in Greenville.

"Just look at the rat's nest on that child's head," said Aunt Be to my mother while I was drying dishes in the kitchen.

I immediately put my hands up to my braids. It was true that they had gotten messy in the travel; Haadha Meti would have had a fit if she'd seen them. But I'd never taken them out on my own.

"Who's going to redo them?" I asked. Under the fuzz of escaped hair, I could still feel the fancy patterns that Haadha Meti had drawn with careful parts.

Mother just sighed and pointed me to a stool.

"I don't want to take them out," I insisted.

My grandmother, seated in her usual rocking chair in the corner, reached for my hand. "Can't it wait another few days? They seem important to her."

Aunt Be ran her hand through the fluff that had escaped from my braids, an unruly, translucent cloud. "It makes her look like a cross between a doily and a sheepdog."

I wanted to argue, but I knew my braids did look awful, if they looked anything like Marmee's. I had avoided the bathroom mirror as much as I could since arriving.

"Well, give her a day, then, to get used to the idea. . ."

Aunt Be frowned. "Church is tomorrow. She can't go looking like this."

"Do I have to go to church?"

Grandmother sighed. "They will have to come out sometime, child. Maybe better now than when they get more tangled."

There was no more room for disagreement. My mother sat on a kitchen chair and pulled up the stool in front of it. Grandmother scooted her rocking chair closer so she could hold my hand.

Mother's unpracticed fingers yanked and tangled in the hair as she undid the braids. It took about an hour to undo six. Aunt Be and even Grandmother had wandered away from the kitchen by then.

"It's not supposed to hurt like that," I said.

Mother's fingers slowed and then suddenly stopped.

"I'm tired," she said. She withdrew her fingers from my hair and clasped one hand over the other in her lap, as if she was holding her stomach in. Her sharp knees dug between my shoulder blades; I could feel the offending, snarled braids, the escaped hair, the dirt at the roots.

Mother put a hand on each of my shoulders, lightly pushing me away. She stood and left the kitchen, her eyes dulled and half-closed, unresponsive even when I called after her.

The dark spaces between the wood slats in the flooring suddenly seemed ominous. The kitchen was very silent, as was the rest of the house: no sounds of cook fires crackling, no kids playing, no neighbors calling out, no animals lowing or grazing. I was very far from home, and my hair was a monstrous mess.

Eventually I stood and went to the back porch. The steps were wide enough to sit on sideways, and I watched fireflies gather in the fields on the other side of the fence. The sounds of crickets kept me company.

I undid each braid slowly, tenderly, loosening each gnarled strand a little bit at a time. It hurt less then, but I was still crying. I couldn't recreate the feeling of Haadha Meti's fingers in my hair.

Marmee came over to watch, and when I finished with my own hair she sat down in front of me so I could do hers. My hands cramped from the repeated motion, and I had to stretch my fingers backwards against my thighs every so often. Marmee hummed village songs and squirmed only a little bit between my knees.

When I was done, we rose to face each other. Marmee's hair, several shades lighter than mine, nearly platinum, crinkled above her wide forehead, swooped down to broaden her cheekbones and spread out around her shoulders, lessening the emphasis of her pointy chin. She looked fierce as a lion. We laughed shakily at each other and shook our heads in wide arcs to feel the looseness of the unruly crimps. I wasn't sure what came next.

When Aunt Be found us, she shooed me into the steam-filled bathroom and shut the door behind me. The water in the tub was almost scalding to the touch, so full it threatened to slop over the green-ceramic edge. I waited, then tested the water again, and my hand came out red and stinging. I used a clothes-hanger I found on the back of the door to pull the plug until the drain gurgled and the water level visibly dropped. When the tub was half empty, I let the plug settle back in and ran cold water until the temperature was right.

All that water seemed like a rich man's dream, like a luxurious waste, but here there seemed to be no limit on it, no effort required to gather it, no careful hoarding. It was so easy to have so much of it.

The ceramic was slippery under my feet, and the water lapped over me in unfamiliar ways, more intimate than swimming in the river because the water responded only to me and nothing else. Eventually, I leaned back far enough to let the water reach my scalp. I scraped away caked dirt with my fingernails and then rubbed in some pink shampoo, blinking hard when the lather reached my eyes. The water was murky beneath the whitecaps of shampoo suds, so I let the water drain again and ran some more. I rinsed, lathered my hair again, and rinsed again, face-down under the faucet, until there was no more trace of Ethiopia.

After Marmee took her turn, Aunt Be combed our hair for us with a skinny pink comb that looked sharp. Surprisingly she didn't pull too much. Then Aunt Be showed us how to fix our hair in one thick braid that started at the crown of our heads and worked its way down to the middle of our backs. Her fingers held our wet hair firmly until it pulled at our scalps. The tight braid squeezed water down my neck as Aunt Be wove it. The braiding didn't take as long as I expected.

"My Dana used to wear her hair like this when she was little," she said. "She cut her hair before she started high school, but I used to braid her hair like this every night."

The braid was so taut it pulled my face backward, in a different angle than I was used to, but my hair still felt loose in only one large braid. By morning, all sorts of hair had fallen into my face. Aunt Be redid the braid before church, but within the hour there were loose pieces again. I pushed the strands back from my face as if they were tree branches blocking my path.

We got to church just before the service started—getting ready had taken on a level of preparation fit for a parade—and people in the pews turned to stare at us as we walked in. There was a multitude of white people, all gawking at us.

After a few songs, there was a lengthy sermon. When my mind drifted after just a few sentences, I counted the kinds of hats the women wore in the pews around us. Cassie fell asleep, and Mary read the hymn book. As the service wound to a close, suddenly I realized the pastor was introducing my family: ". . .our dear sister Betty Mason's daughter, and her husband and family, back from among the dark heathens of Africa."

He made us stand up—all of us, including Grandmother and Aunt Be—and he invited Dad to the pulpit to say a few words. We stood in the pew, not permitted to sit back down, while everyone gaped at us as he spoke. The pastor's phrase repeated in my head several times: I wanted to laugh at his ignorance, calling our village "dark heathens of Africa," when they had been Christians for generations, in a country that traced its Christian roots to the days of the apostles and its Jewish heritage to the days of Solomon.

Dad looked for an instant as if he'd like to set the pastor straight, but instead, he smiled woodenly, and then he stumbled over the unfamiliar church language. The more he looked unsure what to say, the longer he stayed in the pulpit, gripping the sides of the lectern as if hoping he would suddenly find the right phrase to redeem his previous floundering. The suit jacket was too small for him, and the tie knot that sat squarely under his Adam's apple accentuated his nervousness. I watched the tie bob up and down as he spoke, and I wished I could just sit down and be on a level with everyone else again.

Eventually the pastor led the congregation in an "Amen, Brother! Hallelujah!" and then it was over.

After the service, clumps of people passed us, staring and whispering behind their hands, as my sisters and I waited for the adults. There were girls around our age, but they didn't talk to us; their parents merely nodded and smiled and murmured hello.

Aunt Be came over and introduced us to two elderly women. "Girls, say hello to Mrs. DeWitt and Mrs. Newton."

I looked at the floor and nodded. Aunt Be poked me in the ribs and spoke low so the women wouldn't hear. "Shake hands, Adelaide—and look the ladies in the eyes."

I hesitated, then shook the women's wrinkled claws gently, glancing briefly at their faded eyes. Mary and Cassie followed suit. All my life I had been told it was rude to look an older stranger in the face, but I assured myself I would follow the American rules while I had to and shed them as soon as I could make it back home. When the ladies walked away, I gripped my beaded bracelet with my other hand and kept my head down until we left the church and drove back to the haven of Grandmother's house.

It didn't help, in those first few weeks, that Aunt Be was always on our case about something. One morning I answered her question with a simple negative.

"Child, are you completely lacking all manners?" she demanded. "When you speak to an adult, you say *Yes, ma'am*, or *No, ma'am*. Do you hear?"

"That's not what. . ."

"I said, did you hear me?"

"Yes, Aunt Be," I said. I bunched my anger into a fist, feeling pride for the way I kept it in check. Marmee would laugh with me about it later, and the edges of my anger slowly smoothed and hardened as I held on to it.

※

Each time I talked with Grandmother, I learned a new family member's name. Aunt Be's daughter Dana was at boarding school, and she rarely came home. I envied her freedom.

Uncle Henry—the older of Grandmother's two sons—was married to Aunt Candice. They lived closer to town, but Uncle Henry ran Grandmother's farm. On Saturdays Uncle Henry brought his children over to Grandmother's house: my cousins Julia and Bernice and the two younger boys. Their older brother was in college, so he was exempt from the family visit. Julia had long blonde hair and a pointed nose, the only straight lines on her. She was about a year older than me, in her last year of high school. Bernice, whose hair flipped out at the base of her ears, was my age.

Grandmother said she was thrilled to see the four of us young ladies together, and she made us sit on the porch and talk as if it were a social occasion. Julia and Bernice mostly talked to each other and occasionally picked lackadaisically at the beans we were supposed to be stringing.

"I remember that!" Bernice said, looking at the dress that had become Marmee's favorite. "It has a hole in the side seam, doesn't it? Mother said she'd mend it, but I made her get rid of it. It's so funny to see you wearing it now. It looked a lot better on me than on you."

It took me a moment to realize her rudeness was intentional. I wished an adult was nearby to hear her and give her a good talking-to. Why were my parents never near when I wanted them to be?

"Better be nice, Bernice," Julia said mock-seriously. "Mary's a quiet one. I bet she's sly. She might put an African voodoo hex on you."

"No such thing," Bernice scoffed.

Marmee and I made fun of them in our room at night, when everyone else was asleep. Marmee could imitate their voices so well it made my stomach hurt from laughing. Their comments lost some of the sting after we'd laughed at them, but I still felt pushed down, somehow, and like I needed to push back. I missed Kinci; she would have had some good retorts to put my cousins in their place.

Pretty much as soon as we moved into Grandmother's house, Dad was conscripted to help with the farm work. He left the house after breakfast wearing loose overalls that still bore the shape of the store shelf. He returned to the house at lunch time, sweat drenched and exhausted, then went back to the fields until it was time to wash up for dinner. He still wore his Marines baseball cap, but now he carried a bandanna handkerchief in his pocket to wipe the sweat off his neck and face. It was exactly the outfit Uncle Henry wore, like it was a uniform. Dad joked that he was used to a different type of field work—a kind that involved a lot more talking and fewer blisters. He said his old work made for a more interesting presentation at conferences.

"So, what? Did you quit on anthropology?" asked Aunt Be one night at dinner.

"Beulah, don't pester the man!" protested Grandmother. "If you want to ask a question like that, you ask it delicately."

Dad answered anyway. "The university wants me to work on a book. They say I need to have something to show for all that time before they let me teach."

"Who says? Furman?"

"And the others I talked to," said my dad. He asked her to pass the potatoes. "These sure are good potatoes," he said with sudden enthusiasm. "Just think how lucky I am that I get to help them grow!"

Marmee studied him while chewing a huge mouthful. She didn't smile at his cheerfulness. Cassie scratched her nose and asked for the butter. Mother focused on a spot on the table and said nothing.

After that, we didn't ask him about his work again.

CHAPTER 3

WE STARTED SCHOOL more than a month after everyone else. Aunt Be had arranged for Uncle Henry to pick us up in his truck for our first day, so we waited for him at the end of Grandmother's long gravel driveway. Grandmother had told Marmee and me to find the office and talk with the guidance counselor, who would sort out what classes we needed to take. She had told me everything would be all right, not to worry, but I felt fidgety, almost itchy in my stomach and lungs.

Cassie rode up front in the cab. Bernice and Julia had complained that their dresses would get wrinkled, so I volunteered that Marmee and I could sit in the back with the little boys. Billy and Dewey scooted over in the truck bed to make room for us. For once, they weren't wearing overalls. Dewey's hair was still sticking up as usual—wet from where I could tell his mother had tried to comb it down—and the knees of Billy's pants were already dirty.

Uncle Henry waited until Marmee and I settled, then he started off toward school. The road was paved but still dusty; it made me think of the bus leaving Nekemte, and I suddenly felt homesick on top of the nervousness.

My breakfast jumped in my stomach with every bump in the road. I held on to the sides of the truck tightly, hoping I wouldn't have to throw up. The metal under my fingers had small bumps in the paint, almost like a pattern, if only I could read it. The fields around us were mostly shorn, but occasionally there was some late corn or waves of a low plant I didn't recognize.

Dewey nodded at his brother in a dead imitation of their dad. "Tobaccuh's late this year, ain't it?"

Billy nodded back solemnly. "Shore is."

I fought the urge to laugh. When their sisters spoke, I wasn't struck with an accent, but Dewey and Billy sounded like they were speaking a different language. . . only I was pretty sure they meant it to be English. Marmee was staring off at the distance and seemed not to have noticed.

It took us about ten minutes to arrive at school. We pulled up next to a cluster of brick buildings, the main one long and guarded with white columns. On its other side, there was a compact elementary school, a field, and a cluster of playground equipment. Billy immediately jumped out and ran over to the see-saws. Dewey waited until the truck came to a full stop, then picked up his books and his brother's, said goodbye to his father, and walked over to where his classmates were playing running games.

Inside the cab, Julia and Bernice straightened their collars and smoothed their hair, then leaned over to kiss their father. They pushed Cassie out the door and sauntered over to join a group of girls in the shade of a big tree thick with dark leaves. All of those older girls, and the kids running around, and the high school boys standing at the brick wall punching each other, were white.

Uncle Henry tapped on the glass of the cab window to get our attention. He smiled and then waved, as if to remind us it was time to get out.

I took a deep breath. "Come on, Marmee."

We slid out of the truck and stood to the side with Cassie. Uncle Henry pulled away, slowly, so as not to kick dust all over us.

When I put my arm around Cassie's shoulders, I could tell how tense she was. Her eyes searched the kids running around the playground.

"Look," I pointed. "There's that girl from next door that you've been playing with. What's her name?"

"Bunny," said Cassie. Just then, the girl looked over, smiled, and waved. Cassie waved back and ran off to join her before I could even say goodbye.

Marmee's arm was shaking next to mine. I brushed a streak of dust off her skirt and tucked behind her ears some pieces of hair that had escaped from her braid, then I took her hand. My beaded bracelet tugged at my wrist, and I adjusted it back into its place over the tan lines. At the last minute I had decided to leave my pomegranate seeds at Grandmother's for safekeeping, and I felt their absence in my pocket like a worrisome weightlessness.

"It feels so strange to wear one braid," Marmee said, finally looking at me. "My hair feels so loose."

I nodded. "I hate how it keeps falling into my face."

She smiled a small smile. "*Nagaa xinnoo simbirroo,*" she said. That was what Kinci's mother cooed to her when she was afraid or hurt, what Kinci said to her siblings, what I said to Marmee and Cassie when they were crying. *Peace, little bird.* Hearing it here felt like a secret code, like a breath of warm air, like a marching drum. I straightened my shoulders and smiled back at her.

"*Nagaa xinnoo simbirroo,*" I said back to her.

Peace, little bird, I repeated to myself. I just need to get through today, and I will be all right. I will get back to our village and our friends, back among the corn fields and fig trees, goat herds, clay ovens, and thatched roof houses, where I belong. I just have to make it through a little while until then.

※

When the bell rang, Marmee and I watched our cousins and their group. We followed them at a distance, through the open double doors into the yawning hallway.

Inside, the building was lit dimly, with strange bulbs at weird angles. Voices echoed all around us, punctuated by the metallic sounds of small doors opening and clanging shut. The other students knocked into Marmee and me as they went by. Then I realized that the group of girls in front of us had disappeared. There was no one to follow.

I stood there holding Marmee's hand, looking around for something, anything that would give us a clue for where to go. All the other students were standing around metal boxes that lined the walls, some putting things inside, some talking to others in groups, leaning against the metal doors.

"Where's the office?" Marmee asked me.

I shrugged. I found a metal box without a guard and opened it to see what was inside.

"Hey! What are you doing? That's my locker," a boy yelled behind me.

I didn't turn around or stop to apologize; I just pulled Marmee away as fast as I could. When we turned a corner, the next hallway was quieter, and I saw large doors marked "Office."

We asked the woman at the front desk for help, and she summoned a tall, middle-aged woman in glasses, who introduced herself as the guidance counselor. Fifteen minutes later, after a lot of questions we answered mostly with shrugs, she handed us pieces of paper, which she said were our schedules.

She said, "We'll try this and see how that works. It sounds like your schooling has been. . . irregular. But I'd prefer to put you with other students your age, at least at first. Adelaide, I'll give you a typical eleventh grade schedule, and Mary, I'll put you in tenth grade classes even though you're a little young for them. I think you'll fit in better with them as a group. I'll talk to your teachers, and then we'll meet again at the end of the week to see how it's working."

I nodded, even though I wasn't sure what I was agreeing to.

She paused and studied us as if we worried her, then continued. "Just follow this schedule to see what classes you have and when. These are the room numbers and the names of the teachers. If you get lost, just ask anyone and they can point you in the right direction." She looked down at her notebook and shook her head. "I can't believe this is your first day of school ever."

"Only of regular school," Mary murmured.

The guidance counselor looked over her glasses at us, as if she were about to say something confidential, but there was a knock on the door, interrupting her. She changed her expression and sent us on our way. "Ladies, have a wonderful day. Please come see me if you need anything." She opened the door, and there stood a tall, dark-blond boy. His curious gaze met mine before I realized it and looked away. "Come on in, Justin," said the guidance counselor. He nodded at us and smiled, but I felt defensive, like I might be standing in the wrong place again or like I might suddenly make him and that entire hallway full of people turn on us.

The guidance counselor closed the door behind him, and there was nowhere for Marmee and me to go except forward, to the first room marked on our schedules, where the classes had already started.

I sat through four classes in the morning. Before I entered a room, I double- and triple-checked the numbers of the classrooms and picked a seat at the back of the room. A few times someone headed toward my seat, stopped to stare at me, and then sat elsewhere. Teachers alternately made me stand at attention and introduce myself or ignored me completely. The desks were old, scarred wood that had once been painted dark green but were now a chipped mixture of tan wood, green paint, and pencil markings. In one class, my desk had a long list of initials. In another class, there was a drawing of a rocket. The chairs were attached to the right arm of the desk, so I was closed in on three sides. The small backs of the chairs kept digging horizontally into the middle of my spine, which made it hard to sit still. I copied everything my classmates did.

Julia was in one of my classes, and Bernice was in two others, but they didn't talk to me. They barely even nodded at me, but Julia smiled pointedly at the dress I was wearing. I recognized a girl from Grandmother's church, but she didn't talk to me either: she just leaned close to her friends with her hand up to cover her mouth. They glanced in my direction and laughed. I didn't see the blond boy again.

Later on in the morning, there was a black boy in my algebra class—familiarly tall and angular and dark skinned in the multitude of white faces around me. He sat by himself in the row furthest from the door, head down, eyes on his textbook, speaking to no one. I tried to sit next to him, but the only available seat was at the very back. After class, he disappeared before I could talk to him, and I didn't catch his name from the teacher's roll call.

Right after that class I saw two black girls in the hallway, walking closely together through the throng of other students. They were too far away for me to speak to them. Still, just seeing them made me feel more at home—not everyone at this school was white.

I wished again that Kinci was with me, or Maicaah. I imagined the way Kinci's lip would jut out at the strange gestures of the teachers and the way she would put my whispering classmates in their place. I imagined the way Maicaah's arm would feel around my shoulders if he were here and were allowed to hug me again.

But he wasn't with me, and neither was Kinci. I kept my head down, my pencil steady as I traced the letters carved into the desk and tried not to cry, thinking of my friends.

After the fourth class, the crowd moved like animals in the shade. Students lingered in the classroom, talking in groups or leisurely gathering their things.

Bernice stopped by my desk on her way out the door, surrounded by her bevy of friends. "Doing all right, Adelaide? Are you buying lunch or did you pack one?"

"Oh, it's lunch time?" I asked.

Her laugh sounded like nutmeg against a spice grinder, up and down. "You didn't know it was lunch time?" The other girls followed her lead to laugh at me too. "Poor Adelaide," she said. Then they walked away.

May your animals eat bad grass and make you sick with it, I thought.

I took the lunch bag Aunt Be had sent with me and followed the stream of students until I found a door that led outside.

In the crisp sunlight of the yard, a few of the younger students were sitting on the playground equipment. Some boys were playing with a ball in the field. Some girls were gathered under the shade of the big tree.

They were white, all of them. None of them looked my way; they seemed caught up in their own little groups. I wished Marmee had the same lunch period, but we'd compared our schedules when we got them, and nothing overlapped.

Instead, there were the girls who had laughed behind their hands, and the boys who had stopped me in the hallway to ask if I lived with elephants. They hadn't waited for an answer before they walked away making animal sounds.

I looked for somewhere quiet to sit and eat by myself. "*Nagaa xinnoo simbirroo,*" I told myself. I took a deep breath and let it out.

I walked around a building and was relieved when the noise

faded somewhat and I spotted some stairs to a side door, half hidden in the shadow of a tree that grew next to the handrail.

Just then, five black students came around the other corner, swinging their brown bags and laughing. They glanced at me but reached the stairs first and sat down, opening their lunches immediately, as if they owned the spot.

I recognized the boy from my algebra class and the two girls from the hallway. The other girl looked familiar—high cheekbones just like Kinci, almond-shaped eyes and long eyelashes just like Maicaah, Ibsituu's wide forehead. She was wider than anyone from my village, but she was Oromo—she had to be. How had she gotten here? Would she know my village? Who was she related to?

I walked the last few steps quickly, smiling. Here was someone I belonged with, amidst all the strangeness of this place.

When I got closer, the other four stopped to stare at me, but I knew they'd soon understand.

"*Akkam bultan, addee.*" I bent my neck in a formal bow, hoping my good manners would help.

She didn't greet me back. I reached out my hand, in case she thought I was being too formal.

Then, in English, someone asked, "What are you doing?"

The girl who had spoken was thinner. She had short, curly hair and big, blue rhinestone earrings. She looked more Tigray than anything, probably mixed with something else. Her tone was somewhere between suspicious and curious.

The wide Oromo girl didn't say anything. She hadn't taken my hand, either. I lowered it. "I was saying hello," I told the girl with the earrings.

I switched back to Oromiffa. It was kind of rude to speak again before the Oromo girl acknowledged me, but I was too eager to talk with her.

"Is your family well?" I tried greeting her as if we were already friends. She still didn't respond. "Forgive my rudeness," I said. "I am just so glad to see someone who looks familiar. I know I'm white, but I come from a village in Welega, near Nekemte."

She kept staring, unmoving, the planes of her cheeks slack. Her friends had all stopped eating also.

Finally she spoke—in English. "Girl, what in hell are you saying?"

"Who is she?" The girl with the blue earrings lowered her voice and leaned slightly toward her friends, still studying me.

"Ain't that the new girl?" the girl with lighter, tan-colored skin asked the boy next to her.

"Why are you here, white girl? Go be with your own kind!" The Oromo-looking girl shooed me away as if I were a chicken or a goat.

"You're the one who just moved here from Africa." The darkest-skinned boy suddenly leaned toward me, around the tan girl. "Were you speaking an African dialect?"

"You didn't understand?" I asked the Oromo-looking girl.

Her eyes narrowed.

The disappointment was more than I could handle, on top of everything else.

"Are you crying?" The other two girls looked at each other. "Why are you crying?"

"She going to get us in trouble," said the boy from my algebra class.

"We didn't do nothing! Why she crying?"

I turned my back to them and sat on the bottom step, huddled against the railing. I didn't want to cry, not at school, not when the day was still going on, when I had to go back inside in a little bit. But the fact that even they couldn't understand me was worse than anything else so far. The white people were all strange-looking, foreigners, and I didn't expect them to understand me. This girl had looked so familiar, it had been like a taste of home. But the reality was that no one here knew what my life was like. No one had any idea where I'd come from.

I pressed my face into my skirt and hugged my legs, pushing the hard bones of my knees into my cheekbones, my nose, my eye sockets. My breath shook with the effort it took to not cry. The cold metal handrail pressed against my arm. I wished myself miles and miles away from all this strangeness and these strangers.

I felt a hand very lightly touch my back. "Hey, hey, girl. It's okay. It's okay."

Further away, I heard a different voice whisper, "Is she touched in the head? Why she crying?"

I looked up and clenched my jaw so my chin wouldn't waver. "You're just as American as the white kids!"

All five of them stared at me. The girl with blue earrings pulled her hand away from my back. Her voice stiffened. "You thought we were African?"

Then they all burst out laughing. The darkest-skinned boy stuck his chin out. "Damn straight we are."

"You are?" My breath caught, for a second. Then the others laughed harder, and I felt foolish.

"No, we aren't," said the girl with blue earrings. Her voice was kind. "None of us has ever lived anywhere other than Greenville. You're right—we're just as American as the white kids."

The darkest boy straightened. "We are too African. It is our heritage, and we should claim it." He was not as tall as the other boy, nor as tall as Maicaah, but his voice echoed in his chest in a way that commanded attention. His head was closely shaved, and there was a visible start of a moustache. His eyes were serious.

"What part of Africa did you come from?"

The girl with blue earrings rolled her eyes. "Honey, our families have been here since before our great-great-grandparents. Do you understand?"

"What does it matter? *Why* are you sitting with us?" The Oromo-looking girl still had her arms crossed. Her hair was cut short so that it jutted out around her face in the shape of a triangle.

I could tell from her tone I wasn't supposed to be there. "I didn't really want to sit with anyone else."

"You could get in trouble with the other white kids," said the girl with tan-colored skin. "And the teachers." She swept her hair, light brown and straight, over her shoulder. She spoke as patiently as if she was explaining things to a toddler.

"If you sit with us, they won't know what to do with you," said the girl with the earrings.

I looked at the white kids playing ball. "They don't know what to do with me anyway," I said. "I'd rather sit with you. If it's all right with you."

They looked at each other. The boy from my algebra class frowned, and the girl with triangle hair crossed her arms over her chest. The girl with blue earrings shrugged and looked away, and the girl with tan-colored skin smiled. The darkest-skinned boy nodded once and introduced himself as Nathan.

As I hesitantly opened the lunch sack Aunt Be had given me, Nathan leaned his forearms onto his knees and stared off into the distance. "You probably know Africa better than anyone else around here. What part of Africa were you in?"

"Ethiopia."

"King Haile Selassie! I heard he's descended from the Queen of Sheba and Solomon in the Bible. They say the lineage has been unbroken since the 10th century *BC*." The others kept eating their lunches without catching his enthusiasm. "It's not a very big country, right? Did you get to see him? What's he like?"

"Who?"

"The king! Haile Selassie!

"No. . . I lived in a little village. I think the king lived in the capital city."

"What was it like?" asked the girl with the lighter skin and straight hair. Sarah May, she said her name was.

I answered the first things that came to mind. "Open. Warm. Quiet. Brown. Green. Rough. Beautiful."

All of them stared at me. I smiled. It was the first time I'd spoken about Ethiopia in a way that felt true.

"That sounds nice," said the girl with blue earrings, and she smiled as if she'd just decided I was all right.

The boy from my algebra class flicked his gaze away from me, but he looked like he was thinking about a place that was like what I'd described.

The girl with the triangle hair—the one who *wasn't* Oromo—turned her back to me. "I went to New York once. It was so noisy you wouldn't believe. I was glad to go home."

"Show off!" The girl with blue earrings pushed her arm. The triangle-haired girl stiffened and wrinkled her nose like a bulldog. The others laughed.

"I'm going to live in New York someday," said Sarah May, leaning toward me.

The girl with the triangle hair shook her head. "The question is whether Nathan is going to get a good enough job to take care of you there. My daddy says it's expensive, even for lawyers."

"What do you want to do in New York, anyway, besides keep house for Nathan?" asked the girl with blue earrings.

Sarah May crossed her arms. "What you mean by that, Miss Wendy?"

Wendy—with the earrings—feigned innocence.

The boy from my algebra class made kissing noises at Nathan. "No, not Nathan," he said. "We're supposed to call him something else. . ." Wendy and the other girl laughed.

"It's Equiano," said Sarah May, lifting her chin. "After the man who helped end slavery in the British Empire."

"So he's going to trade in his good Bible name to be the same as some old British man?"

Wendy's earrings caught the light as she turned to me. "Nathan wants to be an activist, like the Reverend King." Her mouth was a little wide, always moving, as were her long, thin eyebrows. There was a pencil-sketch of a scar under her right eye.

"Who?" I said. Immediately I wished I had kept my mouth closed and let them talk without me. "I just moved here," I mumbled. "I didn't think there was a king. Who is he?"

"Elvis," said the boy from my algebra class, straight-faced, looking at me from the corner of his eye. Everyone else laughed.

"No, man," said Nathan. "Elvis is old news. Besides, he didn't come up with anything new. He's the white man's king because they don't know any better." Suddenly he caught himself and looked at a point just beyond me. There was a pause again, and he couldn't seem to think of anything else to say.

"Who's Elvis?" I asked.

Again, laughter. At least it broke the tension, even if they were laughing at me.

Wendy leaned forward, still laughing. "Reverend King is a preacher in Alabama who's working for the rights of black people. Elvis is a rock and roll musician."

"Oh," I said. "Thanks."

"You don't know nothing!" said girl with triangle hair.

"Leave her be," said Wendy. "You wouldn't know nothing either if you moved to Africa after living here your whole life, I don't care what Nathan says about it being our homeland."

"This is our chance to learn from someone's first-hand experience in Africa," said Nathan.

"Should I call you Equiano?" I asked seriously.

His chest started to poke out, but Sarah May answered for him. "Nathan's fine. If you called him Equiano around other people, they wouldn't know who you were talking about. Things confusing enough as it is."

I nodded, and the rest of the lunch time Nathan asked me questions about religion, clothing, and agriculture in Ethiopia. It had gone back to feeling like I was describing some other place, not my home.

To tell him about *home*, I would have talked about the cape chestnut tree, the field between our village and the stream, the way the thatch roof of our house looked in the dark, the taste of figs and pomegranates. I would have told him about Kinci and Maicaah and Ibsituu and the others. But he wasn't asking about my home—he was asking about life in Africa.

Still, it felt good to talk about it. I realized it was the first time anyone in Carolina had asked me about my previous life.

In between questions, I learned the name of the tall boy from my algebra class: Judah, whom they called Lion. The wide girl with the triangle haircut was Frederica. By the end of lunch, I wasn't sure I liked Frederica, and I couldn't figure out Lion. I was hopeful, though, about Sarah May, and I knew I wanted to be friends with Wendy. I liked Nathan too, despite his intensity.

When the bell rang, Wendy pointed me to my next class, making sure I knew where it was. When we went separate directions down the hallway, she smiled and waved slightly. I felt I now had one ally against the homogeneity of unfamiliar faces.

After school, I waited for my sisters on the school's front lawn, and we trudged back together. I felt exhausted, and I couldn't wait to take a nap. Marmee and I said little on the walk to Grandmother's, but Cassie had lots of questions. As soon as we got to the house, I went straight to our bedroom.

I fell asleep counting the number of days until I turned eighteen.

CHAPTER 4

In the village there had been a clear difference between sunlight and shade, day and night, but in Greenville the house was bright even in the dark, and there were lights on at school even in the daytime. After a week or so, I started to get used to the different boundary markers of the day: the bells for classes, the weight of the books on my walk to and from school, the stiffness of school clothes versus faded home clothes.

Toward the end of my second week of school, I headed over to join Wendy and Sarah May in the sunshine before classes started for the day. When I was a few feet away, a short blonde girl passed them from the opposite direction. At first I thought she was talking to herself, because she wasn't looking at them.

"You better clean that bench when you get up from it or decent people won't be able to sit there. There's no 'For coloreds only' sign." She kept walking, head high.

Sarah May stared straight ahead and just clasped her hands tightly on her neatly ironed skirt. Wendy was also silent, her eyes lowered.

"What was that?" I asked. I didn't understand why they weren't reacting more strongly. Neither of them even answered. "That was really rude."

Wendy looked as if she'd just caught me in a lie. "*Rude*," she said. "A lot of people are *rude*." She waved a hand in front of her face.

"That's just *Miss* Tara-Lee Kensington," said Sarah May. "My mama work for her family two days a week. Tara-Lee thinks that give her the right to boss me round too."

"If this weren't school," said Wendy, "I'd bite her like my little brother used to do me when he got mad." Sarah May's face still didn't relax.

I couldn't get over the blonde girl's tone. "Do other people talk to you like that, too?"

Wendy was looking at me as if she was holding a shield and I was on the other side. "Where you been, girl? *Everyone* say stuff like that to us, every day since we started here."

"What do you mean, 'started here'? Didn't you always go to school here?" I looked over at the playground, where Cassie was playing tag with other kids.

Sarah May and Wendy looked at each other, deciding who would explain. Wendy squinted at me. "You really haven't heard about all the commotion at the beginning of the year? This is the first year they allowed us here at this school, the first year there are any black kids at any white school in Greenville County."

I thought they must be kidding at first, but they weren't. "What changed?"

Wendy smoothed the creases of her skirt. "Frederica's daddy was tired of it all. It's unconstitutional for them to keep us out of the white schools—the Supreme Court decided that ten years ago. *Ten years* ago. . . but still Greenville County said it's better to keep the schools separate. White kids get newer textbooks, ones that are up to date, desks that aren't totally destroyed, nicer buildings," she gestured at the white columns in front of us. "All that. So Frederica's daddy, he got some other parents together, and they sued the school board to let us come here. And we won. The school district is still fighting with an appeal, but for now, here we are."

I supposed I'd been too caught up in my own adjustment to realize the tension around me. "Did you choose to come or did your parents make you?" I asked finally.

Wendy crossed her arms and straightened her back. "I volunteered. I didn't want to just talk about working for equality and justice, and I didn't want to wait until college to *do* something. Besides, Sterling's a good school, but I felt I'd gotten all I could from it. I wanted more options."

"You aiming to do college, girl?" Sarah May made a clicking sound. "My mama make me work hard at high school because she don't want me to turn out like her, but she can't make me go to no college."

"But you were still willing to switch schools?"

"Oh, I was tired of Sterling." She examined the ends of her hair. "People were mean. . . said I was stuck up. My mama gets my clothes from the Kensingtons. Ain't my fault nobody else in our neighborhood have clothes like these."

"My sister said our stores don't even sell anything like those clothes," said Wendy. "And my sister would know: she works at Shirby Vogue. That store is so fancy, the owners won't even let you look in the windows if your clothes don't look just right."

I thought my cousins were the only ones stuck on clothes. In the village, if someone's clothes were particularly ratty or faded, others might make comments about her mother's laziness, but no one laughed at someone else's good fortune or need. Everyone knew the tables could turn quickly enough. I rubbed my fingers across the beads of my bracelet, missing home.

"Frederica was one of them who used to pick on me the most," said Sarah May.

"She's always been a bully." Wendy waved her hand at her shoulder.

"Frederica? And you're friends with her now?"

They both shrugged. "There's only five of us at this school. We have to stick together. No one else to talk to."

"I didn't really expect to become friends with the rest of y'all," Wendy said to Sarah May. "I guess it was inevitable." She turned to me. "The second day of school, some white boys started picking on Frederica in the cafeteria, calling her ugly names. She was in a corner all by herself and the boys were getting meaner and meaner."

Sarah May smiled. "Nathan stepped in, and Lion followed. Our boys didn't do nothing or say nothing; they just stepped between the white boys and Frederica. Wendy and I walked away with her, Nathan and Lion behind us. All of us together were strong enough to stop it."

"For that day," said Wendy.

"After the first month it mostly died down," Sarah May told me. "I guess too many other schools around the country have done this. They know there's no turning back once it's started."

"A lot of people still angry," said Wendy.

"Why only you five? Did no one else want to come?" I had so many questions.

Wendy shrugged. "Nathan was eager to sign up, and Frederica's daddy convinced his parents to let him. He also convinced my grandparents. As soon as Lion heard about it, he begged his parents to let him come too. Frederica's daddy said the more of us there were, the easier it would be for us. No seniors wanted to come, right before graduation. A couple sophomores and freshmen wanted to switch, but their families were too scared. So we get to be the groundbreakers. If we make it through the year, there'll probably be some more kids next year."

"I see," I said. Then: "You're so brave."

Sarah May and Wendy laughed as if I was joking. "I don't know what to say to that." The bell rang for the beginning of school, and they kept laughing as we walked toward the entrance. But the closer we got to the others thronging the building, their posture changed and their expressions became more closed off. No one else said anything to them on that short walk, but suddenly I realized the tension in the bubble of space that surrounded them.

Once I was aware of it, I saw signs of the hostility everywhere.

In the hallways, people sometimes purposefully jostled them and didn't bother to say *excuse me.* The teachers ignored them. No one other than me ever sat next to them. No one asked if they would lend a pencil. There were glares whenever anyone had to stand near them or pass papers to them in class.

People treated me differently, too, with a mixture of curiosity, standoffishness, and disdain. I wasn't sure if it was because I was new, because I was from a foreign place, or because of who I was friends with, but I didn't sense the same edge of threat directed toward me as toward my new friends.

Only once did I see someone act purposefully kind to them. After lunch one day, Wendy was trying to pull a book out of the mess in her locker. She upset a pile, and six heavy textbooks tumbled out before she could stop them. Some boys walking past laughed as she jumped out of the way just in time. But a blonde boy, in a navy blue football jacket, stooped and picked them up for her. Justin, from the guidance counselor's office on my first day.

"Careful, these could maim you," he said, handing them back to her with a smile.

When he walked away, his wake was marked by whispers traveling down the hallway.

"Justin Macalister," said Wendy in a low voice, watching him rejoin his group. "No wonder all the girls talk about him in the girls' bathroom."

I wanted to ask what she meant by that tone, but she shook her head and shrugged.

Something about his smile in that hallway brought a sudden,

vivid memory of Maicaah, age thirteen or so, looking me in the eyes and speaking soothingly to calm me down, even as he carried my sister. He had gone running out to meet me when he heard me screaming. I was too breathless to explain that Marmee had hit her head falling out of a tree and was too dizzy to walk. He didn't ask any questions, just followed me to where my sister lay, and then he helped her onto his back. The older women had all clucked at the way he had jumped up when I called, but he had made me know everything was going to be all right. He was there; I wasn't alone.

The memory made me miss him wholeheartedly.

The following week, Bernice walked home with me from school one day while my sisters ran on ahead. Bernice said her mother needed some pickling spices from Aunt Be.

"We need a second car," she said. "Then Julia and I could drive it to school. And we wouldn't have to walk everywhere when my dad goes to Atlanta."

My scoff made me sound like Aunt Be. "You live ten minutes from school. That would be such a waste of a car."

"Don't sound so high-and-mighty, Miss. You should be nice to me, or I'll tell Aunt Be on you."

"Tell Aunt Be what?" I retorted, although I knew.

"I'll tell her how you eat with those colored kids. I probably shouldn't walk so close to you." She took a step away. "You might have gotten lice from them."

My anger flared. "Don't you start with me, Bernice Janine."

"Or what?"

"I'll put an African voodoo hex on you," I said.

"You wouldn't dare." I could tell she wasn't sure.

A sudden flash of inspiration. "And I'll tell everyone at school that you wet the bed when you were thirteen." Grandmother had teased her about this once.

"I did not!" Her face became the color of a red corn cob, the way it had been when Grandmother said it.

"You leave me alone, or I'll do it," I said. "People will take my word for it, since we're cousins. You better not say anything to Aunt Be."

"I wasn't serious, anyway," said Bernice. She sulked the rest of the way to Grandmother's and left right after getting the spices.

Not long after that, I became even more convinced of the importance of having Aunt Be on my side.

The more days that passed, the more I worried about how long it would be before I could go back home to the village, home to Kinci and Maicaah and Haadha Meti, the cape chestnut tree, and the stream.

When I was eighteen, my dad had said, I would be an adult, free to do as I wished. All I needed was money for the plane ticket to go back. I started to think about how I could get the money, and I decided I needed to get a job like Lion and Sarah May and Wendy's sister.

I brought it up one night at dinner.

"Dad," I said, waiting until he looked up from the mashed potatoes on his plate. "Could I get a job after school?" Under the table, I clutched the pouch of pomegranate seeds I'd put in my pocket for luck.

"A job?" said Dad.

"Why do you want a job?" asked Aunt Be.

"What kind of job?" said Grandmother.

Mother's attention was slightly enlivened. My sisters were looking at me, too.

"I don't know. . ." I said. "Maybe work as a sales clerk or at a restaurant or something. I thought it would be good to save some money. For after graduation."

"A sales clerk?" said Grandmother. "Honey, you just barely

started wearing American clothes. You wouldn't know a shoehorn from a chandelier."

"Have you caught up yet at school?" asked Dad. "You should probably just focus on that for right now."

"I think a job is a good idea," said Aunt Be. "It would be good for her to get some work experience. It could teach her some responsibility to have to work for her spending money."

Her tone was authoritative enough to be decisive. I was pretty sure my cousin Dana in boarding school didn't have to work for her spending money, and I wasn't sure what that meant about Aunt Be's opinion of her daughter.

"What about Howard's new drive-in?" said Grandmother. "He bought that place over out Poinsett Highway. They haven't opened yet, but he and Sandra plan to sell burgers and French fries and ice cream. His daughters are helping, but the youngest just found out her husband's job is moving. Howard told me the other day he's going to have to hire someone."

"I can carry food to people. I have experience doing that."

"What kind of customers do they plan to get?" asked Dad. "I wouldn't want it to be the wrong clientele."

"Oh, it'll be mostly high school and college students eating there," said Aunt Be. "Who else can stand eating in a car? And Furman's new campus is out Poinsett Highway."

"I'm sure I could do it," I said.

"Well. . ." said Dad. "Let me think about it. I feel strange about the idea of you working somewhere since you're so young. Besides, it's early to start thinking about life after you graduate."

Aunt Be grunted under her breath, and both my parents looked at her. We never talked about it again, but the following weekend, I was working Friday nights and Saturdays at Howard's drive-in, making about thirteen dollars a week. I saved every cent, and I felt like a millionaire. In the village there was rarely paper money, and women never handled it.

I dreamed of Maicaah and Kinci at the forefront of the crowd that would welcome me in Nekemte and walk back with me to the village. The village would sing proper wedding songs, and no one would say anything when they saw Maicaah and me together.

Despite my dreams, the glamour of my job quickly wore away. I hated the smell of burnt meat and charred French fries that stayed in my hair even after I washed it. I hated the sticky floors and the permanent dampness at the armpits and back of my work dress. I rankled against the way people talked down to me and treated me like furniture.

And before long, the money seemed less and less. I bought new shoes and a school skirt, birthday presents for my friends, candy for my sisters and boy cousins—and the money didn't accumulate as quickly as I thought it would. Soon the plane ticket felt like an impossible amount, but I told myself it would work out. It had to.

One day, when Aunt Be and Mother sent me to look for Marmee before dinner, I found her sitting in the horse barn, cross-legged on a hay bale, her skirt bunched up in her lap. The glasses she'd gotten after the start of school glinted oddly; I wasn't yet used to the way they changed her face. She didn't say anything when I sat down next to her. I didn't say anything either.

I'd heard she always sat by herself at school. Our cousin Julia had told me she ate lunch in the corner of the playground with her back against the brick wall, watching the younger kids as they talked and played.

"Look," she said finally, pointing. "You can see the dust motes flying in the sunlight."

I nodded. The light coming in from the barn door was so strong it looked almost solid. "How long have you been here?"

"Since I got home from school."

"I didn't see you after school. Who did you walk home with?"

"No one. Just by myself."

"Why didn't you wait for me?"

"I don't know," she said. "I thought you might have work or something."

Her tone was almost as detached as our mother's. "Aren't there any other kids in your class who walk this way?"

"I don't know," she said again. "I don't really talk to them. They don't seem that interesting. Besides, I like to be by myself."

"Even during lunch?"

"Other people interrupt the pictures I make up in my head." She was still staring at the dust motes and the sunlight.

I wondered if I was interrupting her, right then, but I wasn't going to go away. If I had interrupted her, it was too late anyway. "What sorts of pictures?"

"Pictures of the kids around me on the playground, mostly."

"Like. . . pictures from a camera?"

"Sometimes. Or sometimes I imagine them painted with oil paints. Or watercolor. I imagine myself doing the painting. I pick out what I would like to paint. Then I pick out the colors and choose a brush and decide what sorts of brushstrokes and how to blend and all that."

I didn't know that my sister knew that much about painting. "Where did you learn all that?"

"All what?"

"About painting."

"From school and books and stuff, I guess." She straightened a little, and I could hear more animation in her voice.

I asked, "Have you ever actually painted? With oils, or watercolor?"

"No. But when we were in Rome, I saw someone painting on the street corner."

"Oh." All I remembered from Rome was the Colosseum and our host explaining its history as the sun made the shadows long. There was also a mime in black clothes and a white face—I had started to feel claustrophobic watching him knock his fist against invisible walls. When had there been a painter? What else had Marmee seen that I missed? "Can you describe one for me? One of the pictures in your head?"

Mary looked as if she was assessing my level of seriousness. Her lenses made her eyes look magnified, and the plastic frames angled upward made her seem older.

"Yesterday it was a boy on the tall slide." Her hands moved around to gesture, breaking the stillness. "He was perched at the top, holding on to the sides with both hands. At first I thought he was waiting for his turn, but there was no one at the bottom of the slide. It was hard to tell from where I was sitting, but I think his hands were shaking."

Hay was poking into the backs of my calves. "How old was he?"

She frowned, as if that was the wrong question. "I don't know; probably five. Younger than Cassie."

I nodded, trying to find the right question to keep her talking. "How would you have painted it?"

"From the middle of the slide. In oils, I think. . . like red and orange." She looked at me to see if I was really listening. "I think the background would have been a tannish brown. And maybe a magenta, or darker purple, for the slide. His arms and legs would be orange, and his hands I think yellow with streaks of red. His face would be the most interesting. . . the focal point, you know, with highlights of really pure yellows and reds. I'd want there to be contrast. I think more lines would really show his concentration."

I could imagine the picture, her words filling color into the lines sketched by her hands moving through the air. I wished she could paint it and make it a reality for others to see also. I didn't want to spoil the mood, so I waited for the moment to pass, for the picture to fade back into the sight of the barn.

"I can see the colors so clearly," she continued. "Yellow and brownish red and bright orange. Like the colors of the sun setting in the village, you know?"

Those were exactly the colors I was picturing. I nodded, and she smiled like I hadn't seen her smile in a long while.

"Where do you get paints like that?" I asked.

"Paints like what?"

"Like those oils you were talking about. Or the watercolors."

She sighed. "They don't carry them in the stores downtown. And they're not in the Sears catalogue. I don't think the stores downtown could even order them. Maybe they could."

"What about at school?"

She snorted, sounding like one of the horses. "Mr. Randolph thinks looking at textbooks is all the art education we need."

"Does he know of any way to get the paints?"

"No. I asked him already. Besides, they'd be too expensive."

"How do you know?"

She sighed again. "In London I saw a stationery store that was selling oils for two pounds."

"Two pounds? That doesn't sound like that much."

Mary shook her head. "Each tube. And then there's the paper, a special kind of paper that costs another three pounds. And the brushes. The good ones cost a pound each. And it's better with an easel, which is another two pounds. I don't know what it would be in dollars."

"Oh." That did add up. "Are you sure it wasn't just an expensive store? Maybe it was just because it was London. Everything was more expensive in London."

She shrugged. "I just know they're expensive."

"What about watercolors?"

"I don't know," she said. "I didn't check."

So she'd prefer to have the oils.

"Watercolors are harder to control," she told me. "That's what I've read. And with oils, you can combine colors more easily and predict the result. In Rome, the man on the street would mix the tiniest bit of blue into yellow, and it would make a really pretty light green."

As we headed back in toward the kitchen, I kept thinking about how her face had brightened, talking about her pictures and the paint. Her birthday was a month away, and I determined to find some oil paints, even if I could only afford paper, a tube of red, a tube of yellow, and a tube of green.

Dad said he was working on his book in the evenings. After dinner he retired to the sitting room and closed the door. He stayed in there until after I went to bed, but he never talked about how it was going.

He still attended conferences. Now, however, he was being invited to speak at missions conferences at local churches, instead of academic gatherings. He wanted us to go with him when he spoke, and he bribed us with driving lessons afterward in Grandmother's Crosley station wagon, so I went on the Saturday mornings Howard didn't need me at the drive-in.

At one church, a white haired woman in a floral print dress came up to my sisters and me where we were sitting off to one side waiting for our dad. "I knew your mama from the time she was a baby," she said. "I remember when your family left. You two older girls were itty bitty, and now you're so darling and so grown up. . . I was sorry to hear your mother couldn't be here today. Please tell her hello for me."

A young woman walked over. She had crooked front teeth and a baby on her hip. "Are y'all the girls from Africa?" she asked, bouncing the baby. "You don't look it." She smiled shyly at her own joke. We heard it at least once at every new place we visited.

"No, we aren't!" Cassie looked at me, waiting for me to defend her, but I wasn't sure what she was refuting.

"Cassie, behave," I said. "Yes, ma'am, thank you for coming."

"No," said Cassie. "We aren't from Africa. Greenville is our home, just like everyone else. . . Just leave us alone!" She burst into tears.

She, the one who was actually born there, who had been baptized into the tribe, who had been claimed by the village as a native-born daughter in a way the rest of us never were.

Through her tears, she was still waiting for me to say something. "Adelie, you tell them! Tell them we're from *here*," she insisted. "We belong here."

When I shook my head, finally, not trusting myself to speak, not knowing where to start, she ran off. She ran so hard her skirt flew as if trying to bite her ankles. She didn't talk to me the rest of the day. As soon as we got back to Grandmother's, she ran off to play with her friends from the neighboring farm.

When Cassie washed up for dinner that night, she splashed water from the faucet like it had always been limitless. Her beaded bracelet was gone, the tan lines almost faded from around her wrist.

When I kissed her good night, she smelled of child sweat and cut grass and fried chicken. When she said *good night* back to me, her voice held the same accent as the kids from school.

Later that night, after Marmee had already turned over once in her sleep, I slipped on my shoes, opened my window, and slid out onto the roof of the back porch. I had to walk carefully because the roof slanted downward, but I didn't mind. This had become the place where I could think.

In the moonlight, I took the pomegranate seeds out of my pocket and shook them free of their pouch, holding them in the open palm of one hand. They were so small; all five could have fit on a dime with room to spare. Two of them were flaking, and I picked at the edges of the outer skin. Like picking at a scab—I knew I shouldn't, but it was hard not to. I closed my fingers around the seeds and put them back in their pouch, where I couldn't harm them further.

What if Maicaah were to appear suddenly in Carolina, come to see me, come to take me home? I hugged my knees, imagining it. Maybe someday at work I'd turn to the driver of a new car and it would be him. Maybe he'd found gold or sold a lot of really nice hides at the market, enough money to buy a plane ticket to come see me. Maybe I'd see him walking up Grandmother's driveway, wearing American clothing: coat and tie, hat pushed back on his head. Somehow he would see me on the roof of the back porch, and he'd climb up fluidly and sit out there with me until the sun came up. Maybe he was on his way even now.

I was getting tired of waiting. I felt the need to move, to do something, go somewhere. If I went down the regular way, inside, I'd wake Marmee and maybe even Cassie. So I left the pomegranate seeds on the windowsill and climbed down the trellis at the corner of the porch, careful not to miss my footing or to make too much noise. I jumped the last few feet, landing in the soft grass.

It had been a long time since I'd run. I checked to make sure I didn't hear voices coming after me, and then I ran away from the house, toward the fields, past the barn. It was awkward in my nightgown and shoes. I hitched my gown up over my knees and kept running until my breath was short and my shoes rubbed against my heels.

I was out of practice. I paused, pulled off my shoes, and kept running, carrying the shoes against my chest like a baby.

I ran until I reached a fence. Somehow I'd made it to the end of Grandmother's land; on the other side of the fence was a dark, paved road. The fence posts were leaning in all directions, and the barbed wire between them was rusting. Dad would have to fix it eventually. More of this work that wasn't the kind he wanted to do.

I held on to the fencepost, trying to catch my breath. Parts of my hair had slipped free of the braid; it had been fun to run with my hair streaming behind me. My feet were more sensitive than they had been—I could feel the ground, soft under my feet. It smelled peaceful and comforting. The stars were in dramatically different positions than they'd been in in the village, as if more than a couple of months had passed.

Mother fit in here, that was easy to see. Here, she had a confidence of small gestures—security with the paring knife that she'd never had with the machetes the women in the village used. Here, she could make the beds with crisp sheets tucked into hospital corners; she could peel potatoes and snap green beans with an ease and efficiency of movement that the other mothers, but never she, had had in the village. Here, she greeted her sisters and her childhood friends with more energy than she'd shown toward us in a year. She didn't leave the house very often, but when we could persuade her to, or when someone else arranged to visit, she bloomed and acted almost like her normal self, the way she'd been before the baby came.

Dad still referred constantly to our life in the village. But when he spoke about it, it was in ways that I barely recognized. He made it sound exotic, idealistic, as if everyone was always sitting around, talking.

Maybe that was what the village had been like for him, I suddenly realized. My dad's work had been talking with people; then he'd leave to attend conferences in Europe. Mother had been the one who had to clean the dirt floors, cook over open fire pits, keep bats out of the thatch roof. Dad hadn't had to figure out what to do with grain that mice had gotten into, when there wasn't anywhere we could get other grain. Dad sat with the other men at meal times and was always gone for conferences when the other men were harvesting.

He was even gone when Mother had the baby, when she was sweating and crying out. It was Marmee and I who cleaned up afterward with the village women. We were the ones who kept

Cassie out of the way and took care of Mother and prepared the small, ever-still body for burial. By the time Dad came home, there wasn't even a trace of blood.

And yet, how could we accuse him for doing his job? The very job that had taken us to the village, without which I would never have known Ethiopia?

Going back to Grandmother's house took me longer than I expected. I had run further than I realized, and on the way back I had to stop and catch my breath more often.

I was shivering when I reached the edge of the yard. My feet were especially sore and cold from the ground. I tied my shoes together by the laces and hung them around my neck, then climbed back up the trellis and in through the window. Marmee lifted her head as I snuck in, but she just smiled sleepily and rolled over.

CHAPTER 5

ABOUT A MONTH AFTER I STARTED SCHOOL, I thought I was settling in decently well—well enough to survive until I could make it back to the village. I was proud of how well I was handling everything.

Then Aunt Be stepped in, and everything fell apart.

That day, I walked home with Cassie and the other little kids after school. I hadn't been able to find Marmee, so I figured she'd gone home by herself again. Cassie chased the kids from the farms beyond ours as we passed through the old mill neighborhoods, all the houses matching and in disrepair.

I recited the list of kings and queens of England, which I had to learn for my next history test, but I got lost among the Henrys and the Edwards. When we reached the first open fields of the farms, I tried to recite the passage of Shakespeare we had to memorize for literature class, but the unfamiliar language kept tripping me up. Wendy and Lion both had tricks to help them memorize things like this; I would have to ask them for their tips.

When we reached our long driveway, Cassie hesitated, and I took her books. "Just come home before dinner, mind." She smiled and ran after the neighbor kids.

I went around to the back porch, and Aunt Be was waiting for me at the screen door. "I need to talk to you," she said.

"What is it?" I set Cassie's books on the table by the door. I kept my books, ready to climb the stairs to my room.

She stood with her back to the sink, frowning at me. "Sit down."

"Is something wrong? My mother?"

"Nothing's wrong with your mama. She's upstairs, resting. We don't need to trouble her about this."

I nodded. Regardless of what it was, my mother didn't need it weighing on her.

I sat; Aunt Be stayed standing. She crossed her arms over the waistband of her apron.

"What is it?"

"I got a call today from the mother of one of your classmates. . . it doesn't matter who."

"What'd she say?"

"I heard who you've been eating lunch with at school."

I should have known—it was only a matter of time. "Oh?"

Aunt Be stared at me until I looked at her. "You can't sit with the. . . colored. . . children, Adelaide." Her tone was somewhere between horrified and mad.

"Why not?" I crossed my arms to mirror her. Since she was standing, my elbows weren't even as high as her hips.

"This town has laws against such things. . ."

"No, there used to be laws like that. Then there were sit-ins at Woolworth's and Kress's, right here in town—those cases from Greenville went all the way to the Supreme Court." Aunt Be's mouth puckered. My friends liked to talk about those cases, but I guessed Aunt Be didn't. I pressed my advantage. "Surely if the Supreme Court of the United States says colored people can eat at the lunch counter at Kress's, then I can sit with some colored students on the side steps of the auditorium."

Aunt Be's cheeks turned splotchy. "I don't know where you get your ideas. . ."

"You can go look it up at the library. The same library where high school students like my friends peacefully protested to use the books and were sent to jail for it."

"Young lady. . . !" she said.

I stared at her. I'd never been called that, in that tone, before. She made it sound like I'd cursed God.

". . .you are embarrassing this family and making us the subject of gossip. As part of this family, you have a responsibility to be respectable. As long as you live in this house, you will not sit with those colored people."

"I have parents," I said, "and you're not one of them."

Aunt Be and I were both trembling. "I am an adult," she said, "and you need to honor that. You and your family are here in this house at my generosity, and your ingratitude is not welcome. If your mother wasn't sick, she'd tell you the same thing."

"You're just saying that because you're mean and small minded!" My voice filled the kitchen.

And that's when my dad walked in. With him were Uncle Henry and Grandmother.

"What in the world is going on here?"

I was too angry to explain—the words stuck in my mouth like pinecones, sticky with sap.

"Adelaide is being impudent." Aunt Be jutted out her chin.

My father looked at me and set his mouth. "Adelaide, to your room," he said.

"But. . ."

"Now."

"Let me explain!"

My dad pointed upstairs without any words. I ran up the steps and slammed the bedroom door behind me.

My pillow was damp when I heard him at the top of the stairs, maybe half an hour later. I quickly closed the lid on the box where I'd hidden my pomegranate seeds.

Without asking the circumstances, without letting me tell him about my friends or the other kids at school, without asking me for my side, he told me that I was to obey Aunt Be the way I obeyed him and my mother.

"But, Dad—"

"I don't want to hear it, Adelaide."

"What she's asking me to do. . ."

"That's between the two of you. What I'm telling you is between us, and I'm telling you to listen to Aunt Be. If I hear that you've disobeyed her, you will be in big trouble. With me. No more job. No more driving lessons."

I didn't say anything. I couldn't. I just stared out the window as he left.

I didn't say anything to my sisters when they came in to wash up for dinner. I didn't say anything during dinner or while washing the dishes after. I avoided eye contact with everyone.

As I was washing dishes, Grandmother stood up from her chair and took hold of my chin, making my eyes meet hers. She looked at me, into me almost, for a whole minute. Then she grunted and gave me a hug. She didn't ask any questions, and I didn't offer any answers, but that look made me feel a small bit less alone.

Just the same, I cried myself to sleep that night.

The next day, I walked to school slowly, dragging my feet to get there right before the bell rang. It was tricky to time it right, and I ended up having to run a few blocks when I heard the first bell from far away.

In class, I kept my eyes on my desk. Between classes, I stayed at the edges of the hall, avoiding the spots where I usually stood chatting with Wendy, Sarah May, and Frederica. When lunch time came, I dashed out the side door, hoping to avoid everyone, but

Nathan and Sarah May were standing right by the door. They called after me.

"I need to get something from home," I told them.

"It's so far, girl," said Sarah May. "You'll never get back in time!"

"Borrow a bicycle!" said Nathan.

I pretended that I didn't hear him and kept running. Halfway home, I stopped in a field and ate my lunch there. I ate quickly, without conversation to distract me. The bread tasted stale, and the apple was sour. Two ants chased each other up and down stalks of grass, leaf to leaf. I turned to go back when I'd judged that enough time had passed. I walked quickly so that it would seem like I'd run the whole way home and back.

The next day I did the same thing, but I misjudged how long I'd been gone. I arrived late to class, and Mrs. Svensen wrote me up in her grade book.

The third day, I went to the bathroom straight after class and locked myself in the stall furthest from the door. I thought about going back into the hall to get my lunch, but I didn't want to brave the noise. I heard my cousin Bernice's laugh over all the other voices, and I put my head against the wall. I would stay until the noise died down.

I sat up on the tank of the toilet and put my feet on the lid so they wouldn't be visible under the stall door. The pattern of the floor tiles made interesting shapes. A square, a triangle—there was the hypotenuse. It looked just like the diagram my algebra teacher had drawn on the board, referencing types of angles for the equations that I didn't understand. I kicked my heels against the tank, hard, wishing I could rub out that hypotenuse. Why were there special names for the sides of triangles which only exist if drawn by humans, never in the real world?

I shifted and stared up at the corners, where the walls met the ceiling. *Cube*, I thought. *I am on the inside of a cube.* Cubes, by definition, have no door or opening. *I am trapped inside a cube.*

The door to the bathroom creaked open, followed by quick

footsteps. I released my breath slowly to avoid being heard, and some spots floated in front of my eyes. I breathed quietly, steadily, until the edges of my vision cleared again. The sink faucet turned on, then off. The door creaked open again, and the footsteps faded away.

"*Out, out damn spot,*" I told my interrupted eyesight. That was part of last week's assignment for English class. I had studied it before school and during lunch with Wendy, each of us prompting the other when we got stuck. I quoted as much as I could remember, and then I started again. I breathed quietly to the rhythm of the lines, and I spoke the lines to the rhythm of my heartbeat. But I couldn't think of the rest of the words without Wendy's help. I wished, again, that I was outside on the steps with them, eating my lunch peacefully, normally.

I tried instead to practice the next recitation we had to do. This one was easier for me; I quoted the first twelve lines pausing only a few times:

> *Let me not to the marriage of true minds*
> *Admit impediment. Love is not love*
> *which alters when it alteration finds,*
> *or bends with the remover to remove:*
> *O no! It is an ever-fixed mark*
> *that looks on tempests and is never shaken;*
> *It is the star to every wandering bark,*
> *whose worth's unknown, although his height be taken.*
> *Love's not Time's fool, though rosy lips and cheeks*
> *within his bending sickle's compass come:*
> *Love alters not with his brief hours and weeks*
> *but bears it out even to the edge of doom.*

There were two more lines, but I couldn't remember them. I could picture the last two lines in the textbook, carefully diagrammed and labelled *couplet*, but I couldn't think of the words for the life of me. I couldn't even remember the idea of them, which Nathan had suggested was the best way to remember what came next. Nor could I remember what letter they started with, which was how Frederica always memorized her passages. If I was sitting with them, any of them would be able to help me.

Couplet. "Bears it out even to the edge of doom..." What were those next lines? Why could I see the diagram on the page but not see the words? Couplet. Sonnet. Nothing.

I imagined Maicaah on the world map from the social studies classroom, cartoonishly rising up from Africa to bend toward the U.S., reaching for me in Carolina. The poem said love doesn't bend, but our teacher had explained that meant that feelings wouldn't change. My feelings for Maicaah certainly hadn't. I saw my finger as it had been against his knee, tracing the childhood scar. I felt his fingertips over mine, pressing my finger into his knee. We'd almost been holding hands.

I imagined what I would write to him if I could. "Dear Maicaah," the letter would say. "I hope you are well. I don't like life here. I wish you were here. I wish I *weren't* here but there with you. I wish you could send me some of your mother's coffee and Kinci's enjera and the sound of goats in the morning and the smell of the eucalyptus trees after the rain. Please tell Kinci I miss her and that I'll write to her soon. With love, Adelaide."

I imagined the cartoonish map again, me reaching out of Carolina, holding my letter toward him, reaching across from eastern Africa. Our hands would meet in the middle of the ocean. Our fingers would barely overlap, but he would grip my hand as if to never let go.

My imagination faded, and I was left staring at the bathroom stall door until the bell rang.

That week, it was hard to wake up every morning. I resented the repetitiveness of getting dressed, straightening my tousled bed, eating the same tasteless food. The same fields and animals and rocks in the road on my way to school. The same low ceiling, harsh lights, cloudy windows, noisy hallways, shrill bells. The same dank corners of the bathroom. The clang of lockers from every side, everyone headed to class after class. Day after day.

It was a relief to sleep. I dreamt of Maicaah often, and almost every night in my dreams I climbed the cape chestnut. Sometimes he was there, sometimes I waited for him, sometimes I just sat up there and reveled in the joy of being back home.

Then morning would come, and I would wake up, and I'd be in Carolina again.

CHAPTER 6

IN ALL THAT I HATED about my days, algebra was the worst. I was in the same class as Lion, but we had never sat near each other. When I stopped eating lunch with him and the others, he and I didn't acknowledge each other at all.

In algebra, three people who sat behind, beside, and in front of me were friends. The whole class they exchanged looks or mouthed words to each other or giggled behind their hands at each other's gestures. Sometimes they were so distracting that I could hardly concentrate on what Mr. Dykart was saying. It didn't help that math had never come easily for me. In the village, when we were in charge of our own schoolwork, I tended to rush through the math lessons slipshod, rarely bothering to check my answers.

I was so lost after the first week that I started to make up stories with the letters on the board. When we reached a unit on graphing polynomials, my stories were pretty developed. I was a lot more interested in them than in what was happening on the board.

Unfortunately, Mr. Dykart noticed. He loomed over me and pulled my notebook toward him.

"Miss Henderson, who are Xavier and Yvette?"

"No one, sir," I muttered. I could feel everyone's stares. I rubbed my eraser over the desk, leaving clean streaks free from pencil smudges. Lion's back was to me; everyone else looked at me with either hostility or curiosity.

"Then why are you writing their names over and over on your paper?"

By the clock, there were still twenty minutes left of class. I wished he had kept my notebook and talked to me after class. I wished he had sent me out to the hall or to the principal or anything. All I wanted was to get through the class, survive the year, turn eighteen and return to Ethiopia. Why wouldn't he just leave me alone?

"Miss Henderson?"

"Yes, sir."

"When I ask you a question, I require an answer."

"Which question, sir?" I didn't mean to be impertinent.

"Who are Xavier and Yvette, Miss Henderson?"

The class giggled. I worked to hold in my anger. I didn't need this class. I didn't need the pity or the ridicule of classmates who laughed at me. "They're people I made up."

"Why are you making up people, Miss Henderson?"

There was more laughter. I lifted my chin and looked Mr. Dykart straight in the eyes. "I came up with names to go with the letters of the equations. Sir."

Mr. Dykart glanced from my notebook to the board, as if he'd forgotten what he'd written up there. He narrowed his eyes at me and returned my notebook. "I don't know how they do things in Africa, Miss Henderson"—the whole class laughed at this— "but in Greenville we believe that mathematics and flights of fiction belong on separate sides of the hallway."

The class laughed again. I could feel my face hardening as the tone of my voice sharpened. "I'll work to remember that in the future. Sir."

He seemed to deliberate whether to call me out for disrespect or not. "Please do remember, Miss Henderson."

By then others around me had given up on the lesson as well, and there was more noise than usual in the class. A few people started throwing spitwads and crumpled papers at each other. I watched one, then another, fly between boys, hit them in the legs or the back of the neck.

I couldn't believe it. Who thought to put paper in their mouth, chew it, pull it out, and throw it at someone else? Then I felt something small, wet, and hard hit me just below my ear. I jumped out of my seat with a full-body shudder.

Mr. Dykart whipped around, and the class froze.

"Problem, Miss Henderson?"

I rubbed at my neck to rid myself of the feeling of the paper wet with someone else's saliva. I shuddered again and rubbed my hands against the sides of my skirt.

"I said: 'Problem, Miss Henderson?'"

I wanted to tell on them, tell on the whole odious class. But I didn't know who'd thrown it, and I had no evidence now. "No, Mr. Dykart. I thought I felt something is all."

He let me sit down and turned back to the board. Two minutes later, the spitwads were flying all over the room again. Two passed right in front of my face. I bent down and buried my head in my arms to avoid any more.

I didn't notice when the spitballs stopped or when Mr. Dykart turned around again. Suddenly, in the small space between my desk and my elbow, I saw Mr. Dykart's feet in front of my desk. I sat up.

"Feeling drowsy, Miss Henderson? Perhaps you'd care to go to the board yourself and work out this problem for us."

He did this sometimes, making an example of students, forcing them to the front of the classroom to admit publicly that they didn't know the answer.

"Now, Miss Henderson," he said.

I closed my notebook, stood, and walked to the front. He had drawn an axis on the board and a squiggle line over it, marked with two points where it intersected the axis. He had worked halfway through the formula. His chalk lettering left off in the middle of a line. I picked up the chalk and rolled it in my fingers, watching it turn them dusty white. I'd never held chalk before.

I lifted up the chalk to the place where he'd left off. I looked at the squiggle line and the axis again. There were the letters x, y, m. The interrupted part of the equation already had m and y, so I wrote another number and x. There were giggles from the desks. I went down to the next line and wrote p, some numbers, j, q, and r. I was writing faster now. Next line: g, s, and d. H, k, b. More numbers, w, v, t. Equals... I had forgotten the equal sign. Equals 0.

I paused, then squared the zero. I put down the chalk and dusted my hands.

"How interesting, Miss Henderson," said Mr. Dykart. "Care to enlighten us with an explanation as to why that jumble of letters is equal to zero squared?"

I knew I would be punished worse if I said anything disrespectful, so I said nothing.

"No answer? Well, Miss Henderson, could you please erase your work and state for the class that you simply do not know the answer? The beginning of knowledge is the admission that you do not know and want to learn."

I didn't answer, just erased the board—what I'd written as well as a few half-letters of his writing.

I turned and started to walk toward my seat.

"Not so fast, please, Miss Henderson," he said. He sounded tired.

I stopped and waited, even though my impulse was to stride right on by him out the door and into the hallway.

"Please clarify for the class that you do not know how to work polynomial equations."

I looked at the smug faces in the desks. They looked glad for my humiliation. I wiped my hands on my skirt. I ran my tongue across my teeth.

"Please, any minute now, Miss Henderson."

I thought of everything I knew that they didn't: how to make clothing dye from flowers, how to coax a newborn goat to drink milk, how to bake enjera over a fire, from teff we had planted, which I myself had helped mill. How to cook minnows on a flat rock in the sun. How to tie a skirt so that it stayed put even after walking fifty miles while carrying a baby. How to balance a water bucket on my head so that I could carry it without spilling a drop. How to breathe on a fire, just so, until the black coals burned golden again. How to get my mother out of bed and get her dressed when she couldn't or wouldn't move on her own. How to cry at night, without making any sounds, so no one would worry about me.

But not how to work polynomial equations.

"Miss Henderson, would you like to go to the principal's office?"

I looked Mr. Dykart in the eye. "Yes, sir."

"You would rather go to the principal's office than admit that you don't know how to work polynomial equations?"

I said nothing. He rubbed one of his eyelids with his pinkie. While he wrote the note for the principal, I waited, standing on one foot like the Oromo kids did when they were imitating hunters. The stance felt so different in shoes. I couldn't dig into the ground with my toes for balance, and all I could feel was the inside of my shoes and the pebbled bottom of the shoe against the skin of my calf.

At the principal's office, I was as quiet and respectful as anyone could wish. I told the principal I didn't understand what was on the board. I was still mad, but it was doused with a good bit of relief from being out of that room.

The principal sent me to the library for the last ten minutes of class. I put my head down on a table and was nearly asleep when the bell rang.

When I looked up, Emily Rose Martin was standing in front of me, balancing on one shoe while she scratched the back of her calf with the shoelaces of the other foot. She held her books tightly to her chest, as usual.

I knew her as the smartest girl in our algebra class, who everyone more or less left alone because she was so smart. I hadn't ever talked to her. When I arrived, she hadn't been among those who greeted me out of curiosity or among those who had made jokes at my expense.

"Are you waiting for me?" I asked.

"Mr. Dykart asked me to be your tutor for algebra. We're supposed to meet after school, twice a week, and make sure you're ready for class."

"Why?"

"Mr. Dykart can tell you're not. . . prepared in class. What days are you free after school?"

I wondered if Emily Rose ever smiled, or if she just didn't like the idea of being my tutor. She was part of that class, and maybe she hadn't been the one to throw a spitwad at me and maybe she wasn't one of the ones laughing, but I still didn't particularly want to spend time with her. But my interview with the principal hadn't left me many more options; I wouldn't be able to get through the year like this. I needed help.

"Wednesdays don't work for me," she said. "I have to be home for an early dinner before the prayer meeting at church. Any other day would be fine."

"How about Tuesdays and Thursdays?"

She nodded. "Starting tomorrow?"

"Yes, ma'am," I said. She looked offended, though I hadn't meant to be sarcastic. "I mean, thank you."

She nodded again, the same serious look in her eyes. "I'll meet you here in the library after school." She turned stiffly and walked away, looking like she was trying to take up as little space as possible.

As I switched books at my locker, I did some wishful thinking about the types of things that could come up that would prevent me from having to stay after for the tutoring session. I was sure it would be a repeat of the explanations we got in class, the same frustrating jumble of things I didn't understand—only without the background chorus of whispers and tittering. Maybe a fire would start in the school building and we'd all have to evacuate. Maybe I'd wake up in the morning with a raging headache and a high fever. Maybe there'd be a huge flood overnight and we wouldn't even be able to go to school.

I was somewhat disappointed in the morning when I awoke to a cloudless sky, feeling perfectly fine. It was school as normal, again.

After school, I found Emily Rose sitting very straight in her chair at a table by the window. I watched squirrels dig through the grass for seeds.

"You obviously don't know how to work polynomials," she said. "So what do you know?"

"I know a lot of things," I said. "Where do you want me to start?"

"Can you do addition and subtraction?"

"I'm not a baby. Of course I can add and subtract."

"Multiplication? Division?"

The textbook from which I'd learned long division had suffered water damage en route to Ethiopia, so my division skills were spotty. I nodded anyway.

"Fractions? Decimals?" Her pencil poised next to each item on the list in her notebook.

I sighed. "Look, I started having trouble with math in sixth grade. I did my best to work my way through the textbooks, but they got harder and harder to understand."

Emily Rose's pencil wavered as she looked up. "Why didn't you ask your teacher to explain it?"

Her question showed just how much she didn't understand. "I didn't go to school. We learned at home."

"Your mother taught you?"

"We taught ourselves. Our parents told us to work our way through each of the books we had."

Sometimes my friends all perched with me in a tree, gathered around a school book, and I told them which sound went with which letter and made up stories of what life was like in the places where the book had come from. Sometimes I read from the book to them, but they would get bored. Once I accidentally left a book outside, and my dad made me go back in the dark to find it. I had seen eyes in the trees, and I had screamed as loud as I could.

"You really didn't have a teacher?" said Emily Rose.

"No."

She nodded once and folded her hands. I braced myself to hear her give me up as an impossible case.

"No wonder you're struggling. You're doing very well for all that." She opened the math book, turning to the very front pages.

The rest of the hour, she went over—problem by problem, step by step—each skill I needed and was supposed to already know. She focused on the math book's review that was the first chapter. Some of it I had learned already, some of it I had half-learned, some I picked up from class this year. Some of it I had mis-learned or didn't know at all. Emily Rose explained things clearly. She also paused to ask me questions and watch me work.

Then she assigned me some problems to work on and got up to talk to the librarian. She came back with two new textbooks that she set off to the side. When I was finished with my set of problems, she checked my work and smiled at me.

"See, you've got that down now."

I nodded, glad it was done. Emily Rose made it easier than I expected.

"You're a good teacher," I said, putting away my pencils.

"Thank you," said Emily Rose, surprised. She changed the

topic quickly. "Here, I found some extra eighth and ninth grade textbooks for you." She opened the first one and circled some chapter headings on the table of contents with her pencil. "These chapters are the ones you should focus on. Read the explanations at the beginning of each chapter and then try to do the problems at the back." She kept circling more things. She opened the second book and circled more.

"How am I supposed to do all of those chapters? I can't do three years of math in one."

She barely glanced up. "You'll have to if you want to pass algebra."

"What happens if I don't?"

"Then you'd repeat it. It's a class you have to pass to graduate." She pushed the heavy extra textbooks over to me. I wasn't sure how I would be able to carry those plus my other books without dropping some.

"They could make me stay in high school to finish one class?"

She rubbed her eyelid, same as Mr. Dykart had done. "Just try a few problems from each chapter. If you already know the skill, it'll be easy. Make a note of what you don't understand, and we'll talk about it next week."

I carried that whole armful of books all the way through the old mill neighborhoods. I walked by myself, since I'd had to stay late. Just as I came to the last house, a dog jumped and started barking at me. It startled me so badly I dropped my pile of books. The dog was on the other side of a fence, but I was so tired and upset, I started to cry. I picked up my books and kept walking and kept crying as the neighborhood turned into fields.

A car was coming toward me, a ways away, and I didn't want anyone to recognize me crying like that, walking home late from school with arms aching from carrying those books like a dunce. I stepped off the road and ducked under the fence. I wasn't sure whose cornfield this was, and I didn't care. Julia had said once that only ugly girls carried their own books. I didn't really believe her, but I didn't want them to see me crying, just the same.

Surrounded by dried corn stalks, I hunkered down and pushed my face against the books. The car passed without stopping, but I stayed like that, curled over, huddled in. I was crying harder now. My nose was running, and I had to breathe through my mouth. When I pushed the books off my lap so I could wipe my dripping nose with the hem of my skirt, they landed with a satisfying thud. I picked up the book from the top of the pile—the hideous eighth grade textbook—and I threw it as hard as I could. It crashed into a corn stalk and knocked it diagonal. I picked up the next book and threw it: it twirled corner over edge and landed spine-up, embracing a corn stalk. I threw another book and another one. The pages of my civics book fluttered like it might grow wings, but it landed on top of the others. "I'm not stupid!" I threw another one. "I don't care what you think!" I threw another one that landed practically at my feet. I kicked it, and it skidded a few feet into a corn stalk. "I hate this stupid school and its stupid rules and its stupid teachers and my whole stupid life!" My fingers fisted into the sides of my skirt, and I cried and cried, rocking back and forth.

My throat hurt from yelling and crying. Eventually, I cried more gently. I hugged myself tightly around the middle, and that calmed me more. After a while, I untucked my blouse and used the hem to blow my nose. The dry plants shuffled above me, shadowing me from the blue cloudless sky. "I hate Carolina and I hate the whole United States of America," I said in a whisper. My fingers were brown and gritty from the dirt.

I felt worn out and washed out, transparent somehow, but lighter, too. The plants above and around me made me feel safe, hidden, but I knew I couldn't stay there. Getting up and going back to Grandmother's was more than I knew I could do.

But eventually I picked up the nearest book. I dusted it off, straightened the bent pages, and set it down next to me. I arranged them all in a neat stack. I wiped my face off with my skirt, then I stood and picked up the books again.

"You can make it, little bird," I told myself as I made my way through the cornfields parallel to the road. I was late enough, I knew I'd get an earful either way, and I preferred to stay hidden in the field. *Nagaa xinnoo simbirroo*, I told myself each time I came to another fence and had to climb through it.

Finally I saw Grandmother's house. I opened the front door quietly, crept up the stairwell, and went straight to my room. I could hear Aunt Be, Grandmother, and Mother in the kitchen. I hoped they would be satisfied with a vague answer.

Mary and Cassie were sitting on their bed in our room, looking at a book. When they saw me, Cassie's eyes went wide and Marmee put down the book. "Adelie. . . What happened?"

I turned away and got some clothes out of my dresser. "Nothing. I had to stay late at school to meet with a classmate. Is it time for dinner yet?"

Marmee nudged Cassie in the ribs. "I thought I heard Panther. . . Could you go see if he's brought a present to the back porch?" When Cassie was gone, Marmee leaned against the door. "Aunt Be just gave the five-minute warning for dinner. . . That's a really long time to stay at school."

"Five minutes?" Not long enough to take a bath.

I went to the bathroom anyway and looked in the mirror. My face was streaked—almost striped—with dirt and tears. I washed my face and turned the water brown. When the runoff water was clear, I looked in the mirror again.

There was a line on my neck showing where I hadn't yet washed. For a second, I stared at the line. Which was my real skin color: the speckled brown-and-tan or the smooth white? Which was the layer I was washing away? I blinked and the illusion was gone. I bent to continue washing, turning myself white again.

"Adelie! Marmee! Dinner's on the table!" Aunt Be called up the stairs. Marmee handed me the towel, and I quickly dried my face, neck, hands. Then Marmee followed me down the stairs, and I felt her pick something out of my braid.

"Straw," she said.

We crossed into the dining room together and sat down to eat, just in time.

No one even asked where I'd been. Every time I looked in Aunt Be's direction, I felt angry again about how she'd kept me from my friends, and I felt shame that I'd listened to her.

The next day, I ate lunch with Wendy, Sarah May, Nathan, Frederica, and Lion. I explained about what had happened with Aunt Be and how my dad had threatened to not let me work or teach me how to drive. I told them I was embarrassed I had let that keep me away. I asked if they would let me sit again.

"Please don't hold it against me," I said. "You all are the only people I can see myself being friends with at this school. I thought I could get through the year by myself, but I didn't do very well trying to be on my own. I don't care what my family thinks. They're just being small-minded."

Sarah May smiled. "I'm glad you decided to come back."

"Yeah," said Frederica. "We didn't have anyone to laugh at while you were gone."

CHAPTER 7

Marmee, Cassie, and I came home from school one day and found bikes leaning against the back porch: handlebars spotted with rust, wheels flat against the ground, the foam seats chewed through by mice. We touched them gingerly, pulling them upright and wheeling them a few inches back and forth. Our hands and noses were cold from the walk home, but we stayed outside to look at them. If the bikes were fixed up, it would be faster to go to and from school, and I wouldn't need a ride to work.

Uncle Henry had found them in the shed and promised to fix them for us. So, on Saturday, Julia and Bernice's older brother hefted himself out of Uncle Henry's truck. Henry Junior, home from college for the weekend, had the same round face as his little brothers and the same sideways glance as his sisters. He didn't say much and barely looked at us, but he fixed the tires and oiled the chains quickly. He sanded the worst of the rust off the frames, tested the brakes, and lowered the handlebars. Cassie, Marmee and I sat on hay bales in front of the barn, watching him. We wore slacks, the only pairs we had.

After he replaced the seats, he gestured Marmee and me toward them. "Check and see if these are the right height."

I took the one with the red seat; Marmee gripped the handlebars of the one with the white seat. Henry Junior raised my handlebars a few inches, lowered Marmee's seat a touch, and pronounced it good.

I watched Marmee push hers a few inches back and forward, leaning just a little bit of weight onto the handlebars.

I was amazed at how much better the bikes looked. I wouldn't be embarrassed to ride it to school now. "You really fixed them."

"No problem," Henry Junior said. He seemed to be proud of himself and was trying not to show it. A second passed, and he glanced at our feet, still on the ground. "Do y'all know how to ride them?"

Marmee and I looked at him. "It can't be that hard to learn, right?"

He shrugged and stood in front of Marmee's bike, straddling the tire and holding the handlebars firmly. "Go ahead and sit up on it."

Marmee swallowed, tightened her grip, and swung one leg tentatively over the frame. When she lifted up both feet and put them on the pedals, she wavered back and forth a little, but Henry Junior's grip held her steady.

"It's harder to balance standing still," he said. "You ready to pedal?"

Marmee's face was paler than usual under her glasses, but she nodded.

"Put one of your feet down while I get out of the way, then push down with the other pedal when you're ready," he said. He let go and stepped to the side quickly.

Marmee pushed down on the pedal, but her other leg was in the way, and she landed on the ground, tangled in the bike.

"I'm okay," she said and straightened her scarf and hat. Henry Junior pulled the bike up, and I helped her stand. She was shaking, but she tried two more times with Henry Junior and me on either side of her to help her balance. She couldn't seem to get down the rhythm of pedaling for forward momentum, but the third time she did catch herself from falling, pulling her foot off the pedal in time.

"Your turn, Adelie," she said.

I shakily sat up on the seat and balanced on the pedals as Henry Junior and Marmee gripped the handlebars on either side of me. On the count of three, I pushed down on the pedal, and I was moving forward, moving toward trees. I pushed down with the left foot, then the right, then the left again. The trees got closer, and I heard my cousin and sister shouting at me to turn, to stop. I didn't know how. I tilted myself to the left and put my foot down, landing in a heap. I was laughing when they reached me. I picked myself up, leaning on the bike to support my shaky legs.

"Adelie! That was great!" yelled Cassie. Marmee clapped.

"Good thing you didn't run into the tree," said Henry Junior. "Let me show you how to use the brakes."

Within the hour, I was riding wavy circles around the back yard. Cassie and the dogs ran next to me. The dogs licked my face every time I fell.

The next few weeks, I practiced every day after school. Marmee rode next to me sometimes, looping around the yard beside me on her own bike. Cassie begged me to give her a ride, so we figured out a way she could perch on the very front of the seat with her legs tucked up around her, holding on to the center of the handlebars.

Marmee still fell frequently, and she was afraid to go out onto the road. I tried to wait for her, but I got tired of circling the yard while she practiced her balance. Finally, I headed out alone, in the opposite direction I took to go to school. There were more farms and fewer cars in that direction.

My second time out exploring, I came across a hill. It was hard work to get to the top, and I paused when I reached it. The road ribboned in front of me. There was no one in sight, just some cows in the fields on either side of me, breathing out faint clouds of warm air.

The downward slope looked steep and long.

I gathered my breath, pushed forward, and suddenly I was rolling faster and faster, faster than I'd ever gone on the bike, faster than I could control. The road rushed toward me. I gripped the handles tightly, trying to predict where there would be rocks, trying to control the speed, the movement, the momentum of the bike. I was afraid to use the brakes—I was going too fast; any touch of the brake could make me crash, I thought. I focused on staying upright. The pedals were slack against my feet. Fenceposts flew past me in a steady staccato. The cold wind made my eyes tear up, and I couldn't feel my fingers.

I kept my grip firm and my elbows steady. I guided the bike around the rocks and potholes and balanced the curves successfully. I regained control with some light touches of the brakes and slowed the bike to a coast and then to a gentle stop on the grassy shoulder of the road. I was shaking.

I stepped off the bike and slid it to the ground, then walked over to a fencepost and leaned against it, taking deep breaths. The hill was a good ways behind me; it didn't look at all huge from here. I took another deep breath and laughed at myself.

I reached above the barbed wire of the fence, toward the sky. "I am a strong bird!" I shouted. I laughed again, glad no one was around.

When I headed back, the pedaling was too hard this side of the hill. I had to walk the rest of the way up; it was a lot slower than pedaling. At the top, I saw that the slope on this side was more gradual. I hopped back onto the bike seat and rode forward, gaining momentum until I was humming along, the wind in my face, pulling my hair loose. This time I wasn't afraid of losing control. I reveled in the speed and the grace of it.

I rode my bike to school the next day, carrying Cassie with me, pedaling slowly to keep pace with Marmee's timid balance. After school I didn't see either of them—but I didn't look very hard. I raced home by myself, then went past our farm to find the hill again. I went to the hill every day that week. I learned how to go faster and faster until it felt like I was flying.

Toward the end of November, when it felt like I'd been in school for forever, all anyone could talk about was Thanksgiving. Aunt Be and Grandmother discussed pumpkins and mashed potatoes and sweet corn, and everyone at school and at the drive-in compared their predictions for the football game.

My mother's whole family convened at Grandmother's for Thanksgiving Day. By one o'clock on Thursday, there were six aunts, my mother, my grandmother in her usual chair, three girl cousins, three cousins-in-law, and multiple little kids in the very warm kitchen. My sisters were outside with the other kids; Bernice and Julia claimed they had headaches from the heat and went outside to sit on the back porch. But I had never seen so many women I was related to in the same room. The commotion was exciting. I almost didn't mind being in the same room as Aunt Be.

Grandmother was in her element with all her girls around her. She laughed loudly at their jokes and clapped her hands against her thighs and asked what else she could do from her chair. Mostly, she held babies. At one point she had two toddlers curled up with her and an infant in each arm. Everyone stopped what they were doing to turn and exclaim about Grandmother and her great-granbabies.

I couldn't keep track of who the little ones belonged to. They seemed interchangeable—all small, white and pink, with fair hair, passed between mothers and aunts and cousins and grandmothers. I first held a blue-eyed little boy with a furrowed brow and sharp gums, then an extremely heavy little girl with blonde curls who was sleeping. I almost dropped a tiny one whose weight I misjudged—a wrinkled-looking baby with patchy hair and a scaly scalp, and I tried to phrase questions without giving away the fact that I couldn't remember if I was holding a boy or girl.

Aunt Be's Dana sat on a bench by the screen door, fanning herself like a queen of Egypt. She didn't offer to help, and she watched everything with a bored expression. When she had arrived from boarding school Wednesday night, Aunt Be had fluttered around her like a moth, and Dana kept brushing her away. I had thought Dana was stylish and confident, but now her clothes looked a little silly in the context of the kitchen.

Aunt Be moved around everywhere, fetching things for the other women and wringing her hands. A few times she tried to tell someone she'd get something for them, but they told her it was fine—they knew where things were; they'd grown up here too. Mostly she just got in everyone else's way. When Aunt Eliza Betsy shook a wooden stirring spoon at Aunt Candice, a dollop of gravy slid off the spoon onto the floor. Three women exclaimed at it, and Aunt Be grabbed a dishrag and knelt to clean it up before anyone stepped in it.

"Stop fussing, Beulah!" said Aunt Eliza Betsy. "Leave it be."

"Don't anyone drop anything on me while I'm down here!" said Aunt Be. Three aunts stepped around or over her to continue their cooking.

"Beulah, where's the sugar?" asked Aunt Ginger. She was visiting from Kentucky, and it was the first time I'd met her or my Uncle Howard.

"White or brown?" asked Aunt Eliza Betsy, before Aunt Be could answer.

"Brown."

"What for?" asked Aunt Candice. "Aren't you doing the corn?"

"No, I'm making the dressing."

"In the canister behind the rice," said Aunt Eliza Betsy.

"I never put brown sugar in dressing," said Aunt Be. "How much you putting in there?"

"Leave her alone, Beulah," said Grandmother. "Is that your mother's recipe, Ginger?"

Ginger smiled. "My great-grandmother's. She brought it from France with her, apparently."

"Your family was from France, Aunt Ginger?" asked Dana from her bench by the door. "I'm planning to go to Paris to study photography."

"How grand!"

"Wonderful! Beulah, you must be so proud!"

Aunt Be made a clucking noise and turned to stir the two pots on the stove. The cooks responsible for those pots frowned at her.

"Why France, honey?" asked Aunt Louisa.

"Why do you want to study photography?" asked my cousin Eliza Mae. "Isn't that more like something you do rather than study?"

My mother seemed more silent and more overwhelmed than usual in all of the hubbub. "Here are the potatoes," she said, suddenly standing up with the pot full of whole, peeled potatoes. "Is there water for them boiling?"

I wasn't sure who she was asking. Everyone was in charge of whatever dish she'd claimed. Three different women gave my mother different answers, and she was left standing by the table, holding the pot, looking blankly around the room.

I wasn't holding a baby in that moment, so I took the pot from my mother, emptied the potatoes into a smaller pot, and started boiling water on the last empty burner on the stove. Then I sat down at the table and started quartering the potatoes in the smaller pot. Grandmother patted my back, and when I looked at her, she smiled. Her expression showed pride and fondness, but there was some sadness around the edges too.

The chatter had continued, still discussing Dana's dream of going to France, so I didn't think anyone else had noticed my mother's confusion. But, a little later, Eliza Mae's mother gave me a smile with sadness similar to Grandmother's. I looked back down at the potatoes, embarrassed.

My mother was the lamb of the family, Grandmother always said. She hadn't spoken until she was two and a half, and then she had only whispered. As the youngest of seven, everyone around her had always been older, faster, smarter. Her siblings were always speaking for her, always deciding what she wanted and insisting they knew what she needed. Her sisters had preferred playing Baby with her rather than playing with their dolls. Grandmother said Mother would stand still as a mannequin and let them dress her. She had no problem learning to crawl or learning to walk, but most of the time one of her sisters carried her on their hip. Grandmother said she had seemed happiest when she was in her high chair watching everything while sucking her thumb.

I loved how my aunts spoke to me directly, as if I was one of them. They teased me about "beaus," and they asked about the transition to my new school with the same tone they used to ask Dana about her second year of boarding school. They didn't ask me questions about Ethiopia. I was glad, for once, to put that aside and just be where I was.

They asked my mother about Marmee and Cassie. "Oh, they're fine," she said.

"How old is Mary now?" asked Aunt Ginger.

My mother hesitated. "Thirteen," she said.

"Fourteen," I said. "Fifteen next month."

There was a pause.

"I remember when Adelaide was no bigger than a minute—she couldn't have been more than three months old," said Aunt Eliza Betsy. "We brought over Eliza Mae, and she thought Adelaide was the cutest little doll baby. . . until Adelaide got ahold of one of Eliza Mae's curls and pulled it. Eliza Mae started screaming, and the harder she screamed the tighter Adelaide held on."

"All of Eliza Mae's big brothers were standing in a circle around the two of you," said one aunt. "And they were yelling at you to let go, and you just held tighter still! Your mama made those boys scat, then she sang a lullaby and quieted you down so you let go."

"Your mama thought you hung the moon and all the stars." Aunt Candice smiled at me.

Aunt Louisa shook her head. "She gave those boys what's what for yelling at her baby. . . and the boys ran away like hell was on their heels. I laughed so hard—my sweet mouse of a baby sister yelling at those rowdy boys."

I could see it, my mother a proud new mama—like one of the cousins-in-law over there, proud and protective of her baby—me. I wanted to hear more. I was hungry for those stories: it felt like they were giving back to me something of myself that I didn't realize was missing.

It was like I was discovering something that I had always been a part of, even if I didn't realize it. Something that enveloped me, that I fit into, without even trying.

When it was time for dinner, the six aunts corralled children and husbands, made sure they were clean, and shoved them into the dining room. Grandmother cleared her throat, called for silence, and asked Uncle Jefferson to pray since he was the eldest male. Silence descended suddenly on the room, punctuated by a few squirming toddlers and a baby whimpering in the arms of one of the cousins-in-law.

Then the parade of dishes began—two whole turkeys on platters, mashed potatoes, sweet potatoes, collared greens, five baskets of rolls, two green bean casseroles, fruit salad, jello salad, broccoli salad, mixed greens, corn on the cob, creamed corn, and cranberry sauce. There were twenty-five of us at the joined tables in the dining room and living room. The younger kids, including Marmee and Cassie, had a table in the kitchen.

I sat up straight and kept my napkin in my lap, even crossing my ankles though no one could see them under the table. I had my hair teased at the crown and pinned up in a new way Sarah May had suggested.

Aunt Be had arranged the seating so that I was nearest Dana, Bernice, and Julia. Henry Junior was on my other side, but he was talking to Uncle Jefferson and ignored us. Julia and Dana mostly talked about Dana's boarding school.

"How dull to have to live at a school with all girls," said Julia. "How do they expect you to ever get married if you can't meet boys?"

"Oh, we meet boys," said Dana. "There are all sorts of ways of meeting boys."

"Like what?" asked Bernice.

Dana broke off a piece of her roll and ate it. "I better not soil your innocent ears with my secrets. Wouldn't want to plant any ideas." She looked at me out of the corner of her eye and smiled.

"Why did you go to boarding school?" I asked.

Dana hesitated just a second, as if choosing her answer. "My mother didn't like the schools here. Especially not when the school board said it would allow colored kids in the same class-rooms as us."

"Your boarding school isn't mixed?"

She laughed. "Gosh, no! Those girls and their families wouldn't stand for it in a million years."

"Adelaide likes the colored kids at our school," said Julia.

"She's friends with them and eats lunch with them and every-thing." Bernice looked smug.

"Good for you," said Dana. "I'd have wanted to be friends with them too, if I'd stayed."

How did she know that, without having met them? I wasn't friends with Wendy and Sarah May and Nathan just to rile people like Julia and Bernice. And yet, the way Dana held her fork and knife looked so effortlessly elegant.

"Did you want to stay?" I imitated her hold on the silverware and found it was more comfortable that way.

"I didn't really have an option. Mama was set on it, on sending me somewhere nice and fancy." She shrugged. "I liked my old school. I went to Greenville High, you know, because Mama and I lived off Main Street." It sounded like she was bragging. "But enough about me," she said. "Adelaide, you and Bernice are in the same class, aren't you? How is that?"

"We don't tell people we're related," said Julia.

"As if the whole school didn't already know we're cousins," I said.

"Adelaide's always behind in math class. She had to go to the board and tell everyone she's stupid."

"I bet the boys were glad to have something nicer to look at than the teacher," said Dana. "Although that would be a terrible way to meet someone. . . Can you imagine, a boy who says he noticed you when the teacher made you stand in front of the class? One of my girlfriends met her fiancé while she was cleaning gum off her shoe."

Julia laughed. "I heard about a girl who met her husband when his car hit her parents' car. Her father was driving."

"I met my boyfriend at a jukebox," said Dana. "We both got to it at the same time. He said I could pick my song first if I danced to it with him." Dana smiled around another bite of dinner roll. "How'd you meet your boyfriend, Julia?"

"She hasn't got one," said Bernice. "Mama doesn't like the boys she brings home. Our parents met at a church bonfire. There were two chairs left. Daddy made his friend sit down first so that he could sit next to Mama and say it was the only chair open."

"Why couldn't he just sit next to her and tell her he wanted to sit next to her?" I said.

Dana agreed. "It's definitely not as romantic as your parents' story, Adelaide."

"My parents' story?"

"Don't you know how your parents met?"

I knew the basics—my mother had just graduated from high school and my dad had just come back from the war and gone back to college. They married six months after they met, and they had me two years later. They left for Ethiopia a year and a half after that.

"What's so romantic about it?" I asked.

"You don't know?" She took a sip of her sweet tea. Julia and Bernice were arguing with each other about something else. The conversation at the other end of the table had all the adults and the other cousins engaged.

"Your parents," she said, "met at a parade at the army air base, flags and streamers and airplanes doing tricks in the air. Grandmother and Grandpa took everyone on a picnic. Your mother was playing tag with her little nephews, and she accidentally darted right into the path of a tall officer." Dana smiled at me conspiratorially. "He fell, head over heels—literally sprawled on the sidewalk. Your mother hovered over him, offering her high school first aid training, stuttering and blushing all the while. People started to gather—everyone was staring and concerned. Grandmother and Grandpa chided her for getting in the way of an officer—after all he'd done for the country and all that. Grandmother made an absolute fuss over his uniform: he'd gotten grass-stains on it. Small ones, but grass stains nonetheless. She insisted he let her clean them for him, insisted he come to dinner and let her take care of the pants. A few days later, he came to dinner."

"With the dirty pants?"

"No, I think he cleaned the pants himself."

I tried to imagine my dad doing his own laundry. I could imagine him capable of it, but I'd never seen him do anything related to housekeeping. He'd probably paid for dry cleaning. "How did the dinner go?"

"He showed up with a bouquet of flowers for your mother and

a fruit basket for Grandmother. Grandmother and Grandpa were thrilled with him, regaled him with all sorts of stories about how great your mother was." On the other end of the table, my mother was smiling a little vacantly, staring toward the empty kitchen.

Dana leaned in toward me. "The problem was that your mother had a boyfriend who was very attached to her. That boy heard about the dinner and went raging through town, calling out challenges to the upstart soldier. He tried to make your mother swear to never see your dad again. Uncle Howard heard that boy bullying her and kicked him off Grandmother's property, telling him never to return. The boy finally found your father outside Marshall's drugstore one Saturday night and they fought it out in the street. Your father, the veteran soldier, quickly got the upper hand, and he made the boy promise to never bother your mother again. Then your father came by every weekend and took her for long walks after dinner. They got engaged after two months and were married not much later." She rested her wrists on the table, cutlery aloft over her plate. "At the wedding, he said he'd known as soon as he looked up from the sidewalk, as soon as he saw your mother's shocked face. He said she was so pretty and so unpretentious and charming that he loved her right away. They were married in Great-Uncle Fred's church. When they left for Africa, your mother had a babe in arms and another one barely old enough to walk. Grandmother thought she'd never see any of you again."

I realized how tightly I was holding the napkin in my lap. It sounded like a fairy tale, not my parents' real life. "How do you know all this?"

Dana ate her last bite of turkey. "Grandmother tells that story a lot. She always cries when she gets to the last part. I'm surprised you haven't heard it."

I couldn't imagine my parents like that—eighteen and twenty-ish, tripping over each other at a picnic, fighting for the chance to be together. Somehow it made me sad. I wanted to talk about something else, and soon enough, the conversation moved on to football and school rivalries: topics I didn't care much about.

After dinner, the women cleaned up in the kitchen, and the kids went outside to play. My cousins and I went out to the back porch. Marmee and Cassie had already settled into the porch swing; I made them move over to share with me.

"Cassie, why aren't you playing with the other kids?" I asked.

"They're all boys," she said, frowning. "And they said girls can't play football. Marmee said they were right, but she didn't want to play anyway." The cousins laughed at her. I patted her back and told her maybe she could play something else with them.

Not long after dark all of the visitors headed home, except for Dana. She sprawled out on the couch in the den, reading a novel. Cassie and Marmee played a card game in the window seat, eyeing her repeatedly.

When we all went to bed, I asked my sisters what they thought of her. "She seems nice," said Cassie.

Marmee snorted. "She seems like trouble. The way she rolls her eyes at Grandmother and Aunt Be. . . We would get in so much trouble if we did that."

"But she goes to boarding school," said Cassie. "She probably knows when it's okay to talk back and when it would be bad manners."

"I think it's always bad manners," I said. "They just let her get away with it."

"Maybe if our dad died they would let us get away with it too," said Marmee.

I had trouble sleeping that night and lay staring at the shadows on the windowsill. My thoughts went to Maicaah, and I pulled open the drawstring on the fabric pouch with my pomegranate seeds. I rolled them around in my hand, imagining Maicaah slipping them into my pocket that day. I remembered the time I snuck away from the other girls and the mothers' watchful eyes to keep Maicaah company while he was taking sheep to water downstream. I was maybe ten. We had argued over what names to give our children.

I had known even then that if we could talk about getting married it meant I didn't really belong in the village: people born into the village were considered too closely related to the other village members to intermarry. But I would belong when I married him.

I put the fabric pouch with the pomegranate seeds under my pillow. I fell asleep thinking how much better my story would be than the story Dana had told about my parents. I just had to get back to the village to get my happy ending. Only a year and a half left before I turned eighteen.

CHAPTER 8

AFTER THANKSGIVING, it was too cold to sit outside on the steps during lunch. We found a similar spot inside the auditorium foyer, where we wouldn't bother anyone and no one bothered us. In the auditorium, empty rows of seats faced wilted decorations from the last school assembly, but the foyer had a high ceiling and tall, cloudy windows. One set of double doors led in from outside, and two swinging doors led to the seats; we were in between, on a set of curving stairs that went up to the balcony.

I had missed these lunches over the long weekend, missed the teasing and the laughter and the inside jokes. My friends had all seen each other during the break—at church, in the neighborhood; they had even gone together to get hot chocolate at Kress's on Friday. I had spent the day with my sisters and Dana, when she wasn't reading fashion magazines.

By this time I'd noticed that at lunch my friends spoke differently, when they were talking to each other as opposed to when they were talking in class or in the hallways. Around other people, they sat up straight, with their hands in their laps, and spoke as if their words were starched and ironed, every consonant pronounced crisply. At lunch, when it was just us, they relaxed into words like *Imma* and *fixna* and left out words that weren't needed, like *is* or *are*. They sat differently at lunch time too—slouched and fanned themselves with their hands and smacked each other to punctuate an exclamation. Sometimes they made fun of each other for a certain pronunciation of a word, and sometimes they overcorrected to exaggerated White English on purpose, which usually earned laughter.

Sarah May was the only one who rarely used White English. She barely spoke at all in front of white people, and when she did, she was self-conscious to the point of stuttering. Lion was the opposite; he used formal English sometimes even during lunch, as if he was still practicing. Even Nathan—Black Pride man himself—changed when he was around white people. Sometimes he and the others became more formal even when speaking to me, if I did or said something particularly white.

Then, one day, I noticed that hadn't happened in a while. It felt like a victory that they no longer switched to their White English when they were talking to me. A few days after that, all five of them turned to me and howled with laughter.

"What?" This was more than their usual amusement at my expense.

"You sounded just like my little sister!" Lion's laugh was long hoots in between short gasps for breath.

"You sounded just like a black girl!" said Frederica. "If I'd had my eyes closed, I would have thought you were. . ." Tears squeaked out of the corners of her eyes, she was laughing so hard.

"What?"

"The way you said that," said Wendy. "I never heard a white girl talk like that."

"Say it again! Say it again, Adelie!"

I tried, but now I was self-conscious. "I can't. Not with all of you laughing at me."

Wendy pulled a serious face and covered her mouth with both hands. Lion tried to keep a straight face, but he kept cracking up. Frederica and Sarah May hid their laughter against each other's shoulders. Nathan kept laughing so loud it echoed through the foyer.

I thought back on what I'd said and tried to reform the syllables in the same way: "Hey, Equiano, you gon' eat that?"

They all howled with laughter again, and this time I smiled. Sarah May was hiccupping now. Frederica had tears dripping off her chin.

Then the outside doors opened, and Mr. Dykart came through. The laughter stopped immediately, and both Lion and Nathan sat up straight. In the time it took me to blink, Sarah May had her eyes focused on the ground, and Frederica wiped the tears off her face with her sleeve. Mr. Dykart looked at us suspiciously, and we gave him tight-lipped smiles as he walked by. He nodded at us and continued on through one of the swinging doors into auditorium.

As soon as he was gone, Sarah May hiccupped. We laughed again, quietly this time.

Then someone else whispered, *"Hey, Equiano, you gon' eat that?"* and we were laughing as loud as we had been. We were still laughing when the bell rang and we walked inside for the next class.

That week, Mr. Nielsen assigned a group project.

Social studies had become my favorite class. I loved staring at the maps, learning about types of government, hearing about history and imagining the stories behind the facts. I was rarely even tempted to doodle or write a note to Wendy or Sarah May as I did in my other classes.

"I want each of you to find a partner that you're willing to work with," said Mr. Nielsen. "Make sure you choose well; you'll be working with this person for several weeks, and your grades will be dependent on each other's efforts."

I raised my hand. "Can we be partners with someone in the other section of the class?" There was an uneven number in our section, and maybe this way I could partner with one of my friends rather than someone who threw spit wads or asked me stupid questions about orangutans.

"Talk to me after class and we'll see," said Mr. Nielsen.

I felt a tap on my shoulder and turned around. It was squint-eyed Jimmy Campbell. Half the time, he didn't even come to class; the other half of the time, he sat slumped in his seat, drawing pictures of knives and gore.

"Do you want to work with me?" He seemed to be looking at my left shoulder.

"Sorry, I already have a partner in mind." I turned back, before he could argue, hoping Mr. Nielsen agreed.

After class, Mr. Nielsen asked who I had in mind to work with, and he frowned when I told him. "I don't think that's a good idea. Maybe you'd better work with Jimmy and Edie."

I tried to keep my tone respectful. "I would rather work with Wendy or Frederica, if that's all right. Both class sections are uneven, and if I can work with someone from the other section, that'll even things out."

He squinted out the window for a long minute. "This is exactly the type of thing they were afraid of with integration." He raised a hand to stop me from protesting. "Not that I have anything against them, personally. And it would make the grading fairer if every group has two people. But I don't want to hear about this from the principal or the school board. If you do it, there can't be any problems."

"Yes, sir." I tried to show as little as possible of my disgust at his cowardice.

The next morning before school, I found Wendy by her locker and told her about it. "So we can be partners, if you want! Isn't that great?"

Facing the pile in her locker, she rearranged a book so that its spine faced out. "You're not going to disappear again, when some-one tells you that you shouldn't be in a group with me?"

"What?"

Her eyes were guarded when she looked at me, like she was trying to keep something in or keep something out. Quietly she said, "When your aunt told you not to eat with us, we didn't see you for weeks. How do I know this will be any different?"

I didn't know she still thought about that. "I didn't stop eating with you because my aunt told me not to. It was because my dad told me I wouldn't be able to keep my job if I didn't listen to her."

Wendy fiddled some more with the books in her locker. She didn't look like that difference changed anything.

"I came back to the group anyway, didn't I? Don't hold that against me."

Wendy shrugged. "Look, I have a group for the project. Lion, Frederica, and I already came up with a plan."

"But I don't have a group," I said. "I went to ask permission from Mr. Nielsen specifically so I could work with you."

"Maybe you should have asked me first." Wendy closed her locker.

"I thought you'd like the idea! Why are you so mad?"

Wendy faced me again, and her gaze was as strong as a searchlight. "It's just easier if you let it be, Adelaide."

"Like you let it be by suing the school board for integration?"

She looked around us, but no one had heard. She was mad now: her eyebrows had gathered like thunderclouds and her scar was twitching. "How can you compare this with that?"

"What kind of integration is it if you won't work on a project with someone who's white?"

She shook her head. "You're only thinking about what's best for you."

"And you're just saying no because I'm white."

"That's not why." She paused. "That's only part of it."

"Please, Wendy," I clasped my hands in front of my chest. "I really don't want to work with Jimmy Campbell. Friends save each other from situations like that."

She looked up at the ceiling, pulled hard on her right earlobe, and took a deep breath. "You best not let me down again," she said.

As glad as I was to work with Wendy, it was hard to find a time when we could work together. She had to go straight home after school most days, to watch her younger siblings or help in her grandparents' store. I had algebra tutoring Tuesdays and Thursdays, and I worked at the drive-in on Saturdays. We didn't get much done during lunch. When the deadline got closer, I asked if we could work on it at her house while she watched her siblings.

Wendy groaned. "No, Adelaide, you can't come to my house."

I remembered that it was rude to invite myself. "Oh, sorry. . ."

"It's just, my grandparents wouldn't like it." She looked a little apologetic as she said it, and I felt better about where we stood.

"What about if you bring your brothers to the library? We could work on it there."

So Wednesday afternoon, I found a table at the public library downtown while Wendy picked up her little brothers and sister from the colored elementary school across town. While I was waiting for them, reading ahead in *Ivanhoe* for my English class, I suddenly looked up to see Emily Rose sit down across from me. She smiled a quick smile and put her books down.

"Mind if I sit here? This is my usual table at this library."

"It's kind of in the same place as our usual table in the school library, isn't it?"

She nodded, smiled quickly again, and opened her book.

"Just so you know," I said, "I'll be working on a school project with my friend Wendy. She's picking up her little brothers and sister and meeting me here. In case that bothers you."

Emily Rose looked blank. "Wendy? Does she go to our school?"

I nodded. "She's one of the colored girls."

"Oh. . ." she said. She looked uncomfortable.

"You don't have to leave," I told her. "As long as it won't bother you if we're working on something."

Emily Rose looked at the tables around us, all of which had other people sitting at them. "I like this table," she said finally. "I guess I'll stay."

When Wendy arrived, she looked surprised. I shrugged. Emily Rose looked up as I introduced them to each other, and then I met Wendy's little sister, who looked about nine, and her brothers, who were five and six. Emily Rose went straight back to her book and didn't say anything to the little boy who sat down next to her and started drawing. Wendy used her white-people English and talked so quietly I could barely hear her. When one of the boys accidentally kicked the table leg while he was swinging his legs, she gave him a look and he sat still again. I felt stiff too, and I was glad when it was time to go.

Unfortunately, Wendy and I were nowhere near finished. The project was turning out to be a lot harder than we expected. Emily Rose watched us as we talked about how to divide up the research.

"You're pretty far behind," she said. "It's due next week. You could split it up like my group did. We worked on the outline together, and then I wrote the research paper, and my partner is doing the display board."

"That's a good idea," said Wendy, looking at me instead of at Emily Rose.

Emily Rose nodded and went back to her book.

For the next week, Wendy and I met every day before school to work on the outline, and then I worked on the display board while she typed up the paper. I got Marmee to help me make it look pretty. On Friday I walked to school instead of riding my bike so that I could carry the display board to show Wendy.

"You misspelled *Bismarck*," she said, pointing to the title.

"Did not. . ."

"There's a *c* before the *k*."

"Since when?" I grabbed the book she was pointing at and groaned. "Maybe no one will notice."

"I bet your friend from the library will. She's always correcting the teachers in class."

"Emily Rose?" I said, laughing. I only had algebra and English with Emily Rose; she was mostly quiet in them.

"She's done it twice," said Wendy. "It was pretty funny."

"She's not that bad, really," I said.

Wendy sketched in a *c* on the display board. "My brothers were scared of her. But then again, they were sort of scared of you, too."

"Why scared of me?"

She smiled. "They said you look funny, but I told them you used to have cornrows and they liked that."

On Monday, Wendy and I turned in our project before the first bell rang. Ours was clearly one of the better-done display boards, despite the squeezed-in *c*, and our paper was longer by half than the others. I felt smug as we gave it to Mr. Nielsen together. We had proved him wrong.

Then, as Wendy and I headed to our separate first classes, I mostly felt relief that it was finished. The logistics of working with Wendy outside of school had been harder than I expected, and a part of me had been waiting for someone else to make a fuss over it. It definitely would have been easier if I'd just worked by myself.

It was the following week when our lunch group was interrupted.

"Nathan! Nathan, wait a minute." We were at the end of the hallway, almost out the door.

It was Justin Macalister. Tall, blonde Justin Macalister, who carried himself in a way that made everyone look at him.

I knew who he was now—after he helped Wendy when her books fell out of her locker, I started to hear his name every-where. He played on the football team and wrote for the school newspaper and was in the running to be class salutatorian. His dad was the pastor at Fourth Presbyterian, one of the prettiest churches downtown. And, like Wendy, I'd heard plenty of girls talk about him in the girls' bathroom.

"What does he want?" Frederica mumbled as he made his way toward us.

"No idea," said Nathan.

When Justin reached us, he stopped a little ways from where we stood in a line, facing him with our arms crossed. Justin lifted his navy football jacket off his shoulders, then let if fall again, as if adjusting his mantle. He was on the thin side, but that jacket fitted him nicely.

"Hey, Nathan, how you doing?"

Nathan nodded, but he didn't offer his own greeting. People pushed around us to get through the doorway. A few turned to stare at Justin and broke into talk as soon as they passed us.

Justin cleared his throat. "I wanted to talk to you about something. Do you mind if I eat lunch with y'all?"

We looked at him as if he'd grown a second head. Now I knew why they'd stared at me when I sat down with them my first day.

Justin waited for an answer. People continued to pass us and whisper, but Nathan took his time to study Justin. Nathan's impenetrable expression was kind of frightening; I was glad he hadn't looking at me that way.

"What about?" asked Nathan.

"Your speech in English class," said Justin. He glanced at the rest of us, and it felt like he looked at me longer than the others. His expression seemed to be asking me for something. That I would vouch for him because I was the only other white person? I looked away, unwilling to admit a connection.

"Would that be all right?" Justin asked Nathan again.

Some more people thundered out the door past us. Nathan watched them turn to stare at Justin and us, then he nodded. Justin followed us as we continued to our spot in the auditorium foyer. His blond hair was so neatly parted it seemed ironed into place; it was shiny and showed the ridges of a comb.

Sarah May paused outside the door to the foyer, where the boys had already gone in. She gave me a small, sly smile that I didn't understand.

"What?"

She leaned toward me. "He's awfully good looking."

"So?" I tried not to blush.

She wiggled her eyebrows, and Wendy also had a silly expression when she looked at me.

I rolled my eyes. Now I would never be able to talk to Justin, not with Sarah May looking at me like that. "I'm not the one making a fuss about him," I whispered back.

As soon as we were settled on the steps, Justin and Nathan across from each other on the bottom step, Justin started in on what he'd come to say.

"Nathan, I felt really angry about the way everyone reacted to your speech. I wanted to hear the rest of it, and I think it was wrong of them to make you stop."

Everyone stared first at Justin, then at Nathan. No one took a bite of their food.

"What speech?" I asked.

Suddenly Sarah May and Lion wouldn't look up. Wendy waved at the air in front of her face, as if shooing away dust motes.

"Didn't you hear about it?" asked Frederica. Her speech was crisper than normal white English. "Nathan tried to give a Black Rights speech in our English class, and the teacher made him stop and go to the principal. The class booed him out of the room."

"What?"

I couldn't believe I hadn't heard about this. Why hadn't any of them told me? Had they purposefully talked about it without me?

"It was a good speech," said Justin, "and it had a lot of truth in it. Can I hear the rest of it?"

Wendy and Lion both narrowed their eyes at Justin. Sarah May smiled. A muscle jumped in Frederica's clenched jaw as she stared at the wall.

Lion's deep voice rumbled. "Why didn't you say anything in class?"

Justin looked down and brushed some lint off his pants. They were neatly pressed, like the rest of him. I wondered if his mother did their ironing or if they had someone who worked for them.

Justin looked Nathan straight in the eye. "I should have. I'm sorry."

I was caught off guard. I had never seen someone apologize so clearly without excuses. Beyond that, he was a white boy, apologizing to Nathan.

Nathan just looked at him as if deciding. Justin looked at me, again, as if I would understand and could help him. This time I didn't look away, just watched to see what he would do. Eventually he looked back to Nathan. "I wronged you," he said. "The whole class did, and I apologize for my part in it. It wasn't fair at all."

Nathan nodded. His lower lip jutted out slightly, like it did when he was thinking something over, and I could see a slight scar on the fleshy inside of his mouth. I'd heard he got that scar the first week of school, when some boys jumped him on his way home. Police had stopped the fight pretty quickly, but there was still that scar from a badly bloodied lip.

Nathan nodded again and stretched out his hand. Justin nodded back and shook it.

I felt goosebumps on my forearms, the same feeling I got when the wind picked up before a storm, a promise of power in the air.

"What were you going to say after you quoted Galatians?"

Nathan shook his head slowly. "No, man, I've got to start from the beginning."

He took a stance facing us and patted the sides of his legs a few times as he gathered his thoughts. Then he recited his memorized speech. He spoke about freedom and hypocrisy, about Constitutional rights and poor interpretations. He quoted Martin

Luther King Jr., the Bible, W.E.B. DuBois, and Walt Whitman. He became more and more impassioned as he recited it, waving his arms and straining onto his tiptoes.

We, his audience, cheered and clapped more and more loudly in response. By the end, he was pacing the width of the stairwell, shouting his key phrases so that they echoed through the empty foyer and back. He had us on our feet; we stood on our various steps, cheering as if we didn't care who heard us. He finished with a statement as clear and powerful as a fist in the air. He took a bow in our ringing silence, and then we cheered some more.

Sarah May was beaming. "You're going to take the world by storm, Nathan Ramsey," she said.

Lion clapped Nathan on the shoulder, and Justin looked like he was taking notes on the important points, saving them like ammunition. I wondered who he hoped to use the arguments against. Wendy also was smiling widely, but there was a sadness in her expression that I didn't understand.

Frederica was much more subdued. She had clapped but didn't cheer during the speech; she was the last to stand, and she kept looking toward the doors as if afraid someone might come in at any minute. She was the first to sit down afterward, while the rest of us were still catching our breath.

"Nathan, that was incredible!" I said. "You definitely got your father's gift for public speaking."

There was a twist in the pause, and then Sarah May, Lion, Wendy, and Frederica burst out laughing.

"What? What did I say?"

Nathan was laughing harder than any of them. Justin caught my eye and shrugged.

Finally, Wendy calmed down and turned to me. "Honey, have you ever heard his father speak?" She was smiling around her words.

"No, but I've heard you say he's such a great preacher. . ."

Wendy shook her head. "He is a good preacher, but he stutters something awful. He can't get through two sentences without pausing to say, 'P-pwaise the Lohd!' whenever he needs to catch his breath. He couldn't never have given a speech like Nathan just did—Nathan's in a whole different league."

Nathan ducked his head and laughed with them.

Lion pulled a straight face. "You could say Nathan has his father's gift—Nathan got it instead of his father."

I was too embarrassed to do more than chuckle. I tried to stop myself from checking to see if Justin was still looking at me.

He wasn't. He was looking at his notes. "That quote you used was my favorite part of Dr. King's speech."

"You've read Dr. King's speech?" asked Wendy. "How does a white preacher's son like you come out reading Dr. King's speech?"

"I read it in the newspaper we get from Philadelphia, where my dad grew up."

"How does your daddy feel about you reading it?"

"My dad's the one who gave it to me to read," said Justin. "At first he wanted to read the whole speech from the pulpit. But then he asked two of his elders about it, and they told him he shouldn't—said it was too political and would be divisive and would hurt the church about something that wasn't for the sake of the gospel." Justin straightened his pant leg over his shoe. "My dad and I disagreed about whether keeping quiet about that is more harmful or not to the gospel."

We all stared at him.

"You think your dad should read Dr. King's speech from the pulpit despite what the elders say?" I asked, just to clarify.

"He needs to address it somehow." Justin's expression was serious, his eyes like a summer sky. He looked around at the others, too. "I think everyone needs to talk about segregation and civil rights. This is an evil that has gone on long enough. At this point, for a white person to be silent is to be complicit." Justin ran his hands down his pant legs, calming himself. "Sorry, I get worked up about it. And I'm preaching to the choir. . . Y'all live this. I don't know what to say, other than I'm sorry and I want to stand with you."

We stared at him for a few more seconds, then Lion put an arm around Nathan and clapped Justin on the back. "Nathan, man, I think you found a brother from another mother."

We laughed. It was true. And the more we got to know Justin, as he started coming to lunch regularly, I realized increasingly just how alike the two preacher's sons were—so similar in their idealism and unwillingness to compromise and harsh judgment of themselves and others. But they were different, too. Justin's eyes were indignant but clear with hopeful idealism. Nathan's smile sometimes held a hardness underneath. He seemed older than Justin, though they were both seventeen.

Secretly, I did think Justin was awfully good-looking. He rubbed one of his straight blonde eyebrows when he was thinking, and he held his head diagonally when he was really listening to someone. I got nervous every time I met his eyes or saw him smile. I both desperately wanted to talk to him, to have his attention on me—and desperately wanted to avoid him altogether.

When Justin joined us at lunch the next day, I didn't look at him the whole time. It troubled me that I wanted to look at him at all.

CHAPTER 9

"ADELIE, WHAT DO YOU HAVE against Justin?" asked Wendy as we walked to class after lunch, the second day Justin had joined us.

"What do you mean? I don't have anything against him."

"You hardly talk when he's around, you avoid looking in his direction, and when he asked you that question, you pretended not to hear."

"I was caught up in my thoughts. . ."

"Uh-huh. Look, I'm just saying, he's a catch, and he seems curious about you. Maybe he's interested, or maybe he's just curious, but either way it can't hurt to talk to him."

I opened my locker and hid my face from her.

"The rest of us like him well enough," she said. "From the way he was talking, it sounds like he might want to sit with us permanently. I think he came initially because of Nathan's speech, like he said—don't flatter yourself—but I think he's curious about you as the white girl who's been sitting with us all along." She leaned back against the row of lockers and watched people passing by in the hallway.

"That doesn't mean I have to talk to him."

"What—in Africa you couldn't talk to boys or something?"

I leaned around the door of the locker to face her. "Do you think I lived in a convent in the desert and never saw a person of the male gender until I moved here? I talk to Nathan and Lion all the time."

"So what's the big deal?"

I lifted out my next book and closed my locker. Why didn't I want to tell her about Maicaah? It was like talking about him might profane it.

The hallway was emptying as people headed to class. I hugged the textbook to my chest. "There's. . . a boy. . . in Ethiopia. . . that I care about."

Wendy dropped her chin and stared at me. "You have a boy-friend in Africa?"

The bell rang, and I told her I had to go. "I'm finding you after school," she said. "I'm going to make you tell me about this." I waved her off as I turned toward my classroom.

The rest of the afternoon, I thought about what words to use to tell Wendy about Maicaah. When the last bell rang, I found Wendy in the hallway outside of my classroom. She shadowed me to my locker and convinced me to walk with her to her siblings' school so I could tell her the story. It was a Wednesday, so I didn't have tutoring. I put on my coat, scarf, and mittens, and followed her with my bicycle by my side.

"We grew up together," I said. "He was one of my best friends. We've talked about getting married ever since I can remember, and when I left I promised I'd go back to him."

"What? I didn't know you were planning to go back."

We were walking the opposite direction I normally took, toward downtown Greenville. The houses were nicer this direction—the paint fresher, the yards bigger and more groomed.

"My dad said as soon as I turn eighteen I can decide for myself."

"So. . . what's he like, this boy of yours?"

I smiled, thinking of his shoulders against the broad sky. "He's tall, skinny. . . thoughtful, and resourceful, and a hard worker.

He was the one who always organized our games, and whenever anyone argued, he'd put a stop to it."

"He's still in Ethiopia? His parents didn't leave?"

"No, they're still there."

Wendy's books were strapped together with a belt, and she swung them like a pendulum beside her. "He sounds nice. . ." She looked like she was trying to formulate another question. Finally: "He's black?"

"Of course. He's from the village."

She nodded, looking straight ahead and swinging her books. "He's *African* African? I mean, he's never even been to America? That's what you want? Although, if he were here, you wouldn't be able to be with him, not in Greenville. You'd need to move to the North or something for that to work. It's bad enough that you eat lunch with us and that you're walking with me."

I pulled my bike to the side as a pickup drove past us. I remembered how much trouble I'd get in if someone saw us and told Aunt Be. I could come up with some excuse, or tell her it was a coincidence that we were walking in the same direction.

"It's not that different. I hadn't been to America either, until we moved. Not that I remembered." I kept walking, rolling my bike next to me.

"But you're *from* here," said Wendy.

I stopped and stared at her. "No, I'm not."

"What? You're American—you belong here."

How could she not understand something as basic as that? "No, I'm not. . . I don't."

"Why are you mad?"

I wanted to tell her about the confidence I felt carrying a bucket of water on my head, with as good a balance as the other girls. I wanted to tell her about the feeling of sitting at Haadha Meti's feet while she braided my hair. I wanted her to understand that *I* was the girl who ran through fields of waist-high grasses, who climbed trees and jumped into the stream holding my nose. I was the girl who ran barefoot and washed clothes by hand and roasted coffee beans over a firepit until the aroma filled my pores.

That was me, not this girl who wore her cousins' hand-me-down coat and mittens, who put up with rude customers at the drive-in, who couldn't work polynomial equations, who used up all her perseverance to try to sew a straight, invisible seam in home economics.

I hated that no one looking in through a classroom window would have noticed anything different about me—just another white face amidst my white classmates. I knew I was different. But not even Wendy recognized that about me.

"I didn't mean to make you mad," said Wendy.

I looked at her again, and I could tell she didn't understand. I kicked a rock out of the road. Was it worth it to try to explain it to her? She might never understand, even if I explained it perfectly.

"It's just. . . I know that I look like a white girl from Greenville, but that's not who I am. My whole life. . . all these experiences that have been so important to me. . . no one would ever guess that about me, just looking at me. I don't have anything in common with white girls in Greenville, other than that my skin is white and I live in Greenville right now." I moved my right wrist so that I could feel the beads of my bracelet. It was invisible under the long sleeves of my wool coat and sweater and silk undershirt.

Wendy nodded, slowly. "I can believe that. There's a lot about me no one would guess just looking at me."

I looked at her, a little surprised. Was there anything about her that I'd overlooked? She didn't elaborate, and we talked about other things for the rest of the way to the elementary school.

When we reached the school, I looked around and saw only dark skin, and the fist inside me relaxed a little bit. But then a few teachers saw me and stared, and I quickly felt self-conscious. I stayed long enough to say hello to her little sister and brothers, and then I rode my bicycle home, thinking about Maicaah and life in the village.

Kinci would have had her baby by now, I realized. I wondered if it was a boy, like she thought. Was he healthy? I wished so strongly that I had some way of knowing, of finding out, but I didn't know how to get a letter to her. There was no one to read it to her, even if I did.

That night, after my sisters fell asleep, I held my braceletted wrist and clutched my pouch of pomegranate seeds. I tried to keep the tears in so I wouldn't wake anyone, but the best I could manage was to cry quietly.

As we walked out to lunch the next day, Justin matched Nathan step for step, both of them gesturing as they talked. I hung back, but Wendy caught my eye, as if she could tell what I was thinking. The slight, thin scar on her cheekbone became more prominent as she narrowed her eyes at me. She leaned over to whisper, "Don't avoid him. That'll just make things uncomfortable."

"I told you about. . ."

"So say no if he asks you to marry him, but that doesn't mean you can't sit on the same stairs and have lunch with him sitting close by."

I opened my mouth to argue, but Lion looked over his shoulder to see what we were talking about. I rolled my eyes instead and went with them to our usual spot on the foyer steps. I didn't like eating in the bathroom.

A few times during lunch, Justin made jokes, smiling in my direction. Suddenly it seemed like a good idea to mention Maicaah.

The boys were talking about the football team; we girls were mostly listening to them. "He's the best halfback in the state," Justin was saying. "He's set some records for speed."

"Maicaah is a really fast runner," I said.

Immediately I regretted saying it. The boys stopped their conversation, surprised at the interruption, and stared at me. Frederica and Sarah May looked at each other, then at me.

"Who's Maicaah?" asked Sarah May.

"A boy I grew up with," I said. I took a large bite of Aunt Be's sourdough. Wendy's eyebrows quirked a little bit and she seemed to be struggling to keep a straight face.

"In Africa?" said Justin.

Sarah May got a little bit of a funny smile, looking between Justin and me. Frederica looked pointedly out the window.

"What was that like, growing up there?" asked Justin.

I looked at Wendy; I didn't feel like trying to describe it for him—of course he'd be like the others who didn't understand. "I don't know. What was it like growing up in Greenville?"

Justin looked surprised. His blue eyes were very unguarded. "I've never really thought about it. Everyone's always just known what it was like. It was boring, I guess. Nothing special." When he shrugged one shoulder, his football jacket gaped open over his plaid shirt.

"I'd say the same about life in my village."

"I haven't heard you talk about life there very much, Adelie." Sarah May picked a crumb off the cloth napkin that covered her lap. "Did you run with lions?"

"Not until I met this one," I nodded at Lion. Everyone laughed, and I softened a little. "I did see leopards, though. Everyone knew not to walk into the woods after dark. If you went out as the sun was going down, you had to always walk with other people and make lots of noise."

"Or what?" Frederica was looking at me from the corners of her eyes. You'd think I was telling a ghost story, from the way everyone's body language stiffened.

"They would start screaming—high pitched, off key. . . almost like a baby that burned himself in the fire. If you heard it screaming, you always hoped it had got an animal and not some-one you knew."

They stared at me as if they weren't sure whether I was mak-ing it up or not. I rubbed my eyebrow; I could feel the start of a headache. Telling them about my former life felt like trying to time travel by willpower, like trying to tie together separate ends of the universe.

"There's nothing like that here," said Justin.

"There are other night creatures that we're afraid of here," said Frederica. Her tone was flat with rough edges. Wendy and Lion looked at each other.

"What do you mean?" I asked.

"Night riders," said Frederica.

Wendy made a tsk-sound, and Sarah May pulled her cardigan closed. "Not here, Frederica," said Lion. I couldn't understand where the sudden tension had come from.

Frederica was looking squarely at Justin. "Maybe your people don't have to be afraid of them, but they used to go to my gran-daddy's neighborhood every Friday night at midnight. They drove by our house last night."

No one moved. Wendy, Sarah May, Lion, and Nathan looked as if they knew about this already. I thought she might be talking about ghosts.

Frederica could tell I didn't understand. "White men," she said. "Who wear sheets to pretend no one knows who they are. They attack us in the night."

At that, my breath stayed trapped in my chest. "Is your family okay?"

She turned to look at me, and I could see the anger in her eyes, anger that had a long history and many faces. Anger like a forest fire, that could burn down a continent and not grow tired. "My daddy knows the senator, so they only left things in our yard. Dead animals, rabbits and a deer, strung from a tree. We keep our dog inside the house with us because of things like this, just in case. The dog woke us up, otherwise there's no telling what would have happened. Once they burned a house down on our street. The family barely got the kids out. They beat up my uncle in Taylorsville and burned several barns down on his road."

"Why didn't anyone stop them?" I asked.

"Who'd stop them?" said Nathan, quietly. "The police take their side. The mayor takes the side of the police chief. The state government doesn't want to get involved."

"That's why we live in town," said Wendy. "If anyone tried that in my neighborhood, they'd be surrounded by black men with shotguns, blocking all the exits." Her earrings swung, side to side, as she shook her head. "My grandpa says he'd never want to live out in the middle of nowhere like your family, Frederica."

"We got what we deserved then," said Frederica. Her voice shook, and she started to pack up her lunch with angry movements.

"That's awful, Frederica," said Justin quietly. "No one should have to live in that kind of fear. I'm glad you said something. I think that's what we all have to do now—speak up."

Frederica stopped packing her lunch and studied him. Her hands were still trembling.

"It can be dangerous to speak up," said Lion slowly. "Even for whites, man. Didn't you hear about that white man that got killed in Alabama last week? They targeted him especially because he was white. . . He was on the wrong side."

"I don't know about y'all," said Justin. "But I'd much rather speak up than pretend nothing's wrong, even if it means potentially facing down violence."

"That's what I'm talking about, man." Nathan clapped him on the shoulder.

As they nodded at each other, I saw Sarah May watching Nathan with an intensity that was equal parts fear and possessiveness, as if she knew people would make him a target and she dared them to go through her first. Her protectiveness seemed to come from a fear every bit as strong as Frederica's anger. Who did she picture facing him, when she imagined him hurt? The men at night? The police? Violence during a protest? I never knew.

"Sometimes people put themselves in harm's way for no reason," said Wendy.

Lion said nothing, and I couldn't tell what was behind his calm face.

"Isn't it worth it to speak up for what's right?" I said.

"Injustice needs to be challenged," said Nathan. "Whatever way we can. That's why we're here at this school."

"Challenged the right way, of course," added Justin. "Without violence or hate, but consistently, persistently, as Reverend King says. It's definitely worth the risk of putting yourself in harm's way, if there's any chance it'll change things for the sake of justice."

"Definitely," agreed Nathan. Again, they seemed like mismatched brothers.

"Your parents would have a heart attack if they heard you saying that, Nathan." Wendy kept glancing at Sarah May.

"Sometimes adults let their fear get in the way of what they know is right," said Justin.

"In this town, people talk all kinds of ways of standing up to injustice," said Nathan. "They tell us this town should be integrated, but I don't see them doing anything about it."

"Jesse Jackson did a lot for this town," said Lion.

"And then he left," said Nathan.

"There's Frederica's daddy," I said. "Isn't he doing the lawsuit against the school board?"

"And we're the ones who are living it out," said Wendy.

"Everyone in their own way, right?" I said. "Whatever way we can. Even if it's imperfect, it's worth it."

Sarah May took a large bite of her sandwich. Justin was staring out the foyer window.

"Here's to doing what's right, regardless," I said, lifting my thermos of milk aloft. The others smiled at me and raised their own cups. It was like we were Musketeers from the book we'd read in English class, and I was glad again that I had them for friends.

I soon found it was harder to take a stand when I was by myself.

That Saturday, I came home from my job at the drive-in wanting nothing but a shower to get rid of the smell of grease and the feeling of dried sweat. Marmee was in the bathroom, singing.

"Hurry up already, will you?" I banged on the bathroom door with the heel of my hand.

"She can't hear you," Cassie said from our bedroom.

"I don't care; I just want to get in there." I hit the door again. Marmee kept singing around the sound of running water, sounding like a mermaid. I sighed and went to our room.

"What are you doing?" I asked Cassie. She was lying on her stomach, kicking her heels in the air while she read the newspaper.

"Homework," she said. "I need to find a current event. Once a week someone has to bring in something from the newspaper to present to the class. My day's on Monday."

"What are you going to talk about?" I pulled off my shoes and wiggled my toes.

"I wanted to talk about this article, about the Christmas decorations they're putting up downtown, but Miss Jenkins doesn't like it if she thinks someone picked an article from the front page just because it's easiest."

I nodded, and Cassie turned to the second and third pages of the newspaper. I sat next to her and scanned the headlines. There was something about California's community colleges, something else about a library in Ashville, and then Elizabeth Taylor going to visit her sick father. There were several shorter articles intended to be humorous. I skimmed the article under a picture, about a man who "Didn't Stand Back": a man in Georgia who protected a fifteen-year-old girl from "a mob of Negro youths." I turned the page before Cassie could see it.

"I can't really understand this," she said, pointing at the next page. "Who are 'the Reds'?"

The headline read, "Gen. Harold Johnson Says He Believes S. Viet Nam Can Win Against Reds." The subtitle said, "With Continued Help From U.S."

"The Reds are the Communists," I said. Just the day before, two of my male classmates had shown up in new military uniforms they'd gotten when they enlisted. All day long, teachers and classmates were fawning over them. *Go get those Commies, boys! We're behind you,* I'd heard someone cheering in the hallway.

"I don't know if I could find Viet Nam on a map, if my teacher asked me," said Cassie.

"I probably couldn't either," I said. I paged past the articles about local beauty queens and local sports teams, the obituaries, the classifieds, and the comics. "What's this about?" I pulled the newspaper closer and tried to make sense of the dark picture. The title said "Melee At The White House." The picture below was titled "Washington Police Haul Away a Lie-Downer." The article at the top of the page read, "LBJ Says He Won't Be 'Blackjacked.'" The article in the middle of the page proclaimed, "Tensions Over Voting Rights in Selma Continue."

"Cassie, what about these? This could be really good to talk about," I told her. "It's about civil rights protests in Alabama and Washington, D.C."

"What protests?"

"Some colored people in Alabama are trying to vote, but the state won't let them, so some people are marching. . ."

"Like an army?" Her heels swung around, crisscrossing in the air.

"Except they aren't an army. They're just people. They're walking, a big group of them, trying to sign up to vote like they're supposed to be able to. The police or someone stopped them and. . . hurt some people."

"They were just walking?"

I nodded. "It's a lot of colored people, and the governor didn't like what they were doing."

"Why not?" Cassie was tracing the pattern of my quilt with her index finger.

"They just don't, I guess." I felt at a loss for how to explain it. "Some white people," I said, "think colored people shouldn't be treated the same way they want to be treated. They don't want them to do things white people can do, like vote. Colored people used to have to sit in the back of the bus and on the worst seats of the train. They can't get the same types of jobs, things like that."

"Because they're dirty and stupid," said Cassie, matter-of-factly.

I stared at my sister. "Cassie, where did that come from? You know it's not true."

She looked up at me. "That's what everyone at school says. Even Aunt Be says not to play with blacks because they're dirty."

I was so suddenly angry and upset, I was shaking. My little sister seemed like a complete stranger. "Cassie, you know better than that. Colored people are no dirtier than white people, just because of the color of their skin. We grew up with colored people, Cassie. All your life until now you played with people whose skin was black. Whether or not they bathe isn't determined by their skin color."

"But Aunt Be says. . ."

"I don't care what Aunt Be says. You should know better. White people who say things like that are trying to make themselves look better than colored people. . . even Aunt Be. That makes colored people's lives harder."

Cassie turned back to the newspaper and frowned. "Maybe I better not do those articles," she said. "Miss Jenkins won't like talking about that." She started reading an article about a rescue dog.

I let it pass, but I was still shaky when I finally got into the bathroom for my shower. Why was Cassie so willing to take the side of Aunt Be, when it went against what she knew?

I felt uneasy about how I hadn't argued harder. I should have made Cassie see; I should have explained it better. I should have convinced her. I wished Nathan or Frederica or Justin had been around to help me explain. It was important, but I was at a loss for how to make Cassie understand.

What kind of justice warrior was I, when I couldn't even explain it right to my sister?

CHAPTER 10

AFTER CHRISTMAS BREAK, I thought I might be able to discontinue my after-school tutoring sessions with Emily Rose.

The first day back, I saw her at her locker before school. I left Wendy and Frederica, saying that I'd see them at lunch.

"Hi, Emily Rose. How was your Christmas?"

She seemed a bit startled, but she smiled when she saw me and unclenched the books from her chest. "Hi, Adelaide," she said. "It was nice, thank you. My grandmother came from Charleston, and my aunt and uncle from Atlanta stayed with us too. It was crowded, but I didn't want to come back to school yet. My uncle and I were working on an experiment to produce sodium carbonate from the stones in our garden."

"Did it work?" I asked.

"No, not very well. I think our sulfuric acid was diluted or that the stones from the garden weren't pure limestone."

The bell rang then, so I had to rush my question. "Do we still need to meet after school for tutoring?"

Emily Rose pushed some hair out of her face and shifted the books balanced on her hip. "I don't know how much more

tutoring you need, but maybe we can still meet to work on homework together? That way if you have any questions, I can help. But
we don't have to call it tutoring, if you don't want to."

Her expression was hesitant, but hopeful, as if she was offering something that she wanted me to accept. "Okay," I said before
thinking. "I guess that would be good."

She smiled and rushed away to class. I had wanted to be done
with tutoring to rid myself of the humiliation. But she had said
this didn't need to be *tutoring* any more. Just working on homework together, like two friends. I supposed I could do that.

By mid-January, I was feeling much less self-conscious around
Justin. He had melded into our lunch group, and I had learned
how to talk with him normally without anything terrible happening. So my guard was down when he stopped beside me, one day
on our way out to lunch, as I lagged behind the others to re-tie
my shoe.

"How's your weekend look, Adelaide? Do you have any plans
for Saturday?"

"Just work," I said, feeling suddenly out of breath because of
his tone.

"How about Friday night?"

"I'll probably have to work then, too. We've been busy lately."
I glanced at him. He was backlit by bright clouds and a magno-
lia tree, and everything about him seemed straight angles, from
his jaw to his elbows jutting out because his hands were in his
pockets.

He laughed, a little self-consciously. "Good thing I know
you're not making that up. What about Thursday night?"

"Thursday night? Nothing. Why?" I straightened and took a
step back. He was closer than he'd ever been; he seemed taller
when he was right next to me. Wendy was right: he was awfully
handsome.

"My dad said I could borrow the car sometime. Do you want to go with me to see a movie or maybe get a milkshake?"

My mouth tasted like metal. I didn't know what to say. "I. . . uh. . . I don't know if my dad would let me."

"I'd be glad to meet him. I can come by and ask him, if that would help."

I imagined Justin in my grandmother's house, amidst the flowered wallpaper and the worn tracks in the floor. My grandmother, aunt, and mother would never let me hear the end of it.

"Dads love me," he said, smiling. "So, is that a yes, if he agrees?"

The others were a good ways ahead. I tried to keep my voice even. "What movie?"

"*My Fair Lady* is playing," he said. "I've heard it's funny and that girls like it." He smiled again, and a small, untamed part of me really wanted to say yes.

"Maybe. . ." I said before I caught myself. I looked away, blushing. Suddenly, an idea: "Maybe as a group?" Wendy was the closest, and I called out to her. "Wendy, you free Thursday?"

"What for?" she asked, waiting for us to catch up with her.

"Want to come to a movie?" Wendy looked at Justin. They both shifted uncomfortably. "Can you?" I asked.

Justin ran his hand over the ridges of his hair.

Wendy looked away. "They wouldn't let me into the theater with you." Her voice was flat. "Colored people have to sit in the balcony."

I felt stupid beyond words, but before I could say anything, Justin spoke up. "The drive-in movie doesn't have separate sections."

"They'd never let us in if we were sitting in the same car," said Wendy.

I wanted to hide. Why couldn't I just tell him no?

"I'll figure out a way around it," said Justin, catching my expression. "That rule isn't just, anyway. It should be broken." He looked confident again. "What do you say, Lion? Join us?"

"What you talking about doing?" Frederica turned around to ask as we settled into the steps in the foyer.

I glanced at Justin. He smiled. "Adelaide and I are going to a drive-in movie. We're trying to convince Wendy and Lion to come too."

"Frederica, you're welcome too," I said quickly. "The more, the merrier."

"Y'all doing what?" said Frederica. "Nuh-uh."

"Civil disobedience, man," said Justin, nodding at Nathan. Nathan thrust his chin out and nodded back.

"A sit-in at a movie?" asked Lion. "I like movies, count me in."

"How you going to do it?" asked Sarah May. "You never going to make it past the gate if y'all riding together."

"My cousin works as a ticket-taker," said Justin. "I can talk him into letting us in. We just have to go to his line, and we'll be fine."

"No one will see in the windows?" The lines on Wendy's forehead showed how little trust she had in this plan. Maybe if she wouldn't go, I could use that as an excuse to back out.

"You ever been to a drive-in movie?" asked Nathan. He glanced at Sarah May and smiled. "Not many people looking in the windows of other cars, man. Most people either focused on the movie or focused on what's happening in their own car. The privacy of each car is part of what's. . . encouraged. . . there. Everybody just mind their own business at the drive-in."

Frederica and Lion laughed at Sarah May's blushing. Justin looked a little embarrassed at the insinuation of what might happen inside other cars.

"It's a movement toward greater integration. There's little danger because no one will be bothered, and we're still making a statement. We're being radical by saying this should be normal."

"Maybe this isn't the best idea," I said.

"It's an immoral rule that discriminates against the black race," said Nathan. "No one's done a sit-in at the drive-in yet."

"Don't look at me," said Frederica. She pursed her lips. "I

wouldn't be able to set foot in my church again if anyone saw me going to a movie, sit-in or no."

"My mother and grandmother barely let me out of the house to go with Nathan, and they like him," said Sarah May. "They'd never let me go with a boy they don't know."

"It sounds like a risk," I said. "Is it worth it, for this particular rule?"

"Come on, Adelaide," said Lion. "We'll be like freedom riders."

"This ain't a bus," I said.

Everyone laughed, but the subject of freedom riders made us all sit up a bit straighter. If what I was doing was part of a larger goal, not just an excuse to spend time with Justin. . .

"Wendy? What do you say?" I asked.

"If people find out. . . even if people *see* me in the car with two white kids, they'd get angry."

"Who would?"

She sighed. "Everyone. My granddad and Meemaw. My big sister. My uncles, my cousins. . . It's not just sitting at a lunch counter next to strangers. There's something personal about riding in a car with *particular* white people."

"I thought your family had gotten used to the idea of me," I said.

"You? Well. . . they know you grew up in Africa, so they think you strange enough that it don't really matter."

I opened my mouth to protest, but Justin shook his head before I could say anything. "So it's me they'd be scared of?" he said.

"A white boy? Sure," she said. "Me riding in a car with a strange white boy would be their worst nightmare."

Lion elbowed her in the ribs. "I'd be there too. They know me. It's not like it would just be you and him."

Wendy and I looked at each other. She seemed to be trying to figure out if I wanted her to say yes. I didn't know what I wanted. Finally, I shrugged. "Justin's right—the rules and every-one's opinion aren't fair. We should do a sit-in. Wendy, didn't you listen when Nathan was talking about that Civil Disobedience thing?"

Wendy rolled her eyes. "That book he was quoting from was banned and blacklisted. . . for probably this exact reason, so it wouldn't be used to excuse stupid things like this." The others groaned. Finally, she threw up her hands. "Fine, fine. . . But tomorrow we are all having a lesson about how to behave during a sit-in." She pointed a finger at Lion, Justin, and me. "And I mean all y'alls."

I almost missed Justin's quick wink in my direction. I blinked, looked at my knees, and straightened my skirt over them, wiping my suddenly damp palms as I did so. That wink—as if he'd won me over—made my stomach swoop. It played over and over in my mind, and every time it did, I felt a little giddy, despite myself.

I knew I needed to get my dad's permission before I could go to the movie. And I knew I had to time it just right.

I avoided asking him when I saw him at the fence as I walked home. I merely waved and asked him how the tractor was behaving today. He smiled, said the tractor didn't like its feed and needed a whip to learn who was boss.

My dad still seemed so out of place—he should have been in a classroom instead of on a tractor seat, sweating through his hatband. His nails were now almost permanently ringed in dirt, and the wrinkled, freckled skin at the back of his neck was now continually sunburnt above the collar of his shirt.

Aunt Candice and Uncle Henry were over for dinner, so I couldn't ask Dad then. Instead, I went looking for him after I dried the dishes. He was alone in the living room, his chin sunk down on his chest, snoring in front of the typewriter.

"Dad," I said, standing in the doorway. He sat up with a jerk.

"Yes? What? What's wrong?"

"Nothing, nothing," I said. I felt uncomfortable with his full attention on me like that; I suddenly forgot what I'd meant to ask him. I cleared my throat, stalling.

As I searched for words, his attention wandered to the page scrolling out of the typewriter. Even as he faced me, waiting, he used the corner of his eye to scan back through what he'd written previously.

"I just wanted to ask you about whether I could go see a movie on Saturday with some friends."

"A movie? That sounds fun."

"I can go?"

"Sure," he said. "I'm glad you're making friends and doing fun things."

I nodded, surprised it had been so easy. I turned to go.

"Wait, who are you going with? Are your cousins part of the group?" He scratched his ear.

"No. . . not Bernice and Julia." I shifted. "My friend Wendy is coming." I watched his reaction, to see if there was any recognition, any realization of who Wendy was and what that meant about my breaking the rules: his, Aunt Be's, the movie theater's.

He nodded. "All right. Does she live around here? Can you walk together? Do you need someone to pick you up after?"

"No, she doesn't live close by. Someone else is borrowing his father's car."

"Oh," said my dad, focusing. "A boy? Who is he? Well, I suppose there are two of you girls going. That's better than being alone with him. Glad for that. You keep an eye on him, though."

I resisted the urge to tell him that my cousins were alone with boys all the time, if the rumors I heard at school were true.

"So it's all right?"

"That's fine," he said. He started turning back to the typewriter, then paused. "But I want you to come straight home after the movie." He raised an eyebrow. "And I want to meet this boy when he picks you up. Afterward, I'll be waiting at the door."

"Thanks, Dad." I didn't bother to tell him it wouldn't be like that. I just nodded and swallowed, then left my dad to his work.

I had trouble sleeping that night. I was curious about the experience of a drive-in movie. I had never been to one, and it was one of the things I secretly wished I could understand when others talked about it. I would have preferred to go with Wendy, Nathan, and Sarah May, but they wouldn't have been able to take me—Justin was the one with access to a car.

I also kept thinking about what he'd said about the rules being unjust, deserving of being broken. The way he'd said it made me want to break those rules with him, made me want to sneak in Wendy and Lion, just to see if we could, just to show up injustice.

A sit-in at the drive-in. I told myself this was part of my American experience, something interesting before I returned to Ethiopia. Part of a full, varied experience. I'd be able to tell everyone else in the village about it. It'd be a good story for my and Maicaah's children: about the time I saw a movie as a protest—with a different boy, not their father. Something to tease Maicaah with when he was acting too sure of himself.

A sit-in at the drive-in. I was ready.

CHAPTER 11

WE'D AGREED THAT JUSTIN would pick me up at home, then the two of us would pick up Lion and Wendy on Old Easley Highway by the train tracks.

I was ready and waiting on the porch when Justin's car pulled in the drive. By the time he'd gotten out of the car, I was halfway across the lawn.

"Am I late?" he asked.

"No, I'm just ready to go," I said. "Come on." I started toward the passenger side, but Justin stopped me at the bumper with a hand on my arm.

"Where's your dad?"

"I'll just tell him he missed you."

"Do you not want me to meet your family?" Justin was smiling, but he wasn't teasing.

"I just thought it would be. . . uncomfortable," I said.

"It will be." Without waiting for me, he walked up the porch steps and rang the doorbell. I saw a corner of the lace curtain move, and I was certain my sisters were spying on us.

I sighed, then went to join him on the porch. Everything was quiet inside, so I opened the door and showed him in. Cassie and Marmee scrambled around the corner to the dining room.

Justin called my dad *sir* and talked to him about the weather and school and the farm. He called my aunt, mother, and grandmother *ma'am*, in a tone that made them all smile. Even Aunt Be seemed to admire his crisp blonde haircut and origami profile. He was wearing a blue sports coat, chinos, and a plaid shirt, nicer than he usually looked for school.

I hadn't taken off my coat when we came inside. When a brief silence came up, I took the chance and grabbed Justin's arm. "Time for us to go now. . . We don't want to be late picking up our other friends."

Justin shook hands with my dad and told all the grown-ups it had been nice to meet each of them. I hadn't expected how self-conscious I felt walking away with Justin, under the scrutiny of my entire family. I waved stiffly at my sisters' faces in the window when Justin opened the car door for me.

Then we were alone in the car, Justin and me. The bench seat was wide, and he felt about a mile away but still too close.

"Ready to be a freedom rider?" he asked. He gave me a lopsided smile that put his dimples at their best advantage. "Did I pass the test?"

"Which test?"

"Your family."

I raised a mock clipboard and pretended to tally points like I'd seen the judges do at a school track meet. "Eleven out of seventeen," I announced. "The distance on your long jump was excellent, but your form was poor coming out of the gate."

"Poor form?" he asked. "You might need to redefine your form, if I got excellent distance."

"Take it to the judging panel. They'll hear any and all complaints between two-thirty and three-oh-four on every other Monday afternoon."

"Tough crowd. My last Olympics I won all gold."

"New year, new rules."

"Apparently," he said and laughed again. When he shifted gears, his hand rested on the seat in between us.

It was easier talking with him than I'd expected. A small, secret part of me was almost disappointed when we saw Wendy and Lion waiting by the railroad tracks.

For a while, the car reverberated with loud conversation. Lion leaned forward, more verbal than I'd ever seen him be. Justin gestured broadly, his eyes moving constantly from the road to me to the rearview mirror. I laughed a lot at the jokes he and Lion were making. Only Wendy didn't say much; she kept tugging at her headband.

Then we pulled off the road into the line of cars entering the drive-in theater, and I didn't feel like laughing anymore. My palms were sweating, and I wiped them on the sides of my skirt.

I didn't think anyone in front of or behind us would notice the mixture of people inside, but then the line split into two lanes. When we rolled forward, I kept an eye on the car that was beside us. At first they didn't notice anything, but then suddenly both the man and the woman in the front seat, and two kids in the back, were staring at us. The little girl in the backseat had her mouth open and was pointing, but the adults just scowled.

Wendy and Lion stared straight ahead through the windshield, not making eye contact, just as Wendy had told us to do. Lion was picking at a hangnail on his thumb. In the quiet, I could hear the belts turning in the engine.

Finally it was our turn to pull up to the ticket booth. Justin rolled down his window and waved.

"Everyone, this is Jeremy. Jeremy, this is Adelaide, Wendy, and Judah, whom we call Lion." I could only see Jeremy's shoulders, neck, and chin. He made no effort to greet us in any way, just stiffly mumbled something and handed Justin the ticket.

"Thanks," said Justin.

"Nice to meet you," I muttered.

The parking lot was about a third full and quickly filling up. Justin pulled in to a spot slightly to the right of the center, about midway toward the screen.

Just as we parked, a group of little kids ran screaming by us. They didn't even look inside, they were in too big of a rush toward the playground equipment right beneath the screen. More colored kids Cassie's age erupted from the car parked two spots to our left, and they ran toward the open field next to the playground.

Justin rolled down his window and pulled the speaker in from the post next to his door. He switched it on and turned the volume up completely. Scratchy classical music filled the car. "Can you hear that?" he asked.

"Wish I didn't," said Lion.

"We made it." I turned half around to smile brightly at Wendy. She still looked a bit clammy.

"Yeah," she said. "So far."

Justin turned around also. His knee touched mine in the center of the front seat before I shifted away. "Who wants popcorn or a Coke?"

Wendy's answer was prompt and prim. "No, thank you."

"I'm fine, thanks," said Lion.

"I'd like some," I said. "But am I supposed to say *no thank you*?"

Justin laughed. "Say yes if you want to. I'll go get some."

When he was gone, I turned again to Wendy. "Is it better if we stay in the car, or can we get out too?"

She glanced at Lion. "Well, I need to go to the ladies' 'fore the movie starts. Why don't you come with me." She still seemed shaky.

No one noticed us step out of the same car. "I am perspiring something awful," she said when the car door closed. She fanned herself, and we smiled at each other.

We had almost made it to the bathrooms when a car whipped into the parking space in front of us and stopped a few inches short of hitting me. Two girls spilled out of the back seat and fell to the ground, laughing much more than normal. They seemed unable to right themselves to walk. I recognized them from school—one was Tara-Lee Kensington, whose family employed Sarah May's mother. I didn't know the name of the other girl. They hadn't even noticed us. Wendy and I stepped around them. Wendy's frown was strong in judgment.

"Adelaide Elaine *Hen*-derson!"

My breath caught. Bernice was standing in the open door of the same car, her feet on the running board so that she towered over us. "Who did you come with?" she squinted as if she couldn't see Wendy clearly.

"It's one of the blacks from school!" said the girl I didn't recognize. Her words ran together; she was still tangled up on the ground.

"Don't mind them, Bernie," said a boy from inside the car. An arm with a beer bottle reached out to circle her waist and pull her backward. "Come back inside with me."

"It's my cousin," she said. She braced herself on the ceiling of the car and the door frame, resisting him. "Let go."

"Tell them to join us!" One of the boys in the front seat rolled down the passenger window and leaned out. He was older than us, more like college age. There were two other boys beside him in the front seat. "Come on," he said. "We're not particular—you're both girls. Join us!"

Wendy pulled my elbow. She was looking at the horizon. "Let's go," she whispered.

"We're just on our way to the ladies' room," I said.

"To the ladies', to the ladies'!" the boy from the front seat chanted, swinging his arms like a conductor. "Where all girls must go together. Come join us afterward! Say you will!"

"Sure," I said, trying to get him to stop yelling. "Sure."

There were cheers from the boys in the front seat. "Wonderful!" said the spokesman. "What's wrong with y'all there on the ground? Can't y'all walk?"

Wendy and I took a few steps away. I kept looking back. Tara-Lee was still on the ground, holding herself up with her hands and giggling. Bernice was fighting with the boy behind her, swatting his grabbing hands until she finally jerked herself free. She didn't look at us as she stumbled past us toward the bathroom. She shoved her way inside and pulled the door shut behind her. Several women in line ahead of us, white and colored, made angry sounds, but no one did anything. No one even glanced twice at Wendy and me.

By the time we made it to the front of the line, Bernice still hadn't emerged. I went quickly, then washed my hands slowly. Wendy was waiting for me by the door.

"Hey, Bernice. . ." I called. "Are you still in here?"

She banged open the stall door and went to the sink. She didn't look at me. A heavily pregnant woman walked a toddler into the stall Bernice had left open.

I stepped a little closer. "Bernice, those boys don't seem nice at all. What are you doing with them?" She moved as if she was wading through water, and she smelled strongly of cheap alcohol, the kind Grandmother said should only be used as a meat tenderizer.

"None of your business." She squinted in my direction fiercely. Her skin looked yellowed in the bathroom light.

"Look, I know we don't get along all that much, but. . . I still wouldn't want you to get hurt."

A girl who was about twelve came out of a stall and moved to the sink behind me. I moved a little closer to Bernice.

"You're the one who's going to get hurt," said Bernice. She nodded at Wendy, and her smile was sickly. "I'll tell on you, and Aunt Be is gonna tan your hide. She might even kick you out."

I had the urge to push her. "Aunt Be's not my mother."

Bernice snorted. "The mother you have isn't doing you much good, is she?"

I clenched my fist to keep from slapping her. I was very conscious of Wendy standing by the door, behind me. She would be so angry if I started a fight. "You can drink yourself to hell if you want to," I told Bernice. "See if I care."

I was almost to the door before I stopped and faced her again. "But if you tell on me, I'll tell your father how drunk you and your friends are. I'll tell how that boy was taking liberties with you. See how you like having your hide tanned."

Bernice was the first to break eye contact. I turned and left the bathroom.

On our way back to the car, Wendy seemed to be searching for words. "Your cousin sure is a peach," she said finally. "What was that comment about your mama?"

"Nothing." I wished she hadn't brought it up. I didn't want to talk about my mother. I still wanted to wipe the smugness off Bernice's face.

Lion was leaning against the rear bumper, next to the word *Ambassador* sprawled across the trunk. "It was getting stuffy in there with the windows up," he said.

We leaned against the bumper next to him. In the near dark of the lot, everyone seemed involved in their own group, greeting people who had just joined them, or getting ready for the movie.

Justin was making his way toward us from the concession stand. Every few feet, someone stopped him to say hello. Cartoons had started showing on the screen, and the flow of cars entering had slowed to a trickle. One of the cars pulled in next to us, and two boys jumped out. Even I recognized them as football players.

One, walking backward while he talked, bumped into Lion.

He started to automatically apologize as he turned around, but he stopped when he saw Lion. "Watch where you're going," he said.

The other guys behind him laughed. Lion didn't move a muscle.

Then the football player saw Justin. "Preacher Boy! I didn't know you were going to be here." He clapped Justin on the shoulder, and a little popcorn spilled to the ground. "Wait. . ." He looked between Justin and Lion, Wendy and me. "Are you with this crowd?"

The football player's tone was conversational, but his friends had come up on either side of him—trapping Lion, Wendy, and me against the car. Beside the two football players was Jimmy Campbell, swinging his arms on either side of his legs. There were four of us and three of them, but they were big.

Without looking at the boys' faces, Wendy stepped sideways, to where she was no longer cornered. I took a step to a diagonal, so one of the players had to turn a little. Lion stepped toward another just enough to make him back up without realizing what he was doing. Wendy had told us in her lunch-time lecture, "Don't let yourself get trapped. That makes you an easy target. Watch where you're standing."

Then Justin put an arm around each of the football players, popcorn bucket hanging from either hand. His posture was as relaxed and easy as swinging in a hammock.

"We came to see *My Fair Lady*, same as you chumps. What happened, couldn't find any girls willing to come with you? I thought y'all would find it easier to talk to girls without me around to get all the attention."

For a second, his attitude put in doubt everything I thought I knew about him—how had I ever thought he was serious about this? He must have been acting the whole time. And yet, his ribbing shifted their attention to him, and they forgot about the rest of us. One of the boys stole a handful of popcorn from one of the buckets, and Justin kicked him away. "Go get your own," he said. "The song-and-dance numbers are about to start."

"Man, is that what this movie is?" one of the football players asked the other.

"I thought this was about a girl in danger," said Jimmy Campbell.

Justin laughed at them as the three started arguing. He waved, but they barely saw as they got back in the car and drove away. No other car took their spot.

Back inside the car, my back and legs felt sticky under my dress. Only now did I realize how afraid I'd been. What would we have done if they'd stepped forward, instead of back? They so nearly had us trapped. And Justin. . . Could you really trust someone who could so smoothly get others to do what he wanted?

No one said anything.

Justin handed me a bucket of popcorn, then reached inside his sports jacket to pull out a bottle of Coke. He passed it to the backseat, then pulled out another one and opened it with a quick move of his keys. He passed it to me and took a handful of popcorn. I glanced at the backseat, but Wendy and Lion weren't looking at each other either.

The cartoon ended. The big screen went black, and then some music started. The grayscale logo of WB appeared, and then faded away.

My right elbow brushed against the car door. Justin looked at the Coke in my hand and smiled, asking if I minded sharing. I reached it toward him, my arm fully extended across the vastness of the front seat.

He took a swig, then glanced at the backseat. "Can y'all see all right?"

Wendy and Lion were sitting toward the middle, craning their necks to see the full screen. I could see how it would work for children, but Lion had to hunch down pretty far to see through the windshield.

"It's not the best view," Wendy admitted.

"Come sit up here," I said. "There's plenty of room for all of us."

Wendy and Lion looked at each other. Lion stretched his neck and rubbed the back of it. "I probably will get a headache if I sit like this the whole movie."

I opened my car door. I didn't look at Justin as I slid toward him. Wendy scooted in next to me, holding one of the buckets of popcorn. Lion scooted in next. When he closed the car door, I inched over to give Wendy a little more room. My elbow and knee touched Justin, just barely. Flowers appeared on the screen, overlaid with different names.

Wendy laughed breathlessly. "Feels like we're playing sardines."

Lion leaned back against the seat. "*Is* a lot more comfortable, though. Pardon me if I fall asleep. . ."

"If you snore," said Wendy, "I'm going to pinch your nose closed until you wake up."

"How do you know my snoring won't sound better than the soundtrack? My mama always said I was musical."

"Save that musicality for the bedroom, Lion," I said.

A full second passed, and then Wendy laughed outright, her real, boisterous laugh.

I blushed. "I mean. . ." They were all laughing at me. "I didn't mean. . . I always say the wrong thing." I buried my burning face into Wendy's shoulder.

"Don't worry," said Justin. "It's charming." He reached into the popcorn bucket, and his other hand, meant to hold the bucket steady, landed on mine. It was a few seconds before he had a handful of kernels and pulled his hand away.

"Shh. It's starting," said Wendy.

I took a swig of Coke and tried to forget about tall, blonde Justin, who could smooth-talk his way out of a potential riot, and whose leg was brushing mine.

※

I dreamed about Ethiopia that night, when I finally got to bed—much later than I normally did—after Justin and I had dropped off Wendy and Lion in their neighborhood, after Justin had dropped me off and walked me to the door. He said good night from a few feet away, on the top step of the porch, and then he waved at my father, visible in the lit living room window. I watched him walk back to his car before I shut the door.

In my dream, I was running toward the cape chestnut, but once I got there I realized something wasn't right. It wasn't the tree I was looking for, and Maicaah wasn't there. I heard the ibis call from several different directions at once, and I couldn't tell if it was Maicaah's call echoing or if it was a flock of birds. I was supposed to have looked for him as I went through the village, but I had missed him somehow. He had been in front of me and then he was behind and then he wasn't there when I looked—he was gone. I knew the bell was going to ring soon, in my dream, and I had to leave and couldn't go back to look for him. I had missed my chance to find him. He was gone. Finding the tree had been useless. I tried to shout for him, but I couldn't remember the words in Oromiffa. My shouts froze in my mouth, gibberish, gagging me.

I awoke freezing cold.

After I picked up the blankets I'd kicked off, I pulled out the narrow box from my bedside table, ran my finger over the velvety pouch. In the dark, I was afraid to shake out the seeds, I could so easily lose them. I reached my finger inside the pouch and felt them. The pips were tiny and withered-feeling. I tried to remember the burgundy fruit they'd come from, tried to remember Maicaah eating the pomegranate, the tang of the juice in my own mouth, but I couldn't pull the memories to mind. All I had were the little husks of what had been. I tucked them back away quickly, carefully, before I lost them.

CHAPTER 12

I woke up to Cassie screaming through the house. "Adelie! Mom! Dad! Adelie! Marmee! There's snow!"

My feet were chilled as soon as I swung them over the side of the bed. The temperature had drastically dropped overnight.

"What is it?" said Marmee from her bed.

I pulled on some socks and threw some toward her. I pulled the blanket off the bed and kept it wrapped around me.

Cassie was jumping up and down by the window in the hallway. "Look how it's coming down! Can I go play in it? Adelie, come with me!"

Aunt Be poked her head around the banister at the bottom of the stairs. "It's been an unseasonably warm winter... We were due. Get ready for a holy mess."

Mother went to the window and put her hands on Cassie's shoulders. "I haven't seen snow like this since I was a little girl."

Grandmother leaned on the banister to yell up at us. "Come down and look! The dogs are going crazy."

Marmee peered around Cassie. "The trees look like something from a fairy tale," she said. "What does it taste like?"

"Haven't you ever seen snow before?" My dad asked.

"No!" the three of us said together.

Grandmother made us put on long underwear and heavy coats, scarves, gloves, and scratchy wool hats. Then we pulled on our rain boots and clomped outside. Mother clutched a blanket around her nightgown and stepped outside in her own rain boots.

"It melts!" said Cassie, watching Marmee's outstretched glove.

The front yard was thickly dusted with white, already covering the faded grass. By the garden fence, there was a pile of white like a heap of ashes at the edge of a fire pit. The world was turning whiter by the minute.

"It's caught on my eyelashes!" I laughed—I could see the heavy white flakes wherever I looked.

"It's in your hair," Marmee brushed the tendrils of hair that fell below my hat. Snowflakes streaked the lenses of her glasses, but she didn't seem to notice.

"Look at the dogs!" The farm mutts were chasing snowflakes, trying to bite them and sneezing. Cassie ran after them; their tails wagged harder as she chased snowflakes with them.

I scooped up a handful and brought my open hand up to my mouth. I licked, tentatively. It thought it would taste like ice cream, but it was more delicate and less tangible, more like the absence of flavor than something noticeable for its own sake. It tasted the way I thought patience would taste.

Aunt Be told us they'd just heard on the radio that school was canceled, so we stayed outside to play tag in the snow, our rain-boots slipping around on our feet. I skidded once, and when I fell, the ground was harder than I expected, and the snow was cold against my neck.

"Snow angels!" cried Cassie. She lay down on the snow next to me and slid her arms up and down and kicked her feet out. "Is this how you do it?"

"Stand up and let's see." Sure enough, there was the shape we'd read about.

"It needs a halo," Marmee wove some twigs together to form a crown, which she laid at the head of the snow print.

We played in the snow until our fingers wouldn't bend and our feet hurt from the cold. My nose was running and burned when I wiped at it with my frozen glove. The yard was covered with our footprints and the dogs' prints and our snow angels. When the sun eventually poked through the clouds, everything shone like crystal.

Mother had made hot chocolate and pancakes. After breakfast, Aunt Be stood over the sink watching the snow—as still as I'd ever seen her—and our mom sat down at the piano to play. We'd never heard her play before. It was like the snow had baptized our normal school day morning into something better.

We gathered around Mother slowly, our bodies looser than usual from playing outside, but afraid of bringing our looseness too close to her, as if it might somehow disrupt this good mood of hers. She taught us several songs—her fingers fluttering around on the keyboard more naturally than I'd imagined possible, her voice so much brighter and clearer than usual.

Cassie leaned against her, pressing into her back, and Marmee perched next to her on the bench. I remembered what Bernice had said, and I lifted my chin, thinking how wrong she was—if she could only see this. I sat down on Mother's other side. Her sleeve brushed me when her left hand reached for the farther keys. I couldn't remember the last time I'd seen her smile.

By lunchtime, the sun had melted all the snow, leaving only traces of it in the shadows and ditches. Our snow angels were gone, and our tracks had turned to muddy patches.

After playing for us, Mother had retreated for a nap. When she woke up, her eyes were expressionless again.

Cassie caught Mother in the hallway and threw her arms around her. "Play something else, Mama!"

Mother didn't respond, and she looked down at Cassie like she couldn't remember what she was talking about. She set Cassie back, unknotting Cassie's arms from around her. She went into the bathroom and locked the door.

I followed Cassie down to the den, not sure whether I should say something or distract her. What could I say? Cassie went straight to the piano and sat on the bench. She reached out both hands, fingers over the keys. Her hands were too small to imitate Mother's reach, so, instead, she plinked away with one finger, testing the sounds of the keys. At first she played softly, but before long she was tapping out a loud conglomeration of notes.

Suddenly Mother loomed in the doorway. "That's not how to play," she said. Cassie stopped and pulled her hands back from the keyboard, but Mother had already turned and disappeared.

"Let's go outside, Cassie," I said. She sat, looking at her hands in her lap, and didn't respond. "Come on. Let's get some air." I put my hand on her shoulder, loosely, briefly. I wasn't sure if she wanted to be touched, so I took my hand away and just stood behind her. After a minute she stood, still without looking at me, and I followed her outside. Marmee was sitting on the porch steps, and the three of us together went around back and into the orchard. All the trees were bare and depressing.

"I wish school hadn't been cancelled today," said Cassie.

Marmee and I said nothing. One of the songs Mother had played on the piano in the morning was stuck in my head.

The last few months of the school year passed quickly. Between classes, lunch on the foyer steps, homework sessions with Emily Rose, and my job on the weekends, I was surprised to suddenly realize it was warm enough to move back outside to the side steps of the auditorium during lunch. For a while people whispered about me and Justin, but he didn't ask me to do anything else, and we didn't do any more sit-ins.

I had finally caught up enough in math to be able to understand what Mr. Dykart was talking about. I could follow along and dumbly replicate his steps, but I couldn't understand why it was that way, and that bothered me. Regardless, I knew enough to pass the exams now, and I was no longer afraid of having to repeat the class. I knew I owed it to Emily Rose's patience with me.

A month before the end of school, Emily Rose and I had no motivation to do homework. Instead, she told me about her grandmother's beach house.

She peered at me, shyly. "My cousins aren't going this year, and my parents said I could invite a friend."

"That sounds fun, Emily Rose," I said. She seemed to waiting for a response. Had I missed something? "It sounds real nice."

"So you'll go?"

"Me?"

"My parents said they'd love to have you. I don't want to be the only girl. And it's the beach, so you know you'll have fun."

She was earnest. Didn't she have other friends she'd rather invite? I couldn't just ask like that. "It sounds wonderful, Emily Rose. But I don't know if my parents will let me."

Suddenly, she smiled broadly. "It's the beach," she said. "How could they say no to letting you go to the beach?"

"I've never been to the beach," I said.

"How have you never been to the beach?" she asked. "You've been to Ethiopia and Rome and London and New York and who knows where all else. How have you not been to the beach?"

I shrugged. I still couldn't understand why she'd picked me. Surely she had other friends, but I couldn't think of anyone I'd ever seen sitting with her at school.

When I asked my dad for permission that night, he said it was fine, as long as it wasn't a problem with my job. I told him I was sure I could find a substitute.

Wendy and Sarah May said they were jealous; Frederica told me which beach I should go to that was the best. Nathan said he'd been to Myrtle Beach and to visit his grandmother on Hilton Head, but he'd never been to Charleston. Lion, like me, had never been to the beach. Justin said his mother and sister liked Charleston, but his dad rarely took vacations.

My sisters were astounded that I got to go. Marmee made me promise to bring her back a seashell. Cassie was less enthusiastic. "Everyone in my class has been to the beach except for me," she said. "The only other person who hasn't been is Frankie Knox." She said the name with a derision that clarified the problem. Obviously no one wanted to be in the same category of anything as Frankie Knox.

"Maybe you can go with Mom and Dad next year, Cassie," I said. We were shelling peas on the front porch, which had the double benefit of giving us a breeze and being out of earshot of the kitchen. "Keep asking. They always give in for you, eventually."

"Really?" asked Cassie, as if I'd presented a whole new realm of possibility.

Marmee and I laughed. After a minute, Marmee changed the subject. "For English class I have to tell a story of my most memorable birthday party, but the problem is, I can only think of your birthday parties, Adelie. I wish I could tell the story of your third birthday. That's the one I keep thinking of."

"My third birthday? How do you remember that?"

"People used to tell it a lot in the village. It was one of Haadha Demiksa's favorites."

I'd forgotten that Kinci's mother, who I called Haadha Meti, wasn't as close to Marmee and Cassie. They addressed her the same way all the other kids in the village had addressed her, as the mother of Kinci's eldest brother Demiksa, instead of by her own name.

Cassie put her chin up like she was listening to something far away. "Is Haadha Demiksa the one who braided our hair?"

"One of the ones," said Marmee. They had usually gone together. "Haadha Ibsituu did also."

"Why did we braid our hair when we were in Africa?" asked Cassie. "It took so long. Why didn't we just put it in one or two braids, like we do now?"

"That's how all the other kids in the village did their hair, Cassie. Don't you remember? We did it so we'd be like them."

I tried to remember Haadha Meti telling the story of my third birthday, but I couldn't recall it. "Marmee, what's the story of my third birthday?"

"Don't you remember?"

"I don't remember either," said Cassie.

Marmee's hands paused over her bowl of peas, and she stared off toward the fields. Her glasses made her profile more square, levelled. "I'll tell it the way Haadha Demiksa told it. Let's see. . ."

When she started up again, her voice was lower, and her gestures reminded me of back home. "Haadha Adelie was new in the village then. She didn't know how to wear our clothes correctly and she had strange things in her house that the village had never seen before."

Cassie interrupted. "Our mama is 'Haadha Adelie,' right?" I nodded and motioned at her not to stop the flow of Marmee's story.

"One day, Haadha Adelie wore her nicest skirt and a new head-dress, so that she looked like the mother of a bride. 'Who's getting married?' we asked her, but she didn't understand. 'No one,' she said. 'It's Adelaide's birthday.' 'What is a birthday?' we asked. 'It's when we celebrate the day she was born,' she said. 'Come to our house after midday. You'll see.' She invited everyone in the village. It became the only thing we could talk about; no one could wait to see what she meant. Whenever we greeted someone that day, as soon as we said hello, we asked if they had heard it was Adelie's birthday. The children of the village spent the whole morning peering in the windows of their house. They came back with the strangest tales, telling us about the things Haadha Adelie was doing in her cooking pot over her fire, telling us about how she was using her knife on her long candles to make them the size of short twigs. We all thought the children were lying. Haadha Adelie finally shooed everyone away around late morning, so firmly we thought she was rude. 'Come back after midday,' she said. 'I want it to be a surprise.' Everyone stayed away until after midday, and Adelie went to play with Kinci to get her out of the way as well. When we went back after midday, the house was transformed: bright fabric hung from the rafters like cobwebs; there were piles of inflated rubber in bright colors; both girls wore fancy dresses; and, in the middle of the table, there was a bright pink cake with candles—unlike anything we'd ever seen."

"Two girls? Where was I?"

"Don't interrupt, Cassie. You weren't born yet. Let Marmee continue."

"When we saw the house, again we asked if she was sure no one was getting married. Why all the ceremony? It was an American birthday party, said Haadha Adelie. She and Aaaba Adelie sang songs none of the rest of us had ever heard before, and then we sang some church songs to accompany them. She had presents for Adelie, and games for all the children to play together. Our children asked if she was a princess, and they were reverent with awe toward her.

"The pink cake was sweet and smooth, and, after we ate it, our teeth were pink too. Haadha Adelie said she'd used the clothing dye we made from flowers, mixing some until she liked the tone. On top of the cake, Haadha Adelie had put the small candles— ones that were too small to be of any practical use, bent in their carving, barely more than splinters that dripped wax onto the splotchy pink of the cake. We didn't know what to make of it. Little Marmee," Marmee smiled slightly to acknowledge that, yes, she was referring to herself in third person, the way Haadha Demiksa would have referred to her, "insisted on feeding herself, and she got the cake all over her face and dress. It was a white, lacy dress for special occasions, but after the cake dropped on it, there was no way to get the pink out of the dress. Years later when Cassie was baptized, we were surprised to see that pink dress emerge again—the first baby ever baptized in the village wearing pink."

"It looked better pink."

The three of us looked up to see my mother on the other side of the open window, hidden in the shadows inside the house. We hadn't realized she was listening.

"I made your father bring balloons and powdered sugar from Cairo. I was afraid he was going to get the wrong kind of sugar. It was nearly impossible to find, he said, but another family helped him get some." She shifted toward the light, and we could see her. Her face was expressionless, same as usual, but her eyes were surprisingly intense, focused on me. "I cut myself twice while carving those candles. I used up two different tapers before I had three small candles that weren't broken or stained with blood. Your father said it was ridiculous—Africans didn't celebrate birthdays, so why should we; why was it such a big deal? I just kept carving." I imagined the knife edge sticking into the soft tallow, dragging wax away from Mother's torso—the way I'd seen my father do when carving wood. "I was determined to give my daughter an American birthday party," said Mother. "She was missing out on so much else."

I started to protest, tell her I hadn't missed out. But I stopped. She wasn't apologizing. Her comments weren't really about me.

Mother kept looking straight at me. "That's how I learned the phrases 'what are you doing?' and 'Is she crazy?' Everyone in the village stopped by to watch my party preparations. It was like going back to the first weeks in the village, when the children gathered like flies around the doorway, watching our every move. Sometimes they would stand there and pass a piece of fruit back and forth, like it was a movie theater. We were the movie. And they would giggle. Always. There was no way to stop them from giggling, and I was always the joke."

My mother looked beyond me, to stare out at the fields. She stood there for a long, silent moment, and then she disappeared back into the shadows inside the house.

"I remember the giggling," Marmee said after a minute, pushing up her glasses.

"What?"

"The giggling. Don't you remember? Everything we did was funny to some people."

"My friends never laughed at me," I said. That only happened here.

"Our friends didn't, but their grandparents did. And sometimes their parents. Or some of the other kids."

"I remember them giggling whenever they saw my underwear," said Cassie.

"They thought it was strange that we had to do homework. They thought it was strange that our mother couldn't cook food the right way. They thought our hair was funny, and it was strange that we didn't get married at fourteen. Don't you remember, Adelie? At least once a week something would come up that made us strange."

I stared at my sisters. I didn't remember that. "But we belonged there. The village was our home."

"And now we belong here," said Cassie, as if it were that simple.

"Here people still think we're strange, only now it's because of African things," said Marmee.

I shook my head. "At least in the village we knew how things were supposed to work and what things about us were strange."

Marmee and Cassie looked surprised at the bitterness in my tone.

"People can only hurt you if you let them," said Marmee. "Just don't pay attention to what people say," she told me earnestly.

"Or. . ." I searched for my mother through the window, but she seemed out of earshot. I whispered just the same. "Or I could just go back to where I know how things work, where I fit in."

Cassie looked confused. I couldn't gauge Marmee's reaction. "Where is that?" she said finally.

"The village," I said. "Home."

"You're going to go back?" asked Cassie. "How?"

"I'm saving the money from my job."

Cassie grabbed my hand and held tight. "When are you leaving?" Her eyes were wide.

I petted the hair back from her forehead. She was getting so big. "I'll go when I turn eighteen. I'll be on my own then. But don't say anything to Mother or Dad. I don't want them to know yet."

"Why don't you want them to know?" asked Marmee.

"I'm not sure what they'd say. Besides, it's still a year away, and I don't want to fight about it now."

"But you'll come back to Greenville after, right?" asked Cassie.

My baby sister. Her eyes were flecked yellow-brown in the light, and I was reminded of when she was born and how I had carried her and had kept her from the fire while Mother cooked and had played games with her while I washed clothes in the stream.

"Right, Adelie?"

"Maybe," I said. It was just a little lie. I supposed there was a chance I'd come back, some time.

CHAPTER 13

THE FIRST MONTH OF SUMMER, I worked every day at the drive-in. Not even the bike ride home could fumigate me of the smell of grease and car exhaust. The customers were mostly kids my age, and I quickly got tired of their demands. They tipped horribly, and sometimes the girls blew cigarette smoke in my face when they rolled down their windows. The boys were especially obnoxious, particularly a college-aged redhead who had a crush on me and was always in my way, trying to get me to talk to him.

I missed my friends. Our paths didn't cross, and I couldn't devise a single way to see them.

I left for the beach the first day of July.

Packing my things was strange. My impulse had been to ask Marmee to help me get the suitcases down from the attic, but I didn't have to pack everything I owned, only enough for two weeks. Aunt Be lent me one of Dana's old bathing suits that only pinched mildly.

There were six of us in the station wagon on the drive to Charleston: Emily Rose's little brother and his friend, in the backseat with me and three small bags, and Emily Rose between her parents in the front. The conversation was stilted and uncomfortable; I quickly regretted committing to such a long time surrounded by people I hardly knew. The inside of my bottom lip was raw where I'd been gnawing at it, and my whole back was slick with sweat. But then, as we came to the outskirts of Charleston, Mrs. Martin leaned toward her open window and asked if we could smell the ocean. I smelled salt and something else, as tantalizing as an inside joke. A smell that made me want to fly and do cartwheels—a smell like freedom.

When Mrs. Martin introduced me to her mother, I stuck out my hand and said hello and *how do you do* politely. Then we put on our swimsuits and ran to the water to wash away the car sweat.

The sand stretched as far as I could see in either direction, and in front of me was blue, blue, blue—only blue. It rose and fell with its own strength, churning and roaring and crashing. It was a bit terrifying.

Emily Rose ran toward the water through the section where the grass mingled with sand. The grass was prickly closer to the beach, and then the sand was really hot. Emily Rose's little brother and his friend kicked up sand as they ran helter-skelter past us into the water. The water splashed back around them as they dove into it.

Emily Rose yelled after them and ran in to the waves. I took a deep breath and ran too. The sand became heavier under my feet, and then it was dragging at me. A wave crashed around my ankles, and then another was at my knees. The water splashed my face, salty and cold. Another wave caught me at my waist, and I screamed. Water splashed in my mouth and stung the inside of my nose. Another wave came and broke against me. I lost my footing and fell into it, blind, gagging. Then the wave subsided, and I stood again. Another wave came, and this time, I was stronger than it was.

Emily Rose showed me how to pinch my nostrils so the water wouldn't go up my nose. I discovered I could paddle the same way I had in the stream below the village, could shake my hair out of my eyes the same way. The water felt different on my skin, grittier, more penetrating, more unpredictable, but there were similarities.

I felt like a new life had begun, and I never wanted to leave the ocean.

A few days later, Emily Rose and I lay on our towels on the beach, half-asleep from the sun, hair drying stiffly from the salt. There was a breeze and the sky was blue, and I felt like nothing in the world could be wrong.

"I want to live like this forever," I said.

Emily Rose smiled. "You could," she said. "Maybe when you grow up you'll live on the beach, like my grandma."

I opened one eye and looked at her. "Is that what you want to do?"

"No," she said. "My mother wants to live here, but I don't." She was belly down, with her chin propped up on her crossed arms, frowning at the dune. I closed my eyes again to feel the sunlight against my eyelids.

"What do you want to do?"

She was quiet for so long, I thought she hadn't heard. Her voice sounded far away when she answered, but she was still belly-down, next to me. "Everyone assumes I'll get married by age twenty—to whoever asks me, probably—and we'll buy a house and have kids. No one's ever really asked me what I wanted to do with my life."

The sunlight was blinding, even behind my eyelids. I rested my face sideways to look at her and balanced on my profile the broad brimmed hat Emily Rose had lent me. "Do you have something else in mind?" I asked.

Her voice was barely above a whisper. "Promise you won't tell?" She cleared her throat. "I want to go to college and study physics. I really want to study the universe, how the planets came about, why they go around each other in orbit, what makes them move. I want to know about the sun and the chemical makeup of the stars and how it would change things if even one star were in a different location. I used to stare at the stars when I was little, thinking about how I wish I knew what they were actually like." She was more excited than I'd ever seen her, and her speech came faster than usual. "I want to go to Harvard. There's an astronomer at the observatory there, Cecilia Payne-Gaposchkin, whose thesis was considered the most groundbreaking thesis ever." She dug a stick into the sand, concentrating on that rather than on me. "Dartmouth's faculty is intriguing also, but most of the other universities are focused on more experimental mathematics right now instead of studying the universe."

I shook my head at her, and the hat wobbled on my ear. "So why not go to Harvard, then, or Dartmouth? You're smarter than anyone I know, smarter than anyone who's ever lived in Greenville, I bet. You have to try."

She frowned and kept digging. "It's just a silly dream."

"I don't understand. What's stopping you?"

"My dad thinks college is a waste of time, and my mother says girls aren't supposed to be good at math. Besides, everyone would laugh at me if they knew."

"I didn't laugh."

"You're the only person who's ever thought to ask me what I wanted to do."

"Well, you are good at math, regardless of what people say. Maybe you could get a scholarship."

"Maybe. . ." she said, as if she was humoring me.

"You sound like Sarah May with that polite denial," I said. Emily Rose didn't know who I meant. "Sarah May, one of the colored girls at school. I eat lunch with them." Emily Rose nodded, slowly.

"The one that I met?" she asked.

"No," I said, remembering the uncomfortable time when Wendy and I worked at the same library table as Emily Rose. "I think you'd like Sarah May. You should join us sometime for lunch.

We sit outside, on the steps at the side of the auditorium. It's nice out there."

"I often have to go to club meetings during lunch," she said.

"Oh." I started digging a hole in the sand, but the sides kept caving in. Then I decided to say something. "Emily Rose, do you feel uncomfortable around my other friends?"

She stopped still. "Kind of," she said finally. I waited. She looked up at me, then continued. "It's just. . . I've been taught that they have their place, and we have ours. It's not that they're bad people, it's just that everyone's more comfortable if we keep things separate. It just makes a lot of trouble to mix us together. Besides, I don't think they'd want me to eat with them."

"Load of hogwash," I said. "They put up with me." I was getting mad, and I had to remind myself that I liked Emily Rose.

"I guess I don't understand why they couldn't just stay at their old school. What was wrong with that system? They're going to overrun our classrooms. I've heard talk that at least twenty of them will be at our school next year."

I was at a loss for words, but I knew I couldn't lose the battle with my anger. "Their old school got the castoff materials from the white high schools—old textbooks, desks that were falling apart. It's not nice to be treated like you don't deserve new things."

"So we should increase spending on the black schools. I still don't understand why we have to integrate everyone together."

Again, I struggled to explain it. "But don't you think having separate schools, even having separate groups at lunch, shows that we don't think they're as good as us? I'm not explaining it well; they could tell you about it a lot better than I could. They've got really interesting things to say. You'd like them."

She nodded, vaguely, and pushed her flat palm across the sand to build a wall, smoothed out the top and sides, and poked her fingers into it to make windows. "What about you, when you grow up?" she asked. "Besides live near the beach."

"There isn't a beach near my village in Ethiopia," I said, as it dawned on me that this might be my only trip to the beach, ever. I was still riled up about the thing that Emily Rose had said, but this thought made me sad.

"What's that got to do with anything?"

"For my whole life—until we moved—I thought I'd live in the village forever. I thought I'd marry one of the boys there." She was just looking at me. "His name's Maicaah. He's the cousin of my best friend Kinci." Her expression was still blank. "I'm going to go back and marry him and be part of the village."

"For the rest of your life?"

I squinted at her. "Of course."

"So you want to go back and live there forever? Even when you're older? Never live anywhere different? Never leave?"

I nodded. Why did it sound so constricting, when she put it like that? My throat felt oddly narrow when I swallowed.

"What about your sisters? You're always talking so much about them. Does that mean you'll never see them again?"

"I don't know." I wiped the sweat off my forehead and covered my eyes with my forearm.

"You really don't want to do any more school? Or travel? Sorry. . ." she said, catching herself. "It's just that I don't understand why you'd want that, if you have other options."

I hadn't ever thought of it in terms of an option. Living in the village and marrying Maicaah had always felt like something so obvious there was really no choice involved. It was the natural trajectory of the path I was on. There had been the question of timing, of when my father would give his permission, but it was never a question of whether that was what I wanted or not. I knew it was what I wanted.

When I lived in the village, marrying Maicaah was a way of making it permanent, of grafting myself into village life, of claiming my place there so that no one could ever question again who "my people" were. I still wanted that. And I missed the certainty I felt with Maicaah, the easy confidence there was between us, the way I knew I could rely on him, the way he knew how and when to make me laugh—and also the new, unsettling energy I felt being close to him as we got older, as if anything might happen and how I wanted it to happen with him.

But Emily Rose's talk of options made me think of Maicaah's widowed aunt. She had been too skinny, too ugly, too mean, and too old to remarry. She hadn't even had any special skills to contribute—she couldn't cook very well or weave, didn't know medicine, wasn't very good at tending livestock. She couldn't even bargain very well. Everyone pretended to not notice the way she couldn't look at Maicaah's father or the bruises she always had on her arms and her face. Her family had been relieved when she got sick and died. I hadn't ever thought much about her, but suddenly I wondered what would happen to me if I was Maicaah's widow. Would I have other options if that happened, or would I become a drain on his family?

"You know," said Emily Rose. "You could always settle down in Greenville, if that's what you want. Everyone knows Justin Macalister's half in love with you."

"Oh, only half?" I laughed. "What happened to the other half of him?"

"He's just waiting for you to notice it."

I sat up and brushed the sand off my legs. "Old news. He's moved on by now."

"I think he's still interested in you." She sat up, too, and we started folding the towels and gathering our things. "Adelaide, don't take things so for granted."

Her change in tone startled me. "How do you mean?"

She fidgeted with the towel she was holding. "I mean, don't do something just because it's the answer that comes easiest, because it's the first answer that came to mind. I mean, don't do something just because you can't think of anything else."

Her words stung. She made it sound as if wanting to go back

to the village was because of a lack of creativity. "Says the girl who keeps what she wants to do a secret."

"I like to surprise people," she said. She looked at me out of the corner of her eye, and when she smiled, it was the most confident smile I'd seen from her. Just as quickly, she was straight-faced again, solemn. "You should at least explore your choices. You could be a journalist. Or a historian. Or an anthropologist, like your father."

I rolled my eyes. "Or an ambassador's wife." I thought, suddenly, of the women in their different kinds of traditional dress at the airport in Addis Ababa. I bet they were able to go to the beach when they wanted.

"Or be an ambassador yourself."

I scoffed. "I'm pretty sure government agencies don't hire women for jobs like that."

"Well, they should. . . Everyone knows women are better at being diplomatic."

We went on to talk of other things, but that conversation with Emily Rose stayed with me. It came back to me that night while I was showering, and the next day, while we flew kites. If I had more choices, would that still be what I would choose? Or was Maicaah just my default, an assumption left over from a time when I hadn't had other options, a dream I held on to because I was too stubborn to let it go?

I pushed away the thought and ran up the beach with Emily Rose.

Going back to Ethiopia and marrying Maicaah was what I wanted, and it was what I was going to do. I was sure. Of course I was.

When the time came, I was ready to return to Greenville. I was ready to see my sisters and go back to my job and my spot on the porch roof outside my window.

"Did you grow?" demanded Aunt Be when she opened the front door to greet me.

"Why, do I look taller?" I looked down at myself, but the fit of my clothes wasn't noticeably different.

"Something," said Aunt Be. She smiled stiffly, then helped me carry my suitcase inside.

"You're so brown!" said Cassie.

Marmee didn't comment; she just hugged me. My mother appeared in the doorway, hands in a dishtowel, and smiled. Grandmother hugged me tightly. When my dad arrived home later for dinner, he stood back to keep from getting me dirty and kissed the top of my head.

"Welcome back, Adelaide," he said. "We missed you."

I was glad to be home, back at Grandmother's, again.

At the end of the summer, just before starting my second school year in Greenville, I caught my bracelet on the edge of the window sill as I was climbing out onto the porch roof.

Before I knew what happened, there was a hail storm of yellow and red and purple and green and dark blue beads that rolled between the floorboards and under the beds and settled into the gutters and rolled off over the trellis and landed in the grass below. I tried to catch them as they fell, but there were too many, and they were too small. I was left clutching the string around my wrist with the last few beads—yellow and purple and green— caught in my fist.

I stared at them for a minute, those tiny colored beads, the frayed string that was already unravelling.

One by one I let them fall onto the floor with the rest.

By the time I reached the fields, I couldn't see where I was running, I was crying so hard.

CHAPTER 14

MY SENIOR YEAR STARTED OFF with a roar. My dad had just bought a car, and its motor was not quiet.

"Do you have to drive us to school today?" I asked. "We got there on our own every day last year."

"Last year there wasn't really another option," my dad shouted back. "Besides, this'll keep your new clothes clean for the first day."

"We wouldn't want our dresses to get all wrinkled," said Marmee. I smirked at her, sharing the joke.

We were wearing new clothes—*new* new, not just new to us—for the first time since arriving in Greenville. I had mentioned something at dinner a week ago about needing a new skirt for school, and Aunt Be had chided my dad into paying for a new outfit for each of us for our first day of school.

"You haven't bought them any new clothes since they got here," said Aunt Be. "They are decent, respectable girls from a good family and should look like it. Especially on the first day of school. First impressions are very key," she said. She'd just sent Dana back to school—after her two-week vacation—with a whole trunk of new clothes. Marmee had inherited most of Dana's cast-offs. I was now too tall for them; Aunt Be had been right: I had grown.

So, at the store, I picked out a light blue and yellow plaid skirt with a blue cardigan set and a matching blue headband. It was a little too hot to wear a cardigan, but I wore it anyway and sweated discretely into my sweater. Marmee had a simple pink skirt and a white blouse.

After the beach, I cut my hair, tired of the length of it. It fell now to just below my shoulders. Marmee didn't want to go to the beauty parlor with me, so she still wore her hair in a braid. Cassie still had her two braids, tied with cantaloupe ribbons that matched her dress.

"Daddy, will you be here to pick us up afterward, too?" asked Cassie.

"No, honey," said my dad. "I've got to be in the fields. Can you walk home?"

I sighed. Why did he make such a fuss about us not walking to school if we had to walk back anyway? I slid out the door without saying anything. I was already looking for my friends.

"Adelaide," my dad called. I turned. "Aren't you going to say good-bye?"

"Bye, Dad," I said.

He smiled and waved, then drove off. I pulled on one of Cassie's braids. "Hey, have fun in third grade," I told her.

"Do you think the new teacher will like me?" she asked.

"I'm sure she will," I said. I gave her a quick hug, and she scampered off.

Marmee was already walking toward the wall by the front entrance. "Marmee, who are you looking forward to seeing?" I asked. "Did you miss anyone from school over the summer?"

Marmee thought for a minute. "Not really," she said.

I started to lecture her on the importance of making friends, but I was interrupted by a very short girl in a too-long navy skirt and a cardigan that was unraveling at the cuffs. She climbed up on the wall next to Marmee.

"Hello, Mary Peony," said the other girl. "How was your summer?" Her voice was so quiet, it felt like it was inside my head.

"Hello, Mary Betts," my sister answered. "Have you ever mixed charcoal and watercolor? I tried it yesterday. Look, I brought it to show you."

I smiled, patted my sister's leg as she dug through her satchel, and went to find my own friends.

I'd just spotted Wendy across the lawn and had started toward her when Justin touched my arm.

"Adelaide!" he said, smiling broadly. "How are you? How was your summer?"

He was tanned and more solid-looking than I remembered. I'd forgotten how he could make me blush. "It was fine," I said. "I went to Charleston for a few weeks. It was really fun."

"With Emily Rose Martin, right? I saw Emily Rose downtown a few weeks ago, and she told me about it."

I nodded. It was like looking in the sun to look in his eyes. I hoped Emily Rose hadn't teased him the way she'd teased me. "Did you go anywhere?"

"My mother took my sister and me to Atlanta for a few weeks, but nothing too exciting. I mostly worked at my uncle's law office. Saving up money for college. And maybe a car. Then there was football practice."

"Oh?" I didn't know what to ask next.

"Adelaide! Hey, girl!" Wendy reached us and beamed at me. It felt like forever since I'd seen her, and I threw my arms around her.

She patted my back and moved away quickly, glancing around as if she was embarrassed.

We exclaimed about each other's hair. She'd grown out her hair so that it framed her face; it made her cheekbones look softer and opened up her eyes. She looked older than before.

"Y'all ready for a new year?" Frederica came up and stood next to Wendy, swinging her book bag back and forth around her legs.

Nathan and Sarah May joined us, walking a little closer together than they had before. Sarah May wore makeup, which she said she'd put on in the bathroom here at school because her mother still wouldn't let her wear it.

Our morning classes went quickly. I didn't see Lion until lunch time, and then he was taller than ever, with the shadow of a mustache on his upper lip and a new boxiness to the shape of his hairline.

It was a noisy lunch time. I was so excited to have our spot back again and be together. It felt like we were on top of the world. "Senior year!" we kept exclaiming.

"What prank are we going to do?" asked Justin.

"Prank?" I hadn't heard of this.

"Yes, ma'am. It's a tradition." Apparently, this was a serious issue, but his eyes were still smiling at me. "Several years ago, the seniors put a cow in the bell tower. No one's been able to top that since."

"That wasn't here! I heard it was at Sterling," said Sarah May.

"It *was* at Sterling. . . My cousin's best friend was the one who thought of it," said Frederica.

"Why is that a good prank?" I asked.

"Because a cow can walk upstairs," explained Lion, "But it won't walk back down. Something about how its legs work."

"So what'd they do? Have to take food to it up there?" My sandwich was white bread, too dry, and it stuck to the roof of my mouth as I chewed.

"No, they had to butcher it up there and bring it down piece by piece."

"That's disgusting," I said.

The boys laughed at my horror. "It's true," said Sarah May.

"You can still see bloodstains," said Wendy.

Justin told stories of other pranks and tried to convince us to come up with a good idea.

"Those all sound dangerous. Or expensive," said Sarah May.

"I've got an idea," said Wendy. She looked around at us, lingering on Justin. "No," she said. "It'd never work. You would never be willing to pull it off." She smiled mischievously, and that scar under her eye gleamed.

"You have to tell now," said Lion.

"Girl, you can't play us like that!" said Sarah May.

But her teasing turned a bit more serious. "No, it's too risky, y'all. We might get in real trouble if we did it. Let me think about it and see if there's a way around getting in trouble."

"Why'd you say anything if you didn't want to say anything?" said Nathan.

"Ask me again tomorrow," was all she'd say after that. "It's a good one, though, if we can do it."

For my new schedule, I had three classes with Justin, two with Nathan and Sarah May and Lion, three with Frederica, and only one with Wendy. We tried to switch, but the guidance counselor wouldn't hear of it. Emily Rose and I had four classes together. I had been dreading the new classes, but having at least one friend in every class helped. I just had to make it to graduation—then I would be free of the demands of school.

In one class, when we finished the work early, Emily Rose helped me calculate the money I'd need for a plane ticket to Ethiopia. I realized I needed more hours at work if I wanted to make enough for the ticket, so I started working three days during the week, after school. My birthday would be in April, but I decided it was worth it to stay until after graduation: that would provide a natural transition point. Plus, that gave me another month to earn money toward the ticket.

Soon after the start of the school year, my dad decided to give me real driving lessons, so I would know how to drive his car.

"You never know how it'll be useful," he said. "It's a good skill to have, just in case."

Previously, I'd only steered the wheel in first gear, but now it was all in my power to do a lot more. The loud motor and wide hood made me nervous. My dad shooed my sisters away, and I settled my hands on the steering wheel at ten and two, taking deep breaths.

"All right," he said, closing the passenger door. "Do you know what pedal is which?" He explained the pedals and the gear shift, then showed me how to turn the key in the ignition.

"I know how the ignition works, Dad."

"Well, go ahead and turn it on."

I turned the key, and nothing happened.

"You have to push down on the clutch when you're turning the key," he said.

The motor roared to life. "Now, slowly, ease your foot off the clutch and ease down on the gas." The motor roared, jolted us forward in our seats, and then died. My hands shook at ten and two. "That's all right," he said. "You just went a little too quickly off the clutch. Let's try that again."

Twenty minutes later, the car was crawling down the driveway. I managed to get it ten feet before it stalled again. "Okay, good," my dad said. "That's good progress."

"Can we be done for today?"

"Don't you want to get it down pat and settled?" He sounded disappointed. "You're really close."

"Don't pressure me!" I said, more sharply than I'd intended. My hands still shook, and my elbows felt stiff.

"Why are you yelling?" He was yelling. "I'm teaching you how to drive!"

"I didn't ask to learn! Why do you have to decide everything for me?"

"Why are you complaining about this?"

"You decide everything for me! You decided when we were starting school, and whether I could get a job or not, and when we were coming back from Ethiopia—which you didn't even bother to tell us until the last minute—and even that we were going to go to Ethiopia in the first place!"

He stared at me, as if I'd sprung, fully formed, from the seat next to him. "Anything else?" he asked stiffly.

I wanted to say, *You weren't there when Mother started screaming and the baby came and we needed you.* I stared at the dials of the car radio. One was misshapen, elongated to one side. The red line of the dial bar rested just to the right of the number nine, and the fact that it wasn't centered bothered me.

Finally I said, "I'm going back to the village. As soon as I graduate. I'll be eighteen. You can't stop me then."

He didn't say anything back. He didn't argue or react or respond in any way. After a moment, he opened the passenger door and got out.

I sat there, in the driver's seat, in silence, a long time. Then finally I got out and went for a walk. The car stayed halfway down the drive, where it had stalled, for two days before Dad moved it.

CHAPTER 15

ONE NIGHT AT THE BEGINNING of October, my dad said he wanted to talk to me. I hoped it didn't have to do with my tantrum during the driving lesson. Or that any teachers had complained about my grades—they'd gotten so much better. Surely people had stopped talking about my friends by now.

Marmee saw me heading to the den instead of upstairs, and she asked what was going on.

"It's all right, Mary," said my dad. "We just want to talk to Adelaide. Nothing to worry about."

Marmee didn't look convinced. She headed upstairs, but I could tell from her expression that she was going to stay awake until I told her what it was about.

My mother and my grandmother joined us, so I guessed it wasn't about my tantrum. Aunt Be cleared the last of the dishes, then sat next to my mother on the couch. Through the doorway, the dining room table looked strangely empty, gleaming dark brown in the overhead light of the den.

Had something happened to someone in the village? Were my friends okay? Maicaah? Kinci? It was so easy for minor ailments to turn serious, and they were so far from the hospital.

"Adelaide, we've been struck recently by how much you're growing up," my dad said, looking at his own hands. "You're a senior in high school. You're almost eighteen."

My friends were fine. I swallowed, trying to calm my quickened heartbeat. I took a deep breath, readying my arsenal of reasons why he couldn't stop me from going back to the village.

From the foot of the table, Grandmother cleared her throat and tapped her fingers on the arms of her chair. "Your father told us you plan to go back to Ethiopia as soon as you graduate," she said. "We wanted to know why."

"It's a really dumb idea," said Aunt Be.

Grandmother made a clicking sound and waved her off. "Let Adelaide speak," she said.

"I'll have enough to pay for the ticket. I'm going to live there. It's my home. It's where I belong."

"That's ridiculous," said Aunt Be. "Your *home* is here. We are your family. You would probably be attacked—robbed and worse—if you went to Africa all by yourself."

"You haven't been there. You don't know. . ."

"It's different to go as an adult," my mother said. She had her hands clasped in her lap, and it looked as if she was speaking to them.

"What do you mean?"

My dad nodded. "Even traveling is much harder as a female adult than as a child with her family."

"But I want to go back there to live. . . The village is my family, and I'm tired of trying to fit in here." Couldn't they understand that I just wanted to go *home*?

"The choice is yours," said my dad slowly. "But we want to make sure you're considering all your options."

My mother stared at the rosebud wallpaper. Her expression was slightly worried.

"What do you mean, *options*?" I said. I could sense that my dad had something he wanted to tell me about.

My aunt and Grandmother were quiet. "We've never talked about college," said my dad. "I guess I just assumed you'd want to go and that it would come up naturally. I've never told you about the money set aside." He looked at my mother, and her gaze briefly met his. "The money from my parents' house and land," he said. "We set it aside for you and your sisters. We thought about using it to buy a house here, when we came back, but your grandmother and aunt have been kind enough to let us stay with them until I get a teaching job. Don't get your hopes up about a private school, but there should be enough for about three years of Clemson or somewhere, if you spend it wisely."

I scratched at a stray fiber of the couch's cloth covering. "Can I use the money for anything else?"

My mother's worried expression deepened as she looked at my dad.

"No," he said, after a slight hesitation. "It's only for college."

"Clemson's less than an hour away," said Aunt Be. "So you can come visit on the weekends."

"I'm not sure I want to go to college," I said slowly. "It would mean more school, and I'm tired of it."

"I heard you're doing well in school, Adelaide," said my mother, in her low voice. She didn't look at me, but even so, her acknowledgement made me feel like she was paying attention to me, something I hadn't felt in a long time. It took the fight out of me, and I felt myself almost physically leaning forward, thirsty in a way I hadn't realized until that second.

"College is different than high school," said my dad. "I think you'll like it a lot better. You get to choose what you want to study and what classes to take, and the people around you are different, too. Less immature, more driven."

"Do you know what a privilege this is?" asked Aunt Be. "You would be a fool to let it go by."

My dad took off his glasses and rubbed the bridge of his nose, then put them back on and looked at me. "It's your decision,

Adelaide. We'll leave it to you to decide. But let me say one more thought. You could always go to Ethiopia after college. This could be just another set of experiences before you go back."

All four of them—Grandmother stroking the arms of her chair, Aunt Be surreptitiously picking her teeth, Mother holding on to the top button of her blouse as if she might come undone if she let go, and my dad with his whole body bouncing a little as he juggled his right foot across his left knee—were looking fixedly at me, hoping their persuasion had convinced me. It was too much to think about all at once. They were waiting for an answer from me, I knew, but all I kept thinking of was Maicaah's hand over mine, my fingers pressing into the hollow below his kneecap, as he told me to promise.

"I need time to think about it," I said finally.

"You'll need to send in applications if you want to go to college," said my dad. "You could apply just in case and ask them to retract the applications if you decided not to attend." He put his hands palm out. "We won't stop you," he said. My mother made a sound like a whimper, but he continued. "It's your choice what to do with your life. We can only give you the best advice we have. And we recommend you choose to go to college before you settle down in the village."

"I'll think about it," I said.

"And the trip?" asked Aunt Be.

"I'm going after I graduate. I'll decide whether I'm coming back."

I sat on the roof outside my room for a long time that night. The wind was strong, restless, and the stars were mostly covered up by clouds. I stayed outside until I was numb from sitting in one spot for too long.

It *was* a privilege they were offering me, but did that mean I needed to take advantage of it? I'd never imagined what college would be like, and I wondered if I really would like it as much as my dad thought I would. But I'd promised Maicaah I'd be back. I'd promised Kinci I'd bring her that baseball cap for her son.

How was I supposed to decide what to do?

I wished there was someone I could talk to, someone who understood the two parts of me: village life in Ethiopia—the life that was as familiar as breathing, the life I loved and craved and yet was forgetting; and everything here in Greenville—my sisters and parents, my friends, everything I'd learned, and the choices this life offered. How could I decide between them? Why did I have to?

I knew what I wanted, what I had wanted for such a long time. . . but was I ready to give up all chance for anything else?

A few days later I found on my bed an application for Clemson University.

Under that was a newspaper article talking about a student from City College of New York, a photographer who was an editor of the student newspaper, who had marched with Martin Luther King Jr, from Selma to Montgomery. The picture that accompanied the article showed the white student carrying a camera, surrounded by a crowd of black people, some of whom held signs clamoring for justice. Underneath the newspaper article was an application for admittance to City College of New York.

I looked at the newspaper article for a long time. I wondered who had put it on my bed, and I wondered how much they knew about my friendships that went against Aunt Be's wishes.

When my sisters weren't looking, I started filling out the applications to both schools.

At the end of October, Lion and I started working together after school at the drive-in. Lion had needed a new job, and Cousin

Howard had been looking for someone new for the kitchen. Howard had been very skeptical about hiring Lion, but he said he was willing to try him out based on my recommendation.

Our second week at work, I noticed Lion was acting strangely: avoiding eye contact but smiling each time he looked away. Whatever secret he knew, it seemed like a pleasant one.

"What's on your mind today?" I asked, trying to be casual as I carried in the last stack of dishes and started filling the sink. "The football game tomorrow?" The radio in the corner started playing Sonny and Cher's "I Got You Babe."

"Since when you care about football?" asked Lion. "I didn't think you even knew when the games were." He hung a wet dishtowel over the bar next to the sink and got a new one from the cabinet.

"I know you care. That's all y'all talk about during lunch."

"You bet your Peter Pan pudding I do. Football is where it's at. . . Everyone's gearing up for the Turkey Day game." He waited for me to share his excitement. "The big game, Adelie. On Thanksgiving. Against Greenville High. Adelaide, you should know this! It's a tradition. You really do just tune us out when we start talking football, don't you?"

"I'm listening to you now."

He paused and looked at me out of the corner of his eye. "Were you planning on going?"

"On Thanksgiving? Probably not. Why?"

He shrugged, but I didn't buy his nonchalance. "It just might be an interesting game," he said, burying his hands in the dishwater.

"Interesting in a way that I care about?"

"It has to do with Justin." Lion paused and shifted his weight. "I guess it's not really a secret if I don't know for sure. . . I was watching practice today, and I think the coaches might make Justin the starter. Coach just switched him to quarterback. Ken

Newton is the usual quarterback, and everyone expected him to start because he's a senior."

"Why is that a big deal? Justin's a senior too."

"Justin usually plays running back." He looked again like he was waiting for me to get as excited as he was, but I didn't know one position from another. I started putting away the dry dishes in the strainer.

Lion tried explaining further. "Justin's older brother played QB and was one of the best in the state. The coach switched Justin as an experiment, just to see if he could do it. Now everyone's saying Justin's even better than his brother and we might have a shot at winning the Turkey Day game."

I put a stack of mixing bowls in the cabinet. "Uh-huh." I wondered if everyone was as into football in college.

Lion sighed. "This is a big deal, Adelaide, and I got no one to talk to about it! If you don't listen I may as well talk to the walls."

"Or you could talk to the dishes." I pulled a handful of mixing spoons from the rinse water and put them in the strainer, then grabbed a towel to start drying. "Why can't they play a game that's actually fun to watch? They only run a few feet at a time. It's basically just watching players stand around and talk."

Lion looked too frustrated for words. He made a face at me, then focused his vehemence on scrubbing at the layers of grease caked on a spatula.

"Why don't you play football?" I asked him.

My change of direction threw him. "No way they'd let me on the football team."

"Are you any good?"

Lion laughed. "I'm alright. I can hold my own."

"Would they let you try out? If you could help the team. . ."

He shook his head, suddenly withdrawn. He didn't seem eager to explain this. "Some of them don't even like it that I watch practice sometimes. I hear them grumbling when they come off the field."

I was quiet too for a few minutes. I didn't have to work hard to picture the scene. "What does Justin say when that happens?" I handed back to him a tray that still had ketchup on one edge.

"I think they've been a little rough on Justin, too, but they usually don't say things when he's around." He re-washed the tray, examined it, and then handed it to me again.

"I still think you should try out," I said. "That could be the stand you take at school—you and Justin. Moving toward an integrated football team."

"Justin talks the talk," said Lion, "but I don't know if he would want to take that stand." He looked at me out of the corner of his eye as if deciding which tack to take to change topics. "He's pretty popular with the girls, from what I hear. People say any girl would be lucky to date him."

"I can't believe how many girls are always around him," I said. "He must love the attention." I checked to make sure the sink was empty and then unstopped the drain. "I overheard a group of teachers talking about how he's a golden boy," I said. "How he's the type of person that everyone wants to follow—or become."

Lion swiped the food bits out of the drain-catcher. He knew I hated that part. "What do you think about Justin?"

His tone made me suspicious. "How come?"

"No reason." He glanced at me from the trash can and raised his eyebrows innocently.

"You are such an *igaggi-ni*. . . What do you call it? You know, someone who loves to get involved in other people's affairs."

He laughed. "Busybody? Gossip?"

I wiped the sides of the sink with a cloth, trying to erase all streaks. Why did talking about Justin make me uncomfortable?

The Beach Boys' "Help Me, Rhonda," came on the radio. Lion started to dance to the faster beat, clicking the tongs in the air as he pulled things from the strainer to dry them. He put the tongs away and swung the dishtowel around in loops, shuffling his feet in rhythmic steps. He danced around the center island, then, feeding off my laughter, completed another loop and spun in circles. He swung his hips, too, in a way Aunt Be and even Grandmother would say was shocking.

"What are you doing, Lion? What do you call that?"

"Haven't you never seen dancing, girl?"

"Not like that I haven't. . . ."

The chorus came on again, and Lion held out his hands for me to join him. He guided me through exaggeratedly slow swing dance moves, and then he spun me around and around while the guitars played their bridge.

I was spinning and laughing when the door opened. Lion immediately jumped back, and I stumbled into the prep counter. Cousin Howard—his thinning red hair a spotlight in the doorway—blinked at us over his bifocals. He looked from Lion, to me, to the empty sink and mostly empty strainer.

I was afraid that anything I said would make it worse. I grabbed a dishcloth and wiped at the counter next to me.

Finally, Cousin Howard said, "Adelaide, Sandra needs to see you."

"Yes, sir," I said. "We were just. . . finishing the dishes."

Howard didn't say anything in response. I slipped past him and turned back to see Lion, his face down, his eyes on the counter. "House of the Rising Sun" came on the radio, and Cousin Howard switched it off.

"Sandra will pay you for the days you worked this week," Howard told Lion. "Don't come back tomorrow."

Lion met my gaze briefly over Howard's shoulder. His smooth, dark features were expressionless, as if he never expected anything less than for things to go this way. Without a word, he took off his apron, set it on the counter, and walked out the back door of the kitchen.

Howard passed me in the hallway, yelling at Sandra that they were going to need to find new help.

I ran after Lion and caught up to him on the street. He was

walking fast and didn't look at me. I realized I was still wearing my apron; I untied it and held it bunched up in my fist.

At the cross street, where he was to turn left and I, right, I stopped. I wanted him to stop too, but I was afraid to touch him. "Wait, Lion," I said. He stopped four feet away, his back to me. "I'm sorry."

"It's not your fault, Adelaide," he said. His voice sounded far away. "I should have known better." He still wasn't looking at me. "If you hear of a different job," he said, "let me know. My parents were counting on the pay."

I nodded, even though he couldn't see me. "You too," I said. "I mean, if you hear of a job for me."

He turned back, slightly. "Don't quit over this, Adelaide. You don't have to, and you need the money for the plane ticket."

"I can't go back to work for him after this," I protested.

Lion shrugged. "Do what you want, Adelaide." He turned away again. I heard him mutter, "At least you have a choice," and then he kept walking, leaving the gleam of the streetlight.

The bitterness of his tone, directed at me, felt so unfair. Didn't he realize I'd just walked out with him? Did he think I didn't see how unjust the situation was? Did he think I wouldn't change it all if I could?

I pedaled hard the whole way home, and, the next day, I left a phone message with Cousin Sandra that was more forceful than it needed to be. I threw the apron away in a dumpster rather than return it.

That weekend I was able to get a job at the department store downtown. It paid better than the drive-in and didn't make me smell like food. Lion got a job stocking shelves at the grocery store near school. He didn't tell me what it paid, but I saw how he had to duck his head and say "sir" or "ma'am" to anyone who asked him a question.

His comment about my having a choice rankled, because I couldn't deny it. There also wasn't anything else I could think to do about the difference in the way people like Cousin Howard treated us.

I didn't ever talk with Lion about it again. I also didn't tell my family I was no longer working at the drive-in, and no one asked, so I hoped that meant that Cousin Howard was ashamed of himself.

CHAPTER 16

IN SCHOOL THE NEXT WEEK, all anyone could talk about was football.

"So, y'all are going to the game next week, right?" asked Justin. He was looking at me when he said it. I wondered if he'd felt anything toward either of the two girls who'd been talking to him and looking up at him adoringly in the hallway before lunch.

"I'll go if the rest of y'all do," I said.

Wendy fidgeted with her earrings. "The Thanksgiving football game is *not* the best place to be if the whole school hates you and you're easy to spot in a crowd," she said. No one else met my eyes.

"Why is that worse than usual?" I asked. "Compared to the rest of life at school? Y'all are always easy to spot in a crowd of white people."

"Football games rile up people's emotions, make them go all crazy," said Frederica. "That's one of the things they warned us against before we transferred. There's no telling what a crowd will do. Especially if the team loses."

"We won't lose," said Justin. "Not this game. Come! It'll really show how y'all are a part of things here."

"I won't understand anything if y'all don't go with me," I said.

I wasn't sure if Lion was still mad at me or not, but I tried coaxing him. "Lion, I know you want to go."

"We'll go," said Nathan, nodding at Sarah May. "It's time we participated more fully in all aspects of school life."

"I'll go," said Wendy, eyes fixed on Nathan.

"It would be fun to watch," said Lion.

"You couldn't pay me to go," said Frederica. "Into a crowd of riled-up white people? No, ma'am. Even if nothing happened, my daddy would shoot me for sheer foolishness."

"We can wear scarves with school colors," said Sarah May. "Justin, we'll join your cheering section."

"Pretty sure the whole bleachers will be your cheering section," said Wendy.

Justin smiled and winked at me, like I'd only seen him do once before. Just like that time, I felt my stomach bottom out, and I blushed.

After school that day, Justin was leaning against the bike rack when I came out. "Adelaide, I heard you're no longer working Saturday nights. Have you been to Hinton's?"

"No. . . What's Hinton's?"

He smiled. "It's a restaurant where I'd like to take you. A nice one. I'll pick you up at six."

I fiddled with my bike handlebars and didn't look straight at him. I felt a jumble of conflicting things—excitement, fear, victory, disappointment, eagerness—and, somehow, anger. His offer of a date hadn't been a question. I wanted to pretend I got asked out to dinner all the time by boys like him, that it didn't really matter to me one way or the other; but I did feel flattered.

Then, what he said about the restaurant being *a nice one* struck me. "Do I need to dress up?"

He smiled wider. "Sure. I mean, if you want to."

Was I supposed to know that about Hinton's? "All right."

He put his hands in his pockets and stepped aside. "Great. I think you'll like it. We'll have fun."

"All right," I said again. "Um, I'll see you tomorrow." I rode away cringing, certain I'd said the wrong thing.

"You're going to Hinton's?" Emily Rose's voice rose to a squeal. "I knew he was in love with you," she said smugly.

"What? Why do you say that?" I saw Miss Young the librarian out of the corner of my eye and opened my textbook so it looked like we were studying.

"Don't you know about Hinton's? It's the nicest restaurant in Greenville. By far. It's in a beautiful spot overlooking the river. Super romantic. My parents sometimes go there for their anniversary. What are you going to wear?"

"I didn't know it was *that* nice," I said. I picked at the gold lettering on the side of my pencil. "I don't think I have anything good enough to wear. Should I cancel?"

"What? No. . . You'll be the envy of the whole school, going to Hinton's with Justin Macalister. You'll show those stuck-up mean girls who are always following him everywhere."

I laughed, wondering at her vindictive tone.

She shrugged. "I've never liked those girls."

"But I don't know. . . I don't. . ."

"Don't worry," she said, rolling her eyes. "It's just a date. Let Justin do this nice thing for you." She sat back and smiled as if she were personally proud of something she'd accomplished.

She talked me into using my discount at my job to buy a new dress, and we walked over to the store. We found a violet taffeta dress: knee-length, boat neck, with a straight skirt that ran slimly down my thighs. Emily Rose said she'd lend me a necklace that would go with it wonderfully, and we decided I should wear my hair down. She said I should iron my hair the way my cousins did.

The more we talked about it, the more nervous I felt.

✳

On Saturday, Justin sat down in the living room and talked with my aunt, mother, grandmother, and dad while I finished getting ready. When I came downstairs, everyone stood up. Their stares made me self-conscious, and there was a chance my mother had teared up.

"Well, have fun," my dad said finally. "Adelaide, you need to be home by eleven."

"Yes, sir," I said.

Justin offered his hand to help me down the last few steps. I was wearing new high heels I'd bought with the dress, and I was feeling unsteady.

"You look very nice," he said.

"Thank you." I stepped down next to him, and he moved my hand to his arm and led me out the door. I felt like I needed to say something else. "You look nice also."

It was true—his blond hair was darker than usual, from something he'd used to comb it. He wore a new-looking suit jacket and a maroon tie that made him look older than high school—steady, and respectable.

In the car, the conversation seemed stiff, as if our manners had been ironed with the fancy clothes and my hair. There was none of the joking of the previous time. We talked about the weather and projects for school.

It was even worse at the restaurant. We sat beneath a chandelier, and I kept feeling tempted to stare straight up at it. I felt conspicuously out of place, afraid I'd break the thin water glass or put my elbow in the salad or do something else to show that it was my first time in such a nice place.

"I didn't know there were restaurants this fancy," I told him. "I feel like I don't belong here."

"Really?" he said. He shook his head. "All you need is a rope of pearls and some diamond earrings, and you'll fit right in."

I shook my head back at him, solemnly. "No, I have it on good authority it's either diamonds or pearls. A girl should wear one or the other, but not both together."

He smiled, and it felt like some camaraderie was restored. "Says who?"

"I don't know—maybe I read it in a magazine somewhere. Or maybe Emily Rose mentioned it."

Our waiter approached, and Justin ordered for us. He looked so at home there, among the linen and shining silverware and starched napkins. I could imagine him eating at restaurants like this when he was thirty and forty and, a little gray in his hair, at fifty. The hair would recede from his forehead, lines would grow around his eyes and his mouth, his jawline would soften just a little—I could imagine him still good-looking when he was older. He would be a good man then, too—a good father, a good husband to whatever girl was lucky enough to get him.

The waiter left, and I looked down at my salad, blushing, afraid to meet his eyes in conversation.

After dinner, Justin asked if I wanted to see a play. Greenville High was doing *Macbeth*, he said, and he knew some of the students in it. We had a little time before it started.

"Let's walk down by the river," he said. "If you can manage it. There's not much of a path, but it's really pretty. Especially if you've never seen the falls."

I was relieved to be out of the restaurant. I felt I could speak normally again and move my elbows if I wanted to. I nodded, and we headed toward the sound of running water.

At the edge of the parking lot, Justin kept walking, picking his way down a grassy hill. The river was moving quickly; I heard the falls but couldn't see them. I looked at the hill, looked at my shoes, looked at Justin's outreached hand.

"I don't think I'm going to make it in these heels." My ankles were hurting, as it was, from wobbling on the concrete and gravel. My toes hurt, too, from the pressure.

"Oh." He looked disappointed. "We don't have to go down."

"No, hold on." I took his hand and used it to keep my balance. I lifted my left foot, as modestly as I could, and pulled off the high heel. Then I switched legs and took off the other one. His hand was warm, and he didn't let go when I was standing in my bare feet, holding the silly shoes aloft.

"Are you sure you want to go barefoot? It's kind of cold."

"I'm sure," I smiled. The grass felt dewy beneath my feet, as fresh as freedom. "Show me the falls." The descent was a little steep. I reasoned I needed his hand to help with balance. His skin warmed me, even more so when he shifted to slide his fingers in between mine. I hoped he didn't notice how my palm was sweating.

There wasn't much of a level edge of the bank at the bottom, but there was room enough to stand. The falls were up and to our left—a wide gush of water crashing from rock to rock. It wasn't a steep drop, but there were several levels, almost like wide steps of a giant front porch. The water rushed down the falls, ran whitely through several twists, and hurried around the bend to our right and out of sight. Some of the water escaped the main current and detoured, more peacefully, into the pool right next to us. Further down, a small stream floated under a bridge just before joining the torrent of the river.

"The Greenville falls," said Justin. "Heart of the city. Can you hear the mills? They used to use the water to power the machines. That's part of what really helped develop Greenville, back before the Civil War."

I nodded, and his hand shifted, drawing me a little closer.

"Apparently," he continued, "there's an old Cherokee story about these falls. A powerful young brave threw himself from the top because the woman he loved wouldn't love him back." I shivered, and he pulled his hand away to take off his jacket and give it to me.

"Thanks," I said, but I wasn't sure my shiver had been from cold. I didn't want to think about the Cherokee brave's broken heart. "Oh, look!" I said, pointing in the opposite direction.

A string of ducks—mother and chicks—bobbed in the stream under the small bridge. The fading light caught their coats at just such an angle that it made them glow iridescent green and yellow and blue. The stream below them reflected the sunset—yellow, orange, and magenta—and all those colors contrasted with the purple shadows of the dark under the bridge. I marveled at it, not breathing, and then a second later, the light faded and the sharp colors disappeared. It was as if a switch had been flipped; the moment gone, forever.

"I didn't see it," said Justin. "What was it?"

I shook my head, not trusting myself to put it into words. I kept looking at where I'd seen all those colors, but they were gone. "It looked like something from another world," I said, finally.

He took my hand again. "Come on. We should probably head to the play."

Back at the top of the hill, I wiped my feet as best I could in the less muddy grass before putting the shoes back on. They pinched even more than they had previously.

In the Greenville High auditorium, Justin and I sat slightly left of center of the room. The seats around us buzzed with conversation. There were a good number of older couples—people our parents' and grandparents' age—and a lot of high school students I didn't recognize. The seats were cushioned with a red fabric, and the light fixtures on the walls were painted yellow so that they looked like gold.

"Our school doesn't have anything this nice," I said.

"Greenville High is wealthier. They look down on our school because it's where the mill kids go."

I felt out of place, again, like I was still tone-deaf to the intricacies of the town. "It's starting," I said, glad for the distraction.

It wasn't long before I was too drawn in to care about anything else. It was like seeing a movie, but better, because the actors were people my age, and I could see them breathing, see them responding to each other, see them react to the cough of someone in the audience. I could see the edges of the scenery, too—and it was like we were all playing a game together, to believe into reality the world in which the actors moved. I was afraid bad things were going to happen on stage, and I wanted to warn them, turn them from it while I could.

"Are you all right?" Justin whispered. "You seem tense."

I nodded without answering. I was leaning forward in my seat, afraid to miss a word. Some of the younger actors spoke very quietly.

Then the curtain closed and the lights came up on the auditorium. I blinked and turned to Justin. "What is it? That can't be the end."

"Intermission," he said. He was laughing at me. "So, what do you think so far?"

"It's. . . it's really good." I was sweating under my arms, and I hoped it wasn't noticeable.

"Can you follow the story? You didn't read the play with us in tenth grade."

I pulled my skirt a little closer to my knees, hoping he hadn't noticed how it had ridden up. "There were some lines I didn't understand, but on the whole I can follow it. I don't like what's happening."

He waved at someone who called out to him, then smiled at me. "It's a tragedy. I don't think you're supposed to like what's happening."

People around us were moving down the aisle, headed outside.

Justin stood up in his seat, but stayed next to me, talking to various people who greeted him. I found a loose thread in the seat upholstery beneath my knee, and I wound it around my finger one way and then the other. I wished the play would start again.

The second half caught me right back up in the story. Some of the actors stumbled on their lines, and I was impatient for them to get the words out, I was so worried about what was going to happen. Actors marched out on the stage with swords, threatening a woman and her children. I clutched my hands together, worried for them. Suddenly, the woman screamed—terrifyingly real. I gasped and grabbed Justin's hand with both of mine.

"It's all right, Adelie," he said. "It's just a play."

"I know," I whispered back, but I kept my eyes on the stage. My heart was still beating heavily as I watched the soldiers drag the woman from the stage. I had had no idea that a play could make me feel so much.

Afterward, I felt like I'd marched twenty miles. I didn't talk on the way to the car, and I leaned more on Justin's arm than I'd intended to. I answered his few questions in monosyllables, and then, for most of the way home, he talked about other things.

I kept thinking about the play—the way that the witches' prediction had come true; what could have been done differently; if only Macbeth had listened to his better intentions. . . I wasn't entirely sure what Justin was talking about, but he didn't seem to notice I wasn't really paying attention.

Then, sooner than I expected, we were slowing down, close to my grandmother's driveway. I sat up a little straighter and covered a yawn. I was looking forward to bed. But Justin pulled onto the shoulder of the road and stopped before turning down the driveway.

"What happened? Is everything all right?"

He shut off the car. The moon was very bright, but it only lit the part of his face that was turned toward the windshield. His own nose cast a shadow on the rest of his face when he turned toward me. "I thought we could stop here for a few minutes." He smiled, but I couldn't read his expression.

"What for?" Why was he looking at me like that?

He was looking at my mouth, what I was always trying to get Maicaah to do, and then Justin moved closer and reached his arm around my back. Suddenly his face was so close to mine and then he was kissing me. His mouth was wet and mushy, and it felt like he was trying to slurp me. I jerked back. I barely stopped myself from wiping the back of my hand across my mouth to erase it.

His hand landed on my shoulder, across my back. "What? Did you not like it?"

I didn't know what to answer. I didn't want to tell him that it had been weird and gross.

"Adelaide? What's wrong?" His hand closed around my shoulder, just a little, and his thumb began to move up and down against the fabric of my dress sleeve: short, repetitive, soothing movements. "Did I surprise you?" he asked. He leaned forward a little to look at me. It didn't seem like he was going to kiss me again, but I still drew back. "I'm sorry," he smiled, looking like someone who got caught sneaking a cookie before dinner. He smiled again at me, more broadly. I could feel the air on my lips; why had I never before been this conscious of how much my mouth could feel?

"I like you a lot, Adelaide," he said. "I'd like you to be my girl." He kept looking at me, in the semi-dark, and his thumb kept moving up and down on the front of my shoulder. I could feel the warmth of his palm through the fabric.

I didn't know how to tell him that I was disappointed—that that wasn't what I'd hoped a kiss would be like, that he wasn't who I'd hoped my first kiss would be with.

"Well?" His smile had become more nervous. "Will you say something?" His thumb stopped moving, and immediately I missed how it had felt, that one small gesture. He pulled his hand away. "Don't you like me?" he said.

I couldn't bear how hurt he sounded. "Justin. . ." I leaned forward, wanting him to smile at me again, wanting his hand on my shoulder. I knew I needed to say something. What could I say? "I don't know what to think. . . You did surprise me."

He had turned to me again, and he was sort of smiling. "I thought I was being so obvious."

I shook my head, still confused. I didn't *not* like him. But I wasn't sure I felt toward him what he wanted me to feel.

He took my hand again, on the seat between us, and weaved his fingers in between mine. I was glad he wasn't angry. In fact, his voice sounded extra gentle. "I guess you don't have to give me an answer now," he said. "But will you think about it? About being my girl?"

I realized I was nodding. I stopped. His eyes were so many different shades of blue, one eye lit by the moonlight, one in dimly textured shadow. His expression was so intent, so focused on me. I nodded again, more slowly this time.

He straightened, confident again. "You can give me your answer whenever you're ready." He turned toward the windshield, and the moonlight made his face, and parts of his ears, eerily white. He turned back toward me, grinning. "Can I kiss you again?"

I shook my head, not trusting my words. I smiled, hoping that softened it.

He smiled in return, and his fingers closed around a strand of my hair. He tugged, slightly, teasingly. "It's all right," he said. "Next time."

He started the car then and pulled into the long, gravel driveway. We were halfway to the house when the porch lights came on, and my dad came out onto the porch to greet us. It was half-past eleven, and Justin apologized, but my dad didn't really seem to mind.

※

That night, I dreamed I was drowning. There was a waterfall and someone was jumping and someone else was yelling at me not to jump. There were ducks swimming toward the rapids, and I tried to get them to stop. But the waterfall drowned out the sound of my voice and no one could hear me.

Marmee pinched me and told me I was yelling.

Later, just before morning, I dreamed again. I was playing tag with Justin on an airplane. The seats were full of strangers. He tagged me, and I turned to chase him, but then I noticed the plane had taken off and we were over the ocean. "We're going to Ethiopia!" I told him. "You get to see my home!"

"Your home is Carolina!" My aunt said, popping up suddenly from the seat in front of me. "You don't belong in Africa!"

"Come on, Adelaide," said Justin. "You're still it!"

I chased him down the airplane aisle, but then I tripped and the floor opened up and I was falling through the bottom of the plane. I was falling. . . and I couldn't let Justin fall, too. I shouted at him, but he couldn't hear me.

I turned over onto a hand. Marmee had fallen back asleep with her arm stretched across the space between the beds. I closed my eyes again.

I was in the branches of the cape chestnut tree, with the stream flowing turbulently below, fast, like the river beneath the falls. Maicaah was sitting in the grass with his back against the tree. He was angry. "Why are you angry, Maicaah?" I asked the top of his head. I couldn't see his face.

"Why didn't you wait for me?" he asked. "You brought another boy!"

"But I came back to you, Maicaah," I told him. "Just like I promised."

Suddenly Maicaah was in the tree with me, but all I could see of his face were his teeth, like a leopard's. "You brought another boy!" he snarled.

"It's all right, Maicaah," I told him. "I can marry you both. Polygamy is practiced in certain regions of Africa."

"Which one will you marry first?" asked Maicaah. "You can't marry us both at the same time."

"Why not?" I asked him. "We'll start a new tradition." I was glad his teeth weren't leopard-like any more, but his face was still a blur.

We went to go tell Kinci, and as we were walking, I reached for his hand but collided with my bedside table instead. The jolt and the throbbing made me sit up. I reached out again. . . where was his hand? Then I realized where I was.

The dream, and the events of the night before, came back to me, and I stared at the ceiling trying to put everything back in its place.

I lay awake a long time, thinking, the back of my hand over my mouth.

On Monday, Justin said his coach wanted him to focus on the game for now, but he asked if we could talk after the game on Thursday.

"You know, if we win, I'll get a special pin for the occasion," he said. "And if I had a girl, I could give it to her." His smile showed off his dimples to such advantage. I wondered what it would be like to kiss him again.

I blushed and said we could talk after the game.

So, after the hubbub of Thanksgiving dinner with my family, I caught a ride with my cousins into town for the football game.

I waited in the parking lot for my friends, worrying about what I should say to Justin, worrying about what it was I wanted, and how to decide.

It turned out I was worried about entirely the wrong things.

CHAPTER 17

WENDY, NATHAN, SARAH MAY, AND LION found me on the skinny strip of grass in the middle of the stadium parking lot outside of Greenville High. They'd met at Sarah May's house and walked over together.

People were streaming by us, wearing royal blue and orange or purple and gold. There were balloons tied around the trees and hanging from streetlamps and caught in the chain link fence that separated the field and stands from the parking lot. I was wearing a new red sweater—I'd forgotten that it would clash. Wendy laughed at me and shook the end of her purple scarf in my face.

"Where'd you get that?"

Sarah May had one too.

"Sarah May and I made them. . . I thought you said you had one."

"I thought you were joking!"

Laughing, the five of us joined the stream of animated people headed toward the loudspeakers in the stadium.

It was a warm day for November, too warm for my sweater, really. I could feel my dress sticking to me under the short sleeves. The sun lazed behind clouds on the horizon.

The morning newspapers had announced that 240 Americans

had been killed in Vietnam in the past week, 470 wounded, more than the number of casualties of the entire previous year. My family had talked about it in low voices over the holiday table, wondering if anyone from Greenville had been in the fighting. On the surface, it seemed like it hadn't affected the excitement at the game, but as we walked in, I felt an undercurrent of unease. I heard later that two graduates from my high school had been wounded, and at least one Greenville High graduate was missing.

My friends were walking closer together than normal, a tight, 4-person knot separated from everyone else by at least a foot. I was in the buffer zone between them and everyone else. Even Wendy's enthusiasm had become more restrained by the time we entered the gates. Sarah May's shoulders were sort of hunched over, and Lion kept looking around out of the corners of his eyes. I assumed it was their habitual paranoia; it didn't seem to me like anyone was paying attention to us. I wondered how Justin was feeling, getting ready for his big debut. I second-guessed myself again about what to tell him when we talked afterward.

In the stands there were more people than I'd ever seen gathered in one place. There were high schoolers everywhere—people I recognized from my classes, from the hallways, from the drive-in, from the play at Greenville High; and plenty of high schoolers I didn't recognize at all. There were people I recognized from church, others I recognized from the grocery store and the sidewalks. Women my grandmother's age huddled together near the back, knitting. Little kids ran up and down the bleacher steps. Older kids threw footballs and played hide-and-seek in a little clearing to the side of the bleachers.

We were talking about Wendy's idea for the senior class prank, the same idea she had been teasing us with for the past two months. She wouldn't tell us what it was—she kept saying she was still figuring out the details.

"You're bluffing," I told her. "I don't think you really have a plan."

"I promise I do," she said. She was also only half paying attention.

"And it doesn't involve hurting any animals, right? Because I won't like it if it does."

"No animals," she said.

"We could do something with the principal's cat," said Lion. "I heard he loves that thing more than his children."

"No animals," I repeated.

"We wouldn't have to hurt it or anything. . . just make a cage for it or something and hang it in the hallway."

"Don't hurt the poor cat," said Sarah May.

"I got a better idea anyway," said Wendy.

"So tell us already!"

We were almost to the bleachers. The people in front of us had bought popcorn and were talking with their mouths full.

"Not yet," she said. "Not here."

"It doesn't involve destruction of property, does it?" I asked. We spotted some empty seats and started to climb toward them. "I don't want to get in trouble with the school."

"We wouldn't get in trouble if they didn't know it was us," Lion pointed out.

"No property damage," said Nathan.

"Ain't the white boys going to do something? This is kind of in their field," said Sarah May.

A boy who looked like a freshman turned to stare at us as we walked past. He whispered to the boy sitting next to him. They were dressed like mill kids in the vocational program: clothes a little too small, a little more worn, and not quite right for the season. Those kids usually stuck to themselves.

"Yeah, why do we have to plan something?" asked Lion. "It's not like it'll help class spirit or nothing. And if something goes wrong, we'd get in more trouble than most. I think it's a bad idea."

"But I've got such a good plan!" said Wendy. "It'd be a real waste not to use it. They won't never trace it back to us."

"So what is your plan? Let's hear it."

"Not yet." We settled into our seats: Nathan, Sarah May, Lion, Wendy, and me in a row.

"Come on, this is getting ridiculous, you being all mysterious."

Wendy set her face out toward the football field and narrowed her eyes as if deciding strategy. "All right, fine. I'll tell you after the game."

"Why not now? What's going to change between now and the end of the game?"

"Hold your horses! You'll hear after the game!"

I threw up my hands and let it go, deciding not to give her the satisfaction of any further attention.

More people were turning to stare at us and whisper. Someone a few rows down said, "They was talking about destruction of property. And something about animals. . ." I wished them luck figuring out Wendy's plan if I couldn't. I doubted the senior prank was that big of a deal anyway.

We were nearly at the top of the bleachers, with empty seats on either side of us and behind us. Everyone in front of us was completely decked out in purple, with highlights of gold. Wendy and Sarah May fit right in with their scarves. I was the only one wearing red. People around us gave us funny looks, some pointing at me while trying to hide it. I turned away from them and asked Lion to explain, again, the basic rules of the game.

There was movement on the field, and the teams were introduced. Just when I spotted Justin, camouflaged under the heavy equipment, he and half our team left the field. Someone kicked the ball, and everyone became breathlessly quiet until someone else caught it. Then two people fell on the person with the ball, and everyone on our side of the stands erupted into cheering. With each start and stop of the game, the tension in the crowd grew: people were hunched forward, arms clasped to their chests or hands held over their faces. Twenty minutes later, the breathlessness returned with even more intensity; then deflated with groans, half-hearted clapping, and a few shouts of encouragement. Several minutes later, suddenly the ball soared across the field and all the players were running. Then everyone in the stands was on their feet cheering wildly as someone ran off the field carrying the ball.

I had never seen such a large crowd carry so much emotion. It reminded me of the festival dances in the village, but then the emotion had escalated according to the rhythm of the drums and the prescribed movements. The instruments had carried the frenzy in the dances; now, the crowd carried itself, investing meaning in the movements on the field. The crowd was a living organism responding as one.

Our group was caught up too. Lion and Nathan unconsciously inched forward to the edge of their seats, moving back when they caught themselves. Wendy sat with her arms folded, but her eyes followed every flash of the ball. She stood and clapped, albeit more slowly, when everyone in front of us did. I kept trying to take it all in, trying to figure out the logic of it.

The whistle blew several times, and everyone stared at a yellow flag on the grass and a man wearing white and black stripes. He moved his arms in some sort of signal, and everyone around me immediately was yelling angrily.

"How can he do that? What is he thinking?" Lion put his head in his hands.

Several men around us yelled at the person in stripes. The man in stripes glared back at them, which seemed to make them madder. It was several minutes before things calmed down and play continued. The overall tension in the bleachers had risen, and lots of people were frowning. Groans sounded when the other team scored, and after a few minutes more of play, both the teams walked off the field. The people around us stood and started milling around.

"Intermission?" I asked.

Lion groaned. "They were doing really well."

"So close," agreed Nathan.

Behind us and to the left, someone started yelling in our direction. "Hey, what do you think you're doing here?"

"Same thing you're doing, Jimmy Campbell," I said, half-turning in my seat.

"Don't, Adelaide." Wendy grabbed my wrist. She and the others were looking straight ahead, barely moving as they breathed. "Don't answer back. It just makes things worse."

I sighed and turned back toward the front, trying to ignore the comments from Jimmy Campbell and the girl next to him. Their neighbors joined in, and the words got uglier. I rubbed my sweating palms on my skirt. I couldn't just sit here and take it. I started to get up to face them, and both Wendy and Lion grabbed my arm to stop me.

"Leave it, Adelie," said Lion.

"Are you touching her, boy?"

"Get your hands off of her!"

"Who does he think he is?" The tenor of voices had ricocheted.

Lion drew his hand back from across Wendy, his hands palm out. He didn't look at the men, but his face had gone stiff and his eyes were wide. Sarah May's lips were trembling.

I stood up slowly and tried to keep calm. "Hey," I said. "These are my friends. We're all just students cheering for our football team. You can keep your ugly comments to yourself."

About a third of the people on the bleachers stared at me. It looked like most of the women were gone to the bathroom or the concession stand, and the weight of the crowd had shifted to male. Around the edges of the stands, more people started to point and draw closer, boys and their fathers thickening the ring that was forming around me, my four friends, and Jimmy Campbell.

I looked over the faces in the bleachers, looking for someone friendly, for someone who could help calm things down. All the faces looked hard, set against us.

On the far side of our school's cheering section, I saw Bernice. She was between two boys I didn't recognize; they were leaning forward to talk around her, passing popcorn back and forth, but she was looking in my direction. I couldn't tell if her frown showed worry or disapproval.

Just then, the marching band started playing their song, full of drums and cymbals and heavy brass instruments. The music echoed in the field and redoubled around our ears. I couldn't hear the questions of the newcomers who were still gathering around Jimmy Campbell. Some of those questions seemed directed at me, others at my friends. People kept gesturing at us, the gestures getting more and more animated.

The drums picked up to a double-tempo.

A man in a plaid jacket reached out to grab Lion's shoulder, and I pushed his arm away. I whirled, ready to slap and scratch at anything in any direction, all directions at once.

Suddenly there was yelling from the field, someone running toward us, three coaches behind him. Justin hopped over the fence onto the bleachers, and one of the coaches followed. They pushed their way through the crowd on the bleachers, making people move back, opening up space. The marching band sputtered out mid-song.

"What's going on?" The head coach I recognized from school assembly pushed his way into the middle of the circle and stood in front of me. Justin came next to me and put his arm around me. He smelled of sweat and grass and sour laundry, and I was so glad to have him next to me in that moment. The other two coaches reached us and stood on the other side of the group. I could feel Wendy shaking next to me.

All the attention of the crowd was focused squarely on our row. The coaches seemed larger than life; their barrel chests puffed in and out from running, and they had matching scowls. Even Justin was so much taller than normal, foreign in his shoulder pads and cleats, holding his helmet.

"That boy was harassing the young lady," said some father, pointing at me and Lion. There was mumbled consensus and a few supporting comments from the crowd around us.

I started to explain, but Justin held me against his chest, keeping me quiet. His helmet knocked into my back, and I struggled to pull away. The head coach glanced at me, then turned back to the man.

"Looks to me like there was no harm done. Come on, folks. Why don't y'all just sit on down now so we can have ourselves a football game?"

A few men muttered, but the coach insisted. "We can't play ball like this. I'm sure it was just a misunderstanding." His voice was loud even without a megaphone.

The crowd listened to him. Soon the knot of men had disentangled from around us. Slowly, they returned to their seats. As they melted away, the coach turned to me and my friends. His voice was barely quieter without the crowd. "Why don't y'all go on home? I don't want any trouble at this game. Come on, now. Let's go." He waited until we gathered our things, then the three coaches and Justin walked us down the bleachers and to the gate.

I tried to read Justin's expression, but he was looking at the crowd instead of at me.

"I'm sorry we disrupted things. Thanks for running out to us."

He glanced at our friends, then lowered his voice. "Are you sure you have to go, Adelaide? There's still another half. We haven't beat them yet." He reached for my hand and smiled half-heartedly.

I shook my head and pulled away, mad at him for suggesting it. "I don't want to stay after that."

He nodded and stepped away. "Meet me at Danny's later. We'll celebrate there." He waved at the others and mumbled goodbye, ducking his head as he ran back onto the field. The coaches barely glanced at us before they turned and followed him.

We made it out to the parking lot before anyone said anything.

The band had started up again, and the cheering was like the roar of a hungry animal.

"Is everyone all alright?" asked Nathan.

Lion had his arms around himself. Wendy and Sarah May were leaning against each other, and Nathan rubbed his forehead.

"Let's get some ice cream," said Wendy. The others nodded. I wasn't sure if I was included in the invitation or not, since they didn't look at me, but I didn't want to be alone. I trusted they wouldn't tell me to leave.

A sign in the window of Danny's Drugstore read, "We're Open Thanksgiving!" Below it, a smaller sign said, "Come Here To Celebrate After the Game!" We claimed the booth in the corner and sat there until our shaking subsided. We were nearly finished with our ice cream floats by the time we could breathe easy again. Still, I couldn't really look at the others. I felt guilty—for talking them into going, for answering back when they told me not to. No one said much of anything.

We could tell when the football game finished. First a trickle of people appeared, then the streets and sidewalks were full of people flocking from the stadium. The drugstore filled up quickly. Those wearing purple and gold didn't look happy.

"We shouldn't have lost," one boy said to his girlfriend. "Justin was playing like an idiot. Coach should never have made him QB like that."

"It wasn't Justin's fault," argued the boy behind him. "Those refs were blind as bats."

Nathan leaned across the table. "Come on, y'all, let's go."

"Hold on," I said. Bernice had just come through the door and was headed toward us.

"Are you all right?" she asked, pausing in the aisle next to me. She glanced around at my friends but didn't say anything to them.

"I'm fine," I said. "What happened at the game?"

"We lost, pretty badly. Justin probably won't play quarterback anymore."

"Was it really his fault?"

"I didn't think so, but Coach was pretty upset with him. Sorry you had to miss it." She looked down.

I blinked and nodded thanks. She didn't see the nod—she had already turned away to join a table of girls with the two boys who had been with her on the bleachers. She had only got a few steps away from our table when a guy shoved past her. She stumbled into the back of a chair, but he didn't even see. He kept charging forward and planted his feet in the aisle next to our table.

It was Jimmy Campbell, more aggressive than I'd ever seen him. His eyes looked red, and I guessed that he'd been drinking.

"I want this booth," he said. He was looming over us, blocking the end of the booth.

Immediately, I was mad. "Go find somewhere else to sit, Jimmy Campbell."

"Don't get in the middle of this, nigger-lover. There ain't no hot-shot quarterback with you now." His spit sprayed the table.

Wendy, Lion, Sarah May, and Nathan didn't even look at me. I'd never seen Nathan look so tense.

I fought to keep my voice even. "Go away, Jimmy."

Jimmy slammed his hands down on the table in front of me. He leaned toward the middle of the table and bellowed, slurring. "Get out of the damn booth!"

Everyone in Danny's turned to us. A few chairs scraped back as boys stood up. Bernice scuttled out of the way.

The manager came out from behind the counter, swinging a broom. "That's it. Out. If y'all want to fight, you're not going to do it in here."

He shoved Jimmy toward the back wall and pulled on Nathan's shirt to make him stand.

"We weren't doing anything wrong," I protested. "He was picking a fight all on his own!"

"You girls, too—out, all y'all. You, too," he pointed in my face. "You should know better than this. Out."

Wendy pulled on my arm, and we followed Nathan and Lion out the door. Everyone stared as we pushed open the door and walked out, the manager frowning in our wake, holding his broom.

The door closed behind us.

We stood a minute on the sidewalk and looked at each other. I was angry enough to spit. Foot traffic, still emerging from the stadium, swept by on the street. Nathan re-tucked his shirt, smoothing it where the manager had grabbed him. Then, when Sarah May started crying, he pulled her to him and hid her face in his shirt-front.

About ten seconds later, the door opened again, and the manager pushed Jimmy Campbell onto the sidewalk. Jimmy was yelling and jostling, but the manager just let go of Jimmy's shirt, turned around, and walked back inside.

Jimmy stumbled and hurled another curse, but the door was already closed behind the manager.

Then Jimmy saw us.

What came next happened so fast we didn't have time to react.

In two steps, he reached us, pushed Wendy and me aside, and threw his whole weight into his fist at Lion's face.

Lion fell back, and then Jimmy was on top of him, punching like a wind-up toy and screaming.

Wendy yelled and shoved at Jimmy, trying to get him off Lion. I tried to grab Jimmy's arms, but he was moving too fast. Nathan hugged Jimmy from the back, pinning his arms to his sides. Lion's eyes were closed; his mouth was open, and blood covered his teeth.

The doors of Danny's opened, and people poured out. Two boys Henry Junior's age grabbed Nathan and held him, while a third started throwing punches at his stomach, his face. Jimmy shook off Wendy, and when I tried to grab his arm again, his elbow caught the side of my ribs and ripped my breath away.

People were shouting, "That's what they get. . ." and "No! Stop it!" and "Fight! Fight!"

Two boys I recognized from English class grabbed Jimmy and pulled him away from Lion. "Calm down!"

"Let me go!"

"Stop it!"

A dark-haired boy bent down to check on Lion. He was motionless. Blood was gushing from his nose and split skin above his eyebrow.

The boy on Nathan's right kneed him, and he doubled over. All three of the boys started hitting and kicking him. There were too many people between him and me. . . I couldn't get to him.

Sarah May was screaming a monotone, shrill wail, unvarying.

Nathan was down on the sidewalk now, arms around his head as they kicked him as hard as they could. I could only see him around the legs and torsos of the wall of people standing around his attackers. I tried to catch my breath and stand, to get to him. Wendy tried to push her way through, but they kept shoving her away.

Girls crowded around the doorway of Danny's, some crying, some screaming. Others just watched with their hands over their mouth.

One of the boys in the wall around Nathan's attackers spied Lion on his back. He ran toward him, aiming a kick—and I slammed into him as hard as I could. I knocked him off balance, and he pulled me down with him, grabbing at my hair. I hit the sidewalk, but I saw another boy headed toward Lion. I grabbed at his legs and tripped him, then shoved myself to a standing position. The other boy came back for Lion, and I put my chin down and rammed him, as hard as I could. Someone else stepped forward, and I used my elbows and knees and nails as best I could to keep him away.

More boys pushed through from the street—older boys, dark as Nathan, tall as Lion. About four of them started pulling off the boys who were attacking Nathan. Everyone was hitting everyone. Two other black boys ran to Lion. One shoved me out of the way, and the back of my head smacked into the window of the drugstore. I stepped forward again to try to help lift him, keep Lion's feet from dragging on the sidewalk. They pushed me away again, but then white boys came and they had to drop Lion to fight back.

I forced my way forward, toward my friend. An elbow caught me in the face and knocked me back, but I kept moving toward Lion, trying to keep him from being trampled. I ducked a fist and crouched, then perched over Lion on my hands and knees. Was he breathing? I tried to remember what to do, what to check. There was too much blood. Someone fell across my back, heavy. I rolled him off. A boot heel landed on my hand and pinned it to the sidewalk. I hit the calf of the leg with the heel of my other palm until he stepped off. I cradled my hand to my chest, crouching lower over Lion. His head rocked a little, but I couldn't tell if he'd moved or if someone had jostled him.

Someone yelled, "Police!" and whistles blew, seemingly from all directions at once. Everyone was running away. Onlookers ran down the streets, and police collared boys right and left. There had to have been twenty policemen, suddenly everywhere, separating boys and yelling at them to calm down. They grabbed two black boys and the white boy who'd stepped on my hand. They grabbed the boys holding Jimmy, and they grabbed the boys attacking Nathan. They pulled Nathan off the sidewalk and handcuffed him.

A middle-aged police officer knelt next to me and put his fingers against Lion's neck. He called for an ambulance. Lion's collar and pocket were torn away from his shirt; the fabric was covered in so much blood you couldn't tell it had been purple.

Another policeman helped me stand. He kept asking if I was all right. He put his hand under my chin and made me look into his eyes.

Behind him, I saw a white woman help up Sarah May, and a police officer slid handcuffs onto Wendy's wrists.

I shoved away the hands of the officer who was talking to me.

"What are you doing? Let her go!" I grabbed at the handcuffs on Wendy and tried to pull them off. They were already fastened.

Sarah May was in handcuffs now, too, repeating Nathan's name and crying.

An officer pulled me back from Wendy. "Miss, please stay out of it."

"What are you doing? You can't arrest them!"

I couldn't move my arms—an officer held them against my sides and pulled me back, over to the wide ledge of a planter. He pushed down on my shoulders to make me sit. The pebbles in the concrete planter dug into the backs of my legs.

"Miss, please stay here."

I ran back again. An officer stood in front of Sarah May and Wendy as the other policemen—a whole crowd of them; where had they come from?—led away the boys who could walk. They had handcuffed white boys and black boys, all of whom were splattered with blood. They were yelling at all of them. I tried to get the police officer's attention, make him hear me, make him understand that my friends weren't at fault.

An ambulance appeared. Immediately they loaded Lion onto a stretcher and put him in the back. Other ambulance workers helped Nathan climb into the back—one paramedic held on to the middle of Nathan's handcuffs to help him stay balanced. Sarah May screamed his name again, and Nathan looked at her, his eyes blank, just before the doors slammed shut and the ambulance drove away.

Wendy stared straight ahead, hands behind her waist. Her lip was bleeding and her dress was torn. She seemed oblivious to Sarah May, who had collapsed against her shoulder, crying hysterically. I pulled on an officer's arm to get him to listen to me, that he needed to let them go. He yelled at someone else, and I was pulled away again. I fought back, trying to get free, and they told me to calm down, to cut it out, that it was all right now.

My ears were ringing, and I was still breathing heavily even as the sidewalk emptied of the policemen leading away the boys. An officer stood in the doorway talking to the manager of Danny's, taking notes.

One of the plants in front of the drugstore had been knocked over, and dirt spilled across the length of the sidewalk, trampled by dozens of footsteps.

Girls' faces lined the glass wall of the drugstore. Some were crying. I saw Bernice's face in the crowd, close to where Nathan had fallen. She met my eyes, fear sketched across every feature, and then another girl stepped in front of her.

Another police car pulled up. The officers around Wendy and Sarah May stood, pulling my friends with them. "In you go," they said.

I pushed my way forward again. "You can't arrest them," I blocked their way to the car. "This is all a mistake. . ."

"Miss, please stand aside."

"You don't understand. . ." The officer tried to move me out of the way. Wendy wouldn't look at me. Sarah May's eyes were closed, her cuffed hands clasped under her chin like she was praying; she rocked back and forth. I used all my strength to keep standing in the doorway of the vehicle, to stop them from taking away my friends.

"Someone move this girl. . ." the officer shouted over his shoulder.

A hand pulled at my arm, and then grabbed my waist and hauled me aside—too strong for me to stop him. I kicked at him, and he yelled at me to quiet down. The officer pushed down on Wendy's head to put her in the backseat of the car, then he put Sarah May in after her.

"No! You can't do this!" I tried to lunge forward, but the policeman that held me back was too strong.

"Miss, this is none of your concern."

"You can't arrest them! This is a mistake!"

"I need you to step away from the car."

"You don't understand! Those are my friends!"

"Someone take care of this girl. . ."

He started to close the door. I could hear Sarah May crying, and I yelled at him to stop. He turned his back on me. I pushed my way forward again, blocking the door. "Cuff me, too," I said. I held out my wrists to the officer. "If you take them, you're taking me too. I belong with them."

CHAPTER 18

THE CELL WHERE they put us had a blanket of spider webs in each corner. At least Wendy, Sarah May, and I were together. Sarah May had finally stopped crying. She sat with her knees drawn up against her chest, leaning against my right arm, her eyes closed, mouthing words. I patted her back and murmured, making the words into a lullaby. It was several minutes before I realized I was saying *Nagaa xinnoo simbirroo*. The words in Oromo comforted me.

My left hand, the one that had been stepped on, was swollen and throbbing. My right cheek had a big, painful lump right under my eye. The middle of my skull pulsed whenever I moved my head, and my back gave sharp screams of pain. My throat burned every time I swallowed. My dress had gotten ripped under the arm, and that seam was barely holding together under my sweater.

Wendy stared at the wall and said nothing. Her wrists had bright red marks from the handcuffs. One of her earrings had been ripped out, and blood crusted her earlobe and had dried in drops down the side of her neck. Her hair was a mess, her face was bruised, both of her hands were in rough shape, and she was breathing carefully, like one of her ribs was bothering her.

When we'd arrived at the station, the officer escorting us told us we needed to call our families. He took the handcuffs off while we used the telephone, and then he told us all the rooms were occupied, so we would need to wait in a cell.

It was a long twenty minutes before they came to tell us that our families had arrived. They told us we needed to stay for questioning, but that we could wait with our parents.

As we walked down the hallway to the waiting room where our families sat, I could hear Aunt Be squawking. "We have a lawyer in our family, I want you to know! You better do right by my niece!"

My mother and Grandmother ran to hug me. Mother had been crying. My dad tilted my chin to look at my bruise and kept asking if I was all right. Their hands on me hurt—back, head, hands, face—but more than anything I was relieved to see them. I kept telling them I was fine and that we didn't do anything wrong. I was saying it through tears. My mother kept her arm tight around my shoulders, and my dad handed me his handkerchief. Aunt Be's dishwashing apron was peeking out of her purse, and her hat was pinned on crooked.

A police officer called us to attention. He introduced himself as Officer Garrett and said he was in charge of taking our statements. He was a young-looking thirty-something with brown hair and blue eyes as clear as Justin's. He said he needed to talk to each of us girls individually, with an adult, in a side room.

Wendy was standing close to her grandparents, elbows touching. Both of Wendy's grandparents had their hands clasped in front of them, as if they were posing for a portrait. Sarah May's mother and grandmother were in a tight huddle in the corner, wearing identical terrified expressions.

"What happened to our boys?" asked Sarah May's mother. She was petite, an inch or so shorter than Sarah May. Her red cloche hat matched her nails, but the feather on it was askew. Her face was delicate but firm beneath her fear.

The officer looked at the door and then back to her. "They've been taken to the hospital," he said.

"Is Nathan all right?" Sarah May's voice broke with his name.

"I haven't heard any news on their condition," said the officer. "I'm sorry. If I hear anything, I'll let you know."

I went first for questioning. My dad came with me. My mother stayed outside, Grandmother's arm wrapped around her waist. Mother clasped Aunt Be's hand with both of her own.

"We didn't do anything wrong," I told the officer as soon as the door closed.

Officer Garrett went behind the desk and gestured us to the two chairs facing him. "We just want to hear what happened from your perspective," he said. He picked up a fountain pen.

I stayed standing. "Sarah May wasn't even part of the fight."

"What charge do you have against my daughter?" asked my dad, standing behind the other chair.

The officer sighed. "Please, sit." He waited until we did. "We can charge Adelaide with disorderly conduct for fighting. That's a misdemeanor with a maximum sentence of one hundred dollars and thirty days in prison. We can also charge her with opposing an enforcement officer. That's also a misdemeanor, with a sentence of five hundred to a thousand dollars and up to a year in prison. Those would both go on her permanent record."

Suddenly, I felt ice cold and like I had been chained to the chair. I could feel my dad glaring at me from the corner of his eye.

"But I volunteered for arrest," I said.

"This is all a pretty serious situation," said Officer Garrett, playing with his fountain pen. "However, we don't want to get you in trouble if we don't have to. If you cooperate, we might think about not pressing charges." He waited to let that sink in. "Please, tell me what happened, as you remember it. Where did the fight start?"

"At the football game," I said. I told him how we wanted to show we were a part of things, and how Jimmy Campbell had started yelling at us during half-time, how others had joined in and surrounded us. I told him how Justin and the coaches intervened and then asked us to leave.

"How did you know Jimmy Campbell?" asked Officer Garrett.

"From school. He was in my social studies class last year."

I told him how we went to Danny's, and how we'd been about to leave, before Jimmy Campbell came up to us and started yelling, again. I told him how the manager kicked us out, then kicked out Jimmy. My voice broke describing how he attacked Lion.

"Is Lion going to be all right? They had to take him away in an ambulance. . . I couldn't tell if he was breathing. He's going to be all right, isn't he?"

Officer Garrett was taking notes. "Is *Lion* his given name?"

"It's Judah. Judah Strawder."

I was clinging to my dad's handkerchief so tight, I thought it might stay permanently misshapen.

"We haven't heard yet from the hospital," said Officer Garrett. I wasn't sure I believed him. "What happened next?"

I told him how Nathan had tried to pull Jimmy off Lion, and how more boys from Danny's had joined in, attacking Nathan. I told how other white boys tried to stop it, and then how other black boys joined in from the street.

"And how did you get hurt?" asked the officer.

"Someone was going after Lion again. He was still on the ground, he looked like he was hurt pretty bad, and I didn't want anything worse to happen to him. I tried to keep the other boys from getting to him."

"What were the other girls doing?"

"Sarah May was standing on the side screaming. Wendy was trying to keep people away from Lion and trying to get to Nathan."

"And what's your connection with these individuals?" Officer Garrett asked.

"With who?"

He consulted his notes. "Nathan and Lion and Wendy and Sarah May. Those are the four black students, correct?"

"They're my friends. We're in classes together, and I eat lunch with them every day."

My dad blinked, as if he had just been told the answer to a math problem he'd been working on.

"Why didn't you yell for help?" asked Officer Garrett.

"I *was* yelling," I said. "Everyone was yelling. The police must have heard something, because they came pretty quick." I looked toward the telephone on his desk. "Could you call the hospital and see if they have news on Lion—Judah?"

"I'll let you know as soon as I hear anything," he promised, still writing notes. "What happened next?"

"When the police arrived, everyone who could, ran away, and then the police started arresting everyone and we landed here."

Officer Garrett flipped back several pages on his notes. "Why were you fighting off the officers?"

My dad rubbed his temples.

"They kept grabbing me for no reason!" I said. My throat hurt from so much talking. "I didn't know what they were going to do with my friends."

Officer Garrett glanced up at me without moving his head. "And then you volunteered for arrest?"

"I wanted to stay with my friends." I crossed my arms.

Officer Garrett raised an eyebrow but kept writing. "Has anything like this happened before?"

"With Jimmy Campbell or with anyone else?"

"Either, I suppose," he said.

"Jimmy's never hit them before, that I know of. Not that I've seen. Nathan and Lion got jumped after school one time, before I got there. But I just heard about it afterward. I don't know who it was."

"I see. You moved recently to Greenville, is that correct?"

"Last year, just after the start of the school year."

He straightened the pile of papers. "Where from?" he asked conversationally.

"Ethiopia."

He glanced between my father and me. "Your work took you there, sir?"

"Yes, that's right," my dad said. "I'm an anthropologist." He pushed his glasses up to rub his eyes. The bifocals rested on his thumb and the knuckle of his pointer finger, framing his eyebrows.

"When I did a little college, I took an anthropology class," said Officer Garrett, smiling. "I really liked that class." My dad made an affirming but disinterested sound and didn't follow up.

Officer Garrett asked me a few more questions about my friends and about how things were at school. Then he looked at his notes one more time, nodded, and thanked me. He opened the door and escorted us out.

Sarah May went next. Her mother stood up, holding on to her daughter's hand. Her grandmother stood up, too, and stayed by her seat, wavering. Clutching her purse uncertainly. Her thin bottom lip trembled.

"Would you like to come as well, ma'am?" Officer Garrett asked her grandmother.

I was struck by his courteous tone and his use of *ma'am*. All of us in the room stared at him. Sarah May's grandmother nodded and took hold of Sarah May's other hand. They walked into the office, all three of them together.

In the waiting room, Wendy was in the corner, staring at the floor, next to her grandmother who was staring at the wall straight ahead. Her grandfather had gone to the bathroom. Neither Wendy nor her grandmother looked at me when we came back to the waiting room or when my dad and I told my mother, Aunt Be, and grandmother what had happened.

We didn't have to wait long before a younger officer came into the room and told us we could go.

"What. . . What about the fines and the jail time?" my dad asked.

The officer shook his head. "She hasn't been charged with anything. She can go."

Aunt Be let out a gusty sigh, and my mother hugged me from the side. Wendy was looking over at us, eyes wide. Her grandmother was still staring at the wall.

"What about my friends?" I asked. The young officer just shook his head and said he didn't know.

Neither of my parents, nor Aunt Be, nor Grandmother said anything as we got into the car. Slowly, the relief of my being all right dissipated, and the air seemed spiced with anger, disappointment, and fear.

"What were you thinking?" asked my dad, finally. His hands were white on the steering wheel.

I stared out the window. I didn't know how to answer—what was I thinking *when*? At what point? Hadn't he heard that I'd just been trying to protect my friends?

"How did you get mixed up with this, Adelie?" asked my grandmother. "Those people were all Negro."

"Wendy and Sarah May and Nathan and Lion are some of my closest friends," I said, loud enough so she could hear in the front seat and so Aunt Be could hear on the other side of the backseat. "I eat lunch with them at school."

The moment stretched for a long time with no response.

"Just be glad they're not charging you," said my dad. "Something like this could have ruined your life, Adelaide. Would have made going to college and getting a job a lot harder, could have taken all your money for the plane ticket to Ethiopia. . . I don't know if you realize how serious this is."

I didn't have any energy for arguing, and keeping quiet turned my mouth bitter. I was staring out the window, but I kept seeing Lion's blood on the sidewalk, his face with his eyes closed and his teeth red. I couldn't shake the feeling of hands grabbing me, shoving me, pulling at me.

After a long silence, my mother leaned closer to take my hand and whispered so only I could hear: "Are you sure you're not hurt, Adelie?"

I turned to her, surprised at her touch. Her eyes were fixed on my face. Her hands were clasped around mine, cradling the boot-heel bruise, and she was running her fingers over the points of my nails. "I'm not hurt, Mama."

It occurred to me, suddenly, that my mother might well have been the person who clipped the newspaper article and requested an application form for City College of New York. That made me glad I'd at least filled out the form, shown I was taking it seriously.

My mother gave me a quick smile before turning again to the front. By the time we were at Grandmother's, her usual blank expression had returned, but she kept hold of my hand until we got out of the car.

CHAPTER 19

I SLEPT MOST OF THE DAY Friday, and Saturday I didn't get off the couch. My right cheek and my left hand were purple and blue, and I ached all over, especially my back and my legs. Marmee sat next to me on the couch, reading while I slept. Cassie offered to bring me tea or lemonade, but then she forgot to actually bring it out.

I still hadn't heard about what state Nathan and Lion were in, and I was distraught over it. I tried calling the hospital, but they wouldn't tell me anything, and the police station receptionist told me she didn't know but someone would return my call. I missed church on Sunday, but when my family got back, they didn't have any news about them either.

Wendy was the only one I knew how to reach. She had talked more than once about her grandparents' controversial decision to open their store on Sunday afternoons. I asked my dad if I could borrow the car, and I drove carefully, in first gear almost the entire way, to a part of town I didn't know at all.

The street was empty, and the *We're Open* sign hung crookedly on the front door. Wendy was standing over the washing machines, her head leaning heavily on her hand, her eyes blinking slowly. When I waved through the glass, she straightened. She snuck open the door, holding still the bells, and pulled me inside. Her grandmother was dusting merchandise on the back wall, and her grandfather looked like he was dozing over the accounts book. The only sounds were the hum of fans, the buzz of a single fly, and a faint melody from a back-counter radio.

Wendy pulled me in among the vacuum cleaners, hidden by the washing machines. "What are you doing here?" she whispered.

"I haven't heard any news. . . Are the boys still in the hospital? Is Lion all right?"

Wendy glanced again at her grandparents. I spotted her little brothers and sister in the opposite corner, playing cards. They watched us with wide eyes but stayed where they were.

Wendy's lip had swollen to twice its normal size. Her ear was bandaged with gauze and she moved her hands slowly. "Nathan had to spend two nights in the hospital under police guard. He has three broken ribs, a broken arm, and a concussion, but they sent him home last night." She looked down, and her voice sounded full of tears. "Lion hasn't woken up yet. They think there may be bleeding around his brain."

"Oh, God. . ." I leaned over, afraid I would faint.

Wendy patted my shoulder, slowly, awkwardly. "They told his parents he was responding well to stimuli, which is supposed to be a good sign."

"So he's going to wake up?" I watched her face, trying to read her reaction.

She looked down again. "I don't know. They won't let us visit the hospital, and I haven't heard from his family."

"Wendy Lu? Whatcha doing over there, girl?" Her grandmother's voice was high pitched, shrill.

"Just dusting, Granny," she said. Her grandmother didn't come investigate. Wendy turned back to me. "In church today, everyone was up in arms about how our boys were near beat to death on our very streets, in the middle of a crowd. People are real upset, Adelaide."

"Did they end up charging you with anything?" I asked.

She shook her head, suddenly nervous. "No. . . Are they going to?"

Relief loosened a little of the tangled chain of worry around my stomach. "I think they would have charged us before they let us go, if they were going to charge us. Do you know if they charged the boys with anything?"

"Nathan was questioned, same as us, but I haven't heard if they pressed charges," she shook her head. "Three other boys who joined in the fighting from the street had to spend the night in the jail, and I heard they have to show up for court later."

"Everyone at my grandmother's church was talking about how five white boys had to spend the night in jail, and three are going to have to go to court."

"They're actually pressing charges against some of the white boys?" She sounded surprised.

"Jimmy Campbell's still in jail," I said. "Apparently it's not his first time for public drunkenness and fighting."

"Wendy Lu, what in heaven's name are you doing, girl?" Her grandmother looked between us, standing by the vacuum cleaners. "Who is that?" Her eyes, sunken in her wrinkled skin, were sharp as she looked at me.

"Granny, this is Adelaide. Don't you recognize her from Thursday?"

I tried to smile, but she didn't return it.

"What are you doing here?" The old woman stood up straight, brushing her hands against her brown dress. "I don't want Wendy in no more trouble."

"No, ma'am," I said. "I just wanted to hear about Nathan and Lion, and see how Wendy was doing." I stood up, feeling self-conscious.

Wendy stood up too, next to me. "Granny, Adelie just told me the police are pressing charging against some of the white boys. They had to stay in jail overnight."

"I heard they're holding them responsible for starting the fight," I said. "There may be a trial, and they'll probably have to pay a fine or spend some time in jail, or both." It had been all my family could talk about over Sunday dinner after church.

"The police is holding the white boys responsible?" asked Wendy's granny.

"Yes, ma'am." Wendy's little brothers and sister had gathered around us, and even her grandfather had woken up.

Wendy's granny took hold of my chin to turn my cheek toward the light. "That face of yours looks as bad as Wendy's," she said. "I heard you got that trying to help Lion. They give you something for the ache?" I told her I'd taken a pill, and she grunted in response. "Would you like a Coke?" she asked, suddenly. "No customers in this store anyways. May as well have ourselves a break."

The little kids cheered and started hopping around, and Wendy's granny shushed them. "No call for that kind of carrying on," she said. The kids smiled at each other anyway, and they peeked at me shyly as well. Wendy's granny handed Wendy and me each a cold bottle, and she gave one to the little kids to share.

The sweet, carbonated drink burned a little as it went down my throat. The little boys passed their Coke bottle back and forth with enraptured expressions. They all waved at me as I drove away, even Wendy's straight-faced grandmother. On my ride home, every burp felt like a prize I'd earned.

I knew even before going to school on Monday that the mood there wouldn't be as festive as it had been in Wendy's grandparents' store.

I waited on the corner of the schoolyard for my friends, but they didn't arrive at their normal time. It was just before the bell rang when I saw Wendy and Frederica step out of a car together. They walked quickly through the yard.

"What happened? Why are y'all so late—and together? Where's Sarah May?"

Frederica barely looked at me. Wendy kept walking toward the school door. "Sarah May stayed home," she said. "She was too scared to come."

"You look like hell, Adelaide," said Frederica.

I asked if they had more news about the boys. They said Nathan would be on bed rest for at least two weeks. They still didn't have any updates on Lion.

As we walked to the main building, some people glared at us. Others just looked. A few, further away, shouted ugly things. Wendy stood taller than usual, her shoulders square, her lip still swollen. Frederica looked straight ahead, neither to the right nor the left. It felt like we were walking the gauntlet of the whole school.

We made it up the steps and through the doorway. There was a sense of relief as we passed from the sunlight and spotlight of attention into the relatively empty hallway. The metal lockers were a still, impassive guard.

At the far end of the hallway, four sophomore girls stood talking. They turned toward us and started whispering to each other. More clumps of students, senior girls and freshman boys, junior boys and sophomore girls, followed us in through the doorway, keeping their distance but watching us. The hallway was shrouded in unfamiliar quiet, tensely focused on us. Teachers came out of their classrooms, and when they saw us, they stared too. No one spoke to us directly.

The bell rang, and then everyone scrambled for their books and classrooms, banging their locker doors as usual.

In first period, everyone was whispering and glaring at me and Wendy. A girl at the desk next to me scooted away her chair and desk with loud scrapes.

The teacher called us to attention. He pretended to ignore the tension, and that set the pattern for the rest of the day—everyone seemed angry and afraid, but no one said anything about it directly.

In the hallway after class, again there were the same whispers and stares. When a football player knocked Wendy aside with his shoulder, she had to hold me back from launching myself at him.

Then Emily Rose called my name loudly from across the hallway. She marched through the whispers and into the space that surrounded us. "Good morning." Her voice was stoically cheerful; her books were clutched against her gray sweater very tightly. "How are you today, Wendy?" she asked, pointedly.

"Fine, thank you," answered Wendy. She looked confused.

"Glad to hear it," said Emily Rose.

New whispers started up around us. Emily Rose's cheeks turned pink, but she leaned forward as if she didn't have an audience. "Could I sit with you at lunch today? My mother made macaroons yesterday, and I brought some to share. They're surprisingly exquisite, compared to my mother's usual cooking ability."

And so, at lunch time, Emily Rose joined Frederica and Wendy and me on the auditorium steps, and she shared her mom's macaroons. We were a small, formal group, but I was proud of Emily Rose's willingness to step forward and talk to my other friends.

Aunt Candice, Uncle Henry, and my cousins came over for dinner the next day. I was not in a mood to be nice to them.

"So, Adelaide," said Aunt Candice. "How's the bruise healing? I hear you were in the middle of that kerfuffle with the colored boys. Jimmy Campbell's mother is in my Sunday school class, and we just can't believe the charges her boy and his friends are facing. After being attacked like that."

"Jimmy wasn't attacked," I said carefully.

"Marietta Campbell is a confounded nuisance, and her son is

a bully." Aunt Be patted her mouth primly with her napkin and went back to cutting her chicken.

"Are you defending the colored boys, Beulah?" asked Uncle Henry.

"They have names," I said. "Judah we call Lion. He's the one in the coma. And the other one is Nathan. He's going to be a famous activist in New York." I tried to control my voice from shaking.

"New York?" asked Julia with a scoff. "Where do these people get their ideas?"

Bernice wasn't laughing.

"I heard," said Aunt Candice, "that one of the colored boys. . . made advances. . . at you, Adelaide, and that our boys were protecting you."

"That," I said, "is a heap of steaming hogwash." I was trembling from anger. "Bernice, you saw it," I said. "You were there. You tell them."

Everyone turned to Bernice. "Well?" Julia asked her sister.

Bernice opened and closed her mouth and looked around the table, at her flabbergasted parents, at Aunt Be's stiff back, at Grandmother's worried expression. Then she folded her hands and looked at the tablecloth. She nodded. "At Danny's, Jimmy went up to Adelaide's table and started yelling at them that he wanted to sit there and they needed to leave. Then the manager came and kicked out Adelaide and her friends. Jimmy was still yelling, so he got kicked out too. Then everyone crowded around the window, because they were fighting. Jimmy was on top of—one of the other boys, I don't know his name—and was punching him like he was a snake or something. The colored boy wasn't hitting back. I didn't want to watch after that, but there were too many people behind me, and I couldn't get away from the window."

Silence settled around the table.

"Well. . ." said Aunt Candice, but Aunt Be looked triumphant.

"That's exactly what Adelaide told the police. It'll be right for Jimmy Campbell to be punished. Public intoxication, indeed."

Later, when the lawyers were collecting statements from witnesses, Bernice told it, just that same way, to Nathan and Lion's lawyer. She had hesitated, worried about the effect it could have on the white boys who were accused—Jimmy was her friend Carol's brother and another boy was the boyfriend of her friend Susie—but when it came down to it, Bernice told the truth.

For weeks, the trial was all anyone could talk about, during lunch time and around town.

I overheard a rich, white woman talking to a friend in the dressing room at my work. "I heard it's that state representative who's making sure the trial takes place," she said. "I heard he needs to tell everyone in Washington there's a fair trial for all involved, since people there are saying it was a near lynching." When she said the final word, she didn't give it any breath.

The woman next to her leaned in. "I heard the President himself told him to make sure to hold the guilty parties responsible. I don't know how they can think our boys are guilty. They don't know anything of the reality up there in Washington. . ."

Nathan and Lion had both been charged with disorderly conduct, but those were very minor charges compared to what the prosecutor was seeking for Jimmy Campbell and two of his friends. They faced charges of assault and battery in the first degree for how badly they'd hurt Nathan and Lion—a felony-level charge—plus assault and battery in the third degree for the injuries Wendy and I received.

We waited to hear what would happen at the trial. More than that, we waited to hear news from the hospital about Lion's condition.

CHAPTER 20

IT WAS THE FOLLOWING Tuesday night when the phone rang right before dinner. I was ironing my clothes for school the next day while Aunt Be and my mother finished dinner.

Aunt Be was checking the meatloaf in the oven. "Adelie, would you see who that is?"

I propped up the iron, off to the side, and went to the phone in the hallway by the den. "Hello, this is the Wright residence."

"Hello. . . this is Wendy Evans. Is Adelaide available?"

"Wendy? It's me." She'd never called me before. I bit my lip. What was wrong?

"Adelie! I have news about Lion."

"What happened? Is he all right?"

"He woke up! I just got the news. Lion's awake, and it sounds like the doctors think he'll make a good recovery. He'll probably get to go home in a few weeks!"

I needed to sit down. I slid down onto the floor, pulling the cord with me. "He's going to be all right?"

"He doesn't remember anything of the fight, apparently, but the doctors say that's normal. He's pretty weak from being asleep for two weeks, but he's going to get some treatments at the hospital. There's a chance he might make it home for Christmas. . . Adelaide, are you all right?"

I was crying into the phone. I couldn't help it. "He's not going to. . . He's going to be all right?" Wendy was crying too now. "I'm so glad. . ."

Aunt Be came around the corner, drying her hands on a dish-towel. She looked worried. My mother shadowed her. Wendy explained how the doctors weren't sure about all the long-term effects yet—it would take a while to figure that out. I nodded, as if I understood anything of what she told me.

When I thanked Wendy for calling and got off the phone, I tried to tell my mother and Aunt Be.

"Lion. . . they said. . . they said he. . ." I was crying harder and couldn't get the words out.

Finally, Aunt Be understood what I was trying to say. "Is he all right?"

I nodded and hiccupped. Aunt Be merely nodded and went back into the kitchen, but my mother came nearer to stand next to me. She patted me softly on the shoulder. "I'm glad," she said. She bent down and kissed me on the top of my head.

I stood to hug her, but she was already walking back to the kitchen. I stayed in the hallway a long time and cried until Aunt Be called everyone to dinner. When I made it into the kitchen, my school clothes had been ironed for me.

Nathan came back to school soon after that. He was quieter than normal, with heavy shadows under his eyes, and he winced when he laughed. Sarah May watched him with more than her usual protectiveness. He didn't speak up as much in class, and during lunch time he spoke in a monotone that was unlike him. He no longer argued about Westerns with Justin.

Sarah May told me that Nathan had lost his scholarship to New York University. They hadn't given him a reason, but Nathan was afraid it was because they'd heard about the fight. I was so angry, I wanted to write the scholarship committee a letter to set them straight, but Sarah May insisted it would only make things worse. She said Nathan was looking at other scholarships now and didn't want to spend any more time worrying about that one.

Justin had also missed a week of school. He said his parents had kept him home because they were afraid of things getting ugly again, but he stopped eating lunch with us on the auditorium steps. He walked by once to explain he had to make up work he'd missed in his classes, but he didn't look anyone fully in the eye when he said it. When I saw him in the hallway, his chin was at a lower angle, his shoulders pulled in a little. Girls still looked at him, but they no longer stopped him in the hallway, and boys no longer yelled "Preacher Boy!" whenever they saw him. He and I still hadn't had a chance to talk, and as more time passed, I started to think we never would.

The week after Lion woke up, Emily Rose invited me to a sleepover, along with Wendy, Sarah May, and Frederica.

Frederica frowned. "Do your parents know? About us? I'm not going somewhere where I'll be kicked out because they didn't know that I'm black."

Emily Rose lifted her chin. "They know." She pulled the sleeves of her cardigan down over her fingertips. "Will you come?"

"Foolishness," said Frederica. "You're just asking for trouble. This isn't the right time to stir things up."

Emily Rose shook her head. "This is exactly the right time," she said quietly. "Besides, it's just having friends over to my house for a party. Why shouldn't I?"

"It's being together in the simple, common things that's most radical," said Nathan. He didn't look up from his sandwich. It was the first time he'd spoken all day.

"What does that mean?" said Wendy. "It sounds like a quote."

"It means that basic, everyday things are the last barrier. When it's not strange for us to eat lunch together or spend the night at each other's house or get married—then we'll really see each other as people, over and beyond our differences."

"Fine," said Frederica with a sigh. "I can't exactly say no after that."

So the party was planned for that Friday, the five of us girls, plus a friend of Emily Rose's from her church.

I kept looking over my coat shoulder as the five of us left school. I felt so conspicuous, all of us walking together, our scarf ends blowing in the wind, carrying sleeping bags, pillows, and overnight bags. Stepping off school property like that felt like venturing into unknown territory, like all bets were off and anything could happen to us when we entered the neighborhood. We only had to go a few blocks to the Martins', but it felt like a very long walk. A three-year-old, sitting on his porch steps in coat and mittens, watched us walk by. Frederica was talking loudly. Next to her, Sarah May made hardly any sound.

When we got to Emily Rose's house, Mrs. Martin threw open the door as soon as we set foot on the porch. She greeted the other girls formally, shaking their hands and repeating their names. She gave me a huge hug and told me how nice it was to see me again— it had been so long since the summer. The house smelled of gingerbread and pine tree; Mrs. Martin's apron had bright pink bows that contrasted with the Christmas decorations.

In Emily Rose's room, we talked about teachers and our fellow classmates, music, and boys. Later on we played some card games and told scary stories. We hugged our pillows tight and screamed at every moving shadow and every sound of the trees outside Emily Rose's window. We went to sleep in the early hours of the morning, sprawled in our sleeping bags on the carpet and bed of Emily Rose's bedroom.

I woke up Saturday to the smell of pancakes and mid-morning sun streaming through the blinds. The other girls were still asleep: Wendy, next to me, had slid off her pillow; she was going to have the imprint of the carpet on her cheek when she woke up. Frederica was snoring slightly every third breath or so. Annette, Emily Rose's church friend, had pulled her sleeping bag over her head so I could only see the very top of her brown hair. Emily Rose's spot on the bed was empty. I got up to go look for her.

As I went down the hallway, I heard her mother's voice in the kitchen, upset and more forcefully quiet than normal.

"How did they know, Max? It's not like we advertised that we had all those girls here."

"It doesn't matter. . . It was an empty threat. The police chief has been working hard to stop things from escalating, so that's probably why they didn't do anything real."

"Did you see the yard, Max? It looked pretty real to me." The hallway had no windows, and I couldn't tell what they were talking about.

"They didn't hurt anything or anyone. . . And the sheriff already said he's going to put some extra cars around to make sure the girls get home safe."

"Those men came to our home! They were right on our doorstep in the middle of the night. They were in our yard. . .!"

"We're all right. They were just trying to make us scared."

"Well, it worked! I'm scared. . ."

"We're safe, Molly." I heard a chair scoot back and a muffled sob. The voices became softer. "We need to be brave. You know Emily Rose is making a stand and following her conscience. We need to support her in that."

"What kind of parents are we if we let her put herself in danger?"

"Emily Rose is all right. She's a brave girl, and she's going to be all right."

Just then, Emily Rose came out of the bathroom and smiled sleepily at me. "Good morning," she said, in a normal tone of voice that I heard echoing through the kitchen. "Were you waiting on the bathroom? It's all yours now." She walked into the kitchen, and her parents' voices strained to be cheerful, as if nothing had happened.

I went to the bathroom and stared at myself in the mirror. Last night: the shadows, those sounds. . . We had thought it was only our imagination.

I ran cold water over my hands and splashed it on my face, trying to wash away the sudden fear that made my mind sluggish. I heard the other girls trooping to the kitchen, and after a minute I dried my hands and face and joined them for pancakes.

Emily Rose's mom was a little pale, but she said nothing of the threat or the argument. When we left, the front yard looked trampled, and the front step was so clean it looked bleached. I said nothing to the other girls, but I understood now why more white people didn't take a stand.

The first court appearance for Jimmy Campbell and the other boys was scheduled for the second week of January. After the holidays, we all kept an ear attuned to the predictions, the crumbs of news about the judge, the lawyers, the expected defenses.

Then, the day of the court appearance, we all held our breath.

"When is the judge going to have the trial?" asked Aunt Be as soon as my father opened the newspaper.

"This doesn't say anything yet. . ."

"When is he going to call people for the jury?" I asked.

"I think they have to decide first if they're going to hold the trial here or if anyone who lives nearby would be influenced by what they already know about the circumstances."

I heard the news in my first class after lunch. "Did you hear?" whispered the girl who sat in front of me to her friend. "They pled *no contest.*"

I tapped on her shoulder. "What does that mean?"

She frowned at me and leaned closer. "It means it's all settled.

They have to pay a fee, and then they have to serve a certain number of community service hours. But there's no trial. Can you believe it?"

No one was happy about the absence of trial. Those of us who believed the boys were guilty felt they needed to acknowledge what they'd done. Everyone else thought the boys shouldn't have to pay the fine and should have had the chance to show how ridiculous the charges were.

And so none of us was called to give testimony to what we went through. The boys never admitted any responsibility for the fight, for Nathan and Lion's injuries, for Wendy's and mine. It was as if the matter simply dissolved into indigestible particles that no one knew what to do with. Ever after, whenever the issue came up, I felt a wave of anxiety and fear that I couldn't explain.

I kept thinking we deserved to tell our side, to have people hear what happened. But, if it had been left up to a jury, who knows what they would have decided? Maybe this was as close to justice as we could get.

It was soon after that when Justin found me after school by my bike rack and asked if he could walk me home. I pushed my bike in the space between us.

"So what do you say, Adelaide? I still like you. I'd still like you to be my girl." His hands were in his pockets, his shoulders hunched a little, the way they'd been since the Thanksgiving game. He looked as clean-cut and shining as always, and I knew that it would be easy, in some ways, to say yes, to be with the golden boy always and have his aura surround me, too.

"I really like you, Justin." I swallowed. "But I can't be your girl."

He nodded once, but his face didn't betray what he was thinking. "Can I ask why not?"

For a whole minute, I was silent. I was trying to put it into words, to formulate the thoughts that still hadn't taken solid shape. The wind was so cold on my face, my nose and cheeks were going numb.

"So much of my life isn't here, Justin, and I can't ignore that. I can't stay here."

"You wouldn't have to. I'm not asking you to marry me, just to go steady with me." He laughed a little, but I didn't meet his eyes. "You're really saying no?" His hands were finally out of his pockets, and he crossed his arms over his chest. His voice sounded hard, angry. I wondered if anyone would ever kiss me again in a darkened car under the moonlight. He kept shaking his head, and now he was stepping away. "You know, most girls would love the chance to go steady with me."

The imperiousness in his voice sparked my temper, but I could also hear the hurt behind the words. The anger was just enough to help me not give in to the part of me that wanted to take back everything I'd just said. "I'm really sorry if I hurt you."

When I opened my eyes again, Justin was already walking back the way we'd come. He was kicking at rocks as he went, and they skipped forcefully away, quick as rodents.

I mounted my bike and rode it past the place where, over a year ago, I had thrown my books at the empty corn stalks. I rode past the turn-off to the hill where I'd learned to go so fast on my bike that it felt like flying. I rode past the houses and trees that had become so familiar from seeing them every day. I didn't stop until I reached Grandmother's house.

I went straight to my room and opened the drawer in my bed-side table.

For a long time I sat on my bed and stared at the pomegranate seeds in their velvet pouch. The tan lines from my beaded bracelet had faded. I hoped I hadn't made a huge mistake.

CHAPTER 21

GRADUATION DAY CAME all too soon. I was ready for it, waiting for it, and then it snuck up on me and I wasn't ready. The morning of the commencement ceremonies, I couldn't find anything.

"My dress was right here yesterday!" I rifled through the hangers yet again, standing in front of the closet in my slip and camisole. "Where is it?" I ran my hands against the sides of the closet wall and the sliding door to make sure I wasn't overlooking it somehow.

Cassie was sitting on her bed, watching me run around. "Maybe it fell off the hanger and slid to the floor?"

"Marmee!" I yelled as loud as I could. She was in the bathroom, singing. "Have you seen my dress?"

There was a quick knock on the door, and Aunt Be marched in. "Here," she said, holding out my dress. "I did a little touch-up with the iron."

I tried putting on the pearls Grandmother had insisted I borrow, because she said everyone had to wear pearls on their graduation day, but I couldn't get the clasp to close on the necklace. Cassie was just watching me.

"Cassie, would you ask Mother if I can borrow a pair of her hose? Mine got a run in them yesterday."

"I'm not an errand boy, you know." She went to find Mother anyway.

Marmee came in to the room. "Here, let me," she said. She took the ends of the necklace and did the clasp for me. "You're nervous," she said. "Just sit there for a minute and breathe. It'll be all right." She smiled at me in the mirror, then picked up my brush and started brushing my hair for me. I closed my eyes and tried to relax. I hoped she wasn't making my hair too flat.

"You'll be here next year, Marmee," I said.

"One more year," she said.

"Are you excited?"

She shrugged. "Will you be here for my graduation?"

I opened my eyes and met hers in the mirror. "You'll have an easier time of it," I told her. "You'll already know what it's like."

She seemed about to say something else, but Cassie burst back into the room, followed by Mother and, leaning on her new cane, Grandmother. Grandmother said all sorts of things about how grown up I looked, and Mama handed me a pair of new pantyhose.

Then Dad called up from downstairs that we'd better leave soon, and it was all we could do to finish getting ready and bustle out the door. I forgot the earrings and sent Cassie back upstairs to get them. She complained the whole car ride to the auditorium about how I'd never stop bossing her around. Even when we were a hundred, she said, I would still be telling her, *Cassie, get this; Cassie, do that.*

The road outside of school was lined on both sides with parked cars, and the auditorium was packed with people. Backstage, Mrs. Palmer, the guidance counselor, handed me my cap and gown, and Sarah May helped me carry it to the chairs where she and Wendy had put their things. They helped me put on my gown, and then we helped Emily Rose when she arrived. We exclaimed over Sarah May's makeup, which looked nicer than usual, and she said that her mother had finally given her permission to wear it in public.

Frederica already had her gown on when she came into the room, and she said she'd been in the bathroom. None of us could settle—we kept sitting down, then jumping up to arrange a collar or a bobby pin. The other girls around the room were just as fidgety, and we wondered how the boys were doing in the other room. We kept looking at the clock, trying to guess when they would call us to line up.

And, finally, they did. Our line of girls joined the boys in the backstage hallway, and then I heard the music start out front. Girls all around me squealed; the teachers shushed them; then the two lines were marching forward, and we stood as tall and grown-up as we could when we emerged onto the stage.

There were so many people in the seats, looking up at us expectantly; even the balcony was swarming. I looked for my family, but I couldn't find them. It was pretty easy to spot Wendy's grandparents and siblings—her older sister had come too—and Sarah May's mother and grandmother right next to them. There was a man who could only be Frederica's father, and I assumed the man next to him was Nathan's dad. In the far back, another black family with a lot of kids had to be Lion's family. Lion had said he felt like the graduation was just pretend for him since he had to do summer school to make up the time he'd missed—but he was walking. On the far right of the audience was Emily Rose's family. Her mother's bright orange hat eclipsed everyone around her so that they had to lean to the side to see.

A couple rows ahead of me, Wendy was watching the musicians. Further down that row, Sarah May was waving at her family. A few rows behind me, Emily Rose sat placidly with her hands in her lap, staring straight ahead. Everyone around her was fidgeting or waving at their family. Justin, next to Emily Rose, was talking to the girl on the other side of him. I turned away before he saw me looking. Frederica was frowning with her arms crossed, slouching in her chair. Nathan was clutching the seat of his chair, as if it was musical chairs and someone might try to knock him out of his seat. Bernice, with a dramatic flip to her hair, filed in among the last few students.

Mr. Jenkins, the principal, got up to speak, alternating between facing our parents in the audience and half-turning to look at us on stage, which required craning his head oddly so he could still speak into the microphone. He talked about The Hope of the Future and The Success That Lay Ahead and how we, the graduates of this illustrious institution, would contribute to make Our Great Nation even greater.

Finally I spotted my family: my dad's blue suit and burgundy tie, his head held high above all the women around him. Grandmother's curly white hair, Aunt Be's bouffant, and Mother's nondescript bun that was beginning to change to gray. Cassie was scratching her chest, staring straight up at the ceiling. Marmee watched the people around her. Dana was there, looking bored, and Aunt Candice and Uncle Henry were on Grandmother's other side, with Bill and Dewey and Henry Junior. Aunt Louisa was there, and Uncle Robert, and more cousins. We had a big family gathering planned at Grandmother's later. Everyone was gathering to celebrate me and Bernice, our accomplishment at graduating from high school. I didn't always share their perspectives, I didn't always even like them, but they were my family, here to support me just the same. Rows of people who had been strangers to me two years ago but who had known me my entire life.

Emily Rose was the class valedictorian, with the highest grade-point average anyone at the school had ever gotten. Her neck and hands were bright red, and she had a perfect circle of flush in each cheek, but she walked to the podium with a straight back and straight face, as if it were someone else who was embarrassed. The principal also bragged about the full scholarship she'd won to Duke, where she hoped to study physics. In the audience, her dad wiped his eyes surreptitiously. When she finished her short speech, I stood to applaud. The people sitting around me looked confused at my effusiveness, but Emily Rose saw me and smiled, just slightly, her usual smile in public.

Then Mr. Jenkins and Mrs. Palmer started calling out the names of my classmates, one by one. I didn't know some of the names, though I recognized most of the faces. I played with my borrowed pearl necklace, waiting for my turn.

". . .Jimmy Campbell," said Mr. Jenkins.

Jimmy Campbell, wider than usual in his gown, more slouched than he'd been before, ambled forward, shook Mr. Jenkins' hand, and raised the diploma over his head as the audience applauded and his family cheered.

No one had expected Jimmy to go back to school after the court appearance. He'd missed over a month of school, all in all, and he'd been behind even before that. Somehow, though, he had made it up or worked out something with the teachers. I heard he would be the first person from his family to graduate from high school. He had a job lined up at the mill, I'd heard, and he bragged about how he would be in line for management since he'd earned a diploma; maybe he would be a manager over his dad, he said. I watched him sit down, smirking, and I was glad I would never have to be around him again.

Sarah May was the first of my friends to be called. The principal shook her hand, and she became the first black student in the county to receive a diploma from a white high school. Sarah May lifted her chin, straightened her shoulders, and walked forward in her high heels as if the stage were hers. The general applause was quieter than usual, and I saw a number of people who didn't clap at all, but her mother and grandmother stood and clapped for all they were worth, smiling as if their faces would break. When Nathan stood at his seat and cheered for her, it was the first time I'd seen him smile in weeks.

Wendy came after that, trying to command her face muscles into a smile as she walked. She didn't see her family or me cheering for her—after she got the diploma, she practically sprinted back to her seat.

Then, before long, it was my turn.

"Adelaide Elaine Henderson," said Mr. Jenkins, and I smiled mechanically in response. I could feel everyone's eyes on me, and I wasn't sure I remembered how to walk. Someone behind me pushed, and then I was going forward. My shoes clacked loudly, and the distance to Mr. Jenkins seemed like a dozen miles across the shiny reflectiveness of the stage. I shook his hand, as we'd been instructed, and thanked him when he gave me a diploma. I smiled out to the audience, who were a blur, and I kept walking, eager to get out of center stage.

Then I heard the cheering and saw that all my friends were waving and clapping for me—Wendy and Emily Rose and Sarah May and Lion and Nathan and even Frederica. Bernice, too, was clapping and cheering. I laughed and waved, and my friends smiled back at me.

As I sat down, I caught Justin looking over at me. He gave me a closed-lip smile, distant but not angry. When his turn came, I cheered for him along with most of the school.

There was a reception on the lawn after commencement, and I introduced my parents to some teachers. Grandmother and my aunts and uncles had gone back to Grandmother's already, taking my sisters with them.

"Adelaide made impressive progress," said Mr. Dykart, smiling at me over his glasses as he shook my dad's hand.

I smiled back, and we kept Xavier and Yvette just between us.

Wendy, Frederica, Sarah May, Lion, Nathan, and their families were all on the edge of the reception, in the corner of the yard furthest from the food. Their black skin contrasted with white dresses and gray suits, and the little kids chased each other through the legs of the adults. There was a perimeter of about two feet between their group and anyone around them. Then Justin crossed the perimeter, reaching out to shake hands. He pulled a tall man and a stiff-looking woman into the cluster, introducing them to everyone in turn.

When my parents finished talking with teachers, we went over so I could introduce my parents to my friends. Frederica's father shook my dad's hand, and Nathan's mother complimented my mother on her gray, toile-covered hat. Wendy's grandparents said nothing, but they shook hands solemnly. Sarah May's mother mustered a smile. And my friends, each of them, shook hands with my parents and said how glad they were to have gone to school with me these past two years. I laughed and told their parents I felt the same way.

Then my dad got to talking to Frederica's dad, looking as if he was about to take notes. My mother stood off to the side, smiling vaguely, ready to leave. Meanwhile, all of us new graduates gathered in a circle. We laughed about how nervous we'd been, how glad we were that it was done, how much we couldn't believe that the day had finally come and we were finished with high school.

And then, all too soon, we were saying goodbye. I hugged Lion, gingerly, so as not to bump his head that was still too tender for jarring. I told him to be good in summer school and to send me a postcard from Orangeburg. He told me, next time I was washing dishes at a diner, to be sure to wash the spatulas at the seam of the handle, since that's where all the yucky stuff collected. I laughed and told him he still owed me dancing lessons.

I hugged Nathan, too, and Sarah May. Nathan was headed off to New York in a month; he hadn't found another scholarship, but he planned to go anyway and see what work he could find. Sarah May's mother had insisted that she couldn't go to New York unless she was married and Nathan could provide for her. Sarah May had fought hard against that prohibition, but she eventually got herself a job at a store downtown, down the street from the department store where I worked. Sarah May hugged me and told me to come find her this summer and we could go for a milkshake. Wendy had told me she guessed Sarah May would sneak off within the year, as soon as she had enough saved for a bus ticket. It took eighteen months before she had saved enough for half a year's rent, but as Wendy had predicted, Sarah May packed her bags and left a note in the middle of the night so that her mother couldn't stop her.

Frederica didn't want to give me a hug, I could tell, but it seemed too distant to shake hands. I stood next to her, put my arm loosely around her, and squeezed slightly. She patted my back, and we pulled apart. She had said she had the most boring summer ahead, with no plans whatsoever, and she couldn't wait for college to start in the fall. She was headed to Howard University, in Washington, D.C., which her dad wanted for her much more than she did. Still, she said, she was glad to be leaving Greenville.

Finally, the only one left was Wendy.

"It's not good-bye," she told me. "I'll see you around."

I nodded, but I didn't say anything. Instead, I gave her a hug and squeezed hard. Of all my friends, I was most sad to leave her. She'd been the first to be kind to me here. "You'd better see me," I said. "You won't have anyone else to laugh at." She hugged me back, and I wanted to laugh and cry at the same time.

On the drive home to Grandmother's house, we passed fields that were high with sweet corn. The pearls weighed heavy on my neck and my dress itched against my ribcage, but I didn't mind terribly. It had been a good day, and I was proud of myself.

CHAPTER 22

I LEFT FOR ETHIOPIA on a Monday morning. The sun followed us the whole drive from Greenville to Atlanta. I bought my ticket at the airport, handing over the twenty-dollar bills my dad had helped me count out beforehand. The woman behind the counter had a Georgia accent, different than the one I'd gotten used to.

"Flying alone?" she asked. She looked at my face, then scanned me, her expression a little suspicious. "How old are you?"

"Eighteen, ma'am."

Her gloved finger circled the date of birth on my passport. "I guess it says that right here, doesn't it. Well, good for you." She glanced at where my sisters, my parents, Aunt Be, and Grandmother were waiting outside the rope line. "Your family's not going with you?" she asked. "You're going halfway around the world to Ethiopia, all on your own, at eighteen?"

I drew myself up to my full height. The woman couldn't have been older than twenty-five, and I was taller than her. I didn't appreciate her condescension. "I grew up there. I'm going home."

She glanced again from my family to me, then she handed me my tickets. Her practiced smile didn't completely cover her skepticism. "All right, honey, have a good trip."

※

It was harder than I expected to say goodbye to my family. Cassie clung to my hand, pulling on it as she leaned backward. She'd gotten so tall and heavy. Would I recognize her when I returned?

Aunt Be kept asking if I'd remembered to pack different things: my toothbrush, my underwear, the mosquito net Uncle Henry gave me from his old army gear. I patted her arm and told her not to worry. I had a feeling Dana, who was home for the summer, would give her enough to worry about soon enough.

My dad handed me the navy blue hard-sided toiletry case that had been my birthday present from Aunt Candice. "Anything else you need, Adelaide? Are you all set?"

"I'm set," I said. I took confidence from how steady that sounded.

Marmee, Grandmother, Aunt Be, and my mother each gave me a hug. Grandmother kissed my cheek and squeezed my hand as she stepped back. Cassie hugged me so hard around the middle that I had trouble breathing, but I didn't mind.

"Be good," I told her.

Marmee poked her head around Grandmother, where she was hiding. "Get me a bracelet, like the one you had."

I smiled, but it felt like my face was cracking. What if I didn't come back? "I will." I could send it, right?

"Don't forget the notes for my book," said my dad. "I'm counting on you."

"I have your questions right here," I told him. I patted my purse, where I'd placed his notebook page full of questions.

"All right, then. Have a good trip." My father gave me a final hug and released me.

I stepped back, letting go, getting one last good look at them. Just as I was turning away, my mother stepped forward.

"Wait, Adelaide," she said in her quiet voice. She opened her purse and dug through it. Finally she pulled out a yellowed, wrinkled envelope. "Here," she said, holding it out to me. It had my mother's name on the front, in my grandmother's handwriting.

I thanked her, automatically, before I peeked inside. It was several hundred dollar bills, of the old kind. They looked unused.

My mother stared into my eyes in her intense way. "My parents gave that to me when I went to Ethiopia. They said they wanted me to have a way to come back, if I needed to." I looked down at the envelope, trying to understand what that meant. She continued. "I want you to have that option now. You can get a return flight. If you choose to."

"Thank you," I said again. I felt more confused than anything. She had had the option of leaving Ethiopia all along? I kept staring at the envelope and the money until my mother gently guided my hand to put the envelope in the pocket in my purse's lining. "Keep that safe," she said. "When you get a chance, put it in your passport belt." I nodded and zipped the lining pocket closed, then zipped my purse closed and put my hand over it.

"One more thing," said my mother. She pulled from her purse a copy of our family photo that we'd had taken at a picture studio the day after my graduation. "Will you take this to the hillside?" she asked, not meeting my eyes. I knew what she meant: the little, lonely grave. I took the photo and hugged her.

And then I was walking away, and they were waving, and I waved back until I boarded the plane and couldn't see them any more.

In later years, after I'd traveled the world over, I would wonder at how uneventful that return trip to Ethiopia was. Everything went smoothly: my layovers in New York, London, and Cairo were relatively short, my luggage made it on every flight with me, and nothing was taken from my bags when they passed through customs.

Soon enough, I was in Addis Ababa, and I could hardly stand the joy. I was in Ethiopia; I was so close to home, so close. I had to make dinner conversation and be polite to the family with whom I was staying, but all I wanted to do was find a bus to take me to Nekemte immediately.

The next morning I made it to the bus station. There were no chickens in the aisle this time—just strangers, many of whom stared at me impassively and continuously. Two different couples spoke Oromiffa, but I could only overhear snatches of what they said. When we finally started moving, I couldn't keep my eyes off the windows: the terrain outside became more and more familiar, and the hills became ones I knew and recognized as my own.

But there was no one to greet me in Nekemte.

I received my suitcases from the driver and tugged them to the side of the road. Other passengers gave me backward glances as they dispersed. The bus driver glanced at me as if unsure whether I was all right, but his shyness won out, and he drove off without speaking. I stood on the side of the road, and the bus disappeared in a cloud of dust.

I kept searching around me for a familiar face. I was sure my dad had written ahead to tell our village, through a letter to a priest in Nekemte, that I would be here. Where was my welcome?

"What are you doing?" A four-year-old girl stared at me, bumping an empty water pail against her legs. It was the first time anyone had spoken to me in Oromiffa since I'd arrived.

I told her I was looking for people from our village and asked if she'd seen anyone from there today. She shook her head. "How do you know people from that village? You're a *firanji*."

"I look like a *firanji*," I told her. "But I belong to the village. I lived there from when I was a really little girl."

I used to know most of the market town children by sight if not by name, but I didn't recognize her—too young, I supposed.

It made me sad. "Do you have older brothers or sisters? I might know them."

The girl didn't respond. She turned and ran off without another word, the water bucket bouncing at her side. I sat down by the well to wait.

When I finally saw a familiar face, it was Demiksa, Kinci's older brother, with two small children and a goat.

I called out to him, and he turned and headed toward me, warily. He was ten feet from me before he realized who I was. Then he laughed so loudly he startled his children; he ran to me, took my face in his hands, kissed both cheeks, and hugged me to his chest. He called me *obboleetti*: sister.

Demiksa carried my luggage for me, both suitcases across his back. He kept telling his children—who, like the girl in Nekemte, were too small to remember me—that I had returned, what a miracle! We saw two men from a neighboring village, and they ran on ahead with the news.

The village came out to greet me as soon as we were within eyesight. Everyone came toward us—grandmothers, babies, goats, Abraham, Gameda, Bontu, Tlahoun, Haadha Meti. The village elders. The mothers of my other friends. Cassie's friends. Kinci, looking glowing. Maicaah, his face more angular, his jawline more pronounced, his eyes more shadowed. It suited him. His quick smile was still the same one that made my heart stop.

I was surrounded by people, all of them clasping my face to kiss it, mingling my tears with their own.

I was home.

Later, when the women brought out platter after platter of food, I took my first bite of enjera in almost two years. It was my childhood returned to me, spongy and tangy. I couldn't help the tears.

The smell of the food—and the coffee beans, afterward—told me this was real. For so long, I'd dreamed of being here, and now I really was back.

Smells that had never registered consciously before, that I never thought to miss, also struck me now with the force of their familiarity. The subtle, sharp vibrancy of the field grass—the soft, cushiony dirt the children kicked up—the quaver of the fire eating through hardwood. Thatch and wool, with their own smells, as well the scent of the rain and the sun and the river and sweat and bodies. I wanted to throw my arms around everything, to hold it close to me, to lay face down in the dirt and weep for gladness that I was here again.

I tried to catch Maicaah's eye across the clearing, but he kept looking at his mother just when I looked at him.

When the feasting was over and the shadows were stretching toward nighttime, I realized the women were having a whispered argument about where I should stay.

Kinci had her hands on her hips. "She's my sister!"

"But you have less room than I do," her mother said.

Other women argued various claims and benefits for the privilege of having me stay with them. Haadha Meti won out in the end, despite Kinci's stubbornness.

When we trooped to her hut, I saw that my parents' old house had become a roosting place for village chickens, and one third of the roof had fallen in, right over where my parents' bed had been. My mother's Carolina sunflowers were a thicket of stalks and flowers, threatening to take over the doorway. It was so disorienting to walk past without going in.

That night I had trouble sleeping. I'd forgotten how scratchy it was to sleep on a cot made out of hay. It kept poking me. I heard bugs and critters moving in the dark, and my eyes still stung from the cookfire. I told myself I had plenty of time to readjust.

※

Over the next few days, I was able to visit everyone and hear all the news from the last two years. Ruth, one of Marmee's closest friends, had died in childbirth with her firstborn. The baby had died too. I saw Ibsituu's mother before I heard her story—half of her face had gone slack; she turned her head away to hide it as much as possible. A fever, others whispered to me later, so sad. Most of the girls I'd grown up with had two children, living in villages where they'd gone to meet their husbands; the boys I'd played with had taken brides to fill the vacancies left by their sisters. A number of the boys and men were gone, too—to the city to find work, their parents told me. They had left the new daughters-in-law and young children behind.

I went to Kinci's hut and sat in the doorway while she made dinner. She had refused my help with the cooking, so I was alone for once with my thoughts and watched the village freely.

I couldn't believe that everyone was grown up, old now. Where were the kids who had chased ostriches with me and shared their unripe figs? I could still see their skinny legs, their narrow feet scratching the other leg, their hands with pink mosquito-bite rings—but now the games and the fruit belonged to other children. Kinci still twirled her braids like she used to. But she also smoothed the hair of a little boy who was almost two, the boy who had been born after I left, who now walked on his own and had a toothy grin and could talk enough to say *bay-ball* when he wanted the cap I had brought him.

Kinci was pregnant again: round, heavy, bigger than she'd been when I left. She cradled her womb with her free hand, as if to hold up its weight. I had trouble remembering that this wasn't the same pregnancy, that she wasn't still waiting for the baby about whom we had whispered over the corn husks.

I saw no trace of those fears in Kinci now. She teased her little boy, clucked at him impatiently, picked him up with one hand, interpreted his whimpers with confidence. I watched her adding spices to the wat, tasting it. She moved the same rhythmic way she always had, but she moved more quickly now. Before, she was merely helping her mother—now, she was the mother. She was a new Kinci, foreign to me.

Sitting in the doorway, I asked more about her family, Haadha Meti, her father, her sisters, her grandmother, Demiksa and his wife and their children. I was afraid to ask about Maicaah; I still hadn't spoken to him.

She told me about her grandmother's accident—she was kicked by a horse and couldn't walk. "They put her in charge of the village's weaving," said Kinci.

"She's always hated weaving," I said.

"I know." When she smiled, I saw the friend I knew.

But then a log fell in the fire, and she was back to tending to her duties.

"Grandmother complains a lot," she told me matter of factly. "My little sister helps her, but they're resentful of each other. I hate for my Moti to see her like that. She used to be so happy and laugh. . . Now she sucks her lip and has grown thin."

"And your cousins?"

She knew I meant Maicaah. She stirred the beans and wiped sweat from her hairline. "They are all well," she said. "Amene will be married in the spring."

"So soon?"

"She will be fifteen," she said.

I nodded. "I still think of her as being a child," I said.

"Remember how she cried over that goat?"

We smiled, and again I felt like maybe things weren't irreparable. We shared so much history, even if the past two years were different.

"My aunt wants Maicaah to marry soon," she said abruptly. She bent down to the pot while she said it. Then she straightened, with effort, but still didn't look at me. "He's been growing his herd.

He has enough to build a house now. She's afraid if he doesn't marry soon he'll go seek his fortune in the city."

I wanted to ask if she remembered the promises she'd been witness to, the plans she'd been a part of when we were children. I wanted to ask if she had encouraged him to wait for me, if she had found excuses to help his mother be more patient. . . but this new state of hers stopped me from asking. In the past two years, I had learned to ride a bike and gone to see a movie at a drive-in and discovered the ocean and ridden in a police car, and I had as few words to tell her about these experiences as she had to tell me about motherhood and marriage and the past two years for her. Before, we had always done everything together, down to getting matching braids. Now I felt too shy to ask her questions.

I held my breath and forced the words out. "Does he talk about me at all?"

She stirred her pot and didn't answer for a minute. "He works so much now, I hardly see him." She looked at me and then spoke in a rush, pushing out her thought. "You were gone so long, Adelie. He didn't know if you were coming back—none of us did, not for sure."

I ran my hand over the rough wood walls. Kinci's house was so much smaller than I remembered, smaller than Grandmother's kitchen, by far. The smoke was thick and stung my eyes. Surely that was why they were watering.

Kinci stirred her pot steadily.

Everything here felt as engrained as if my marrow was constructed with the same wood and straw as the thatch-roof houses. Everything in Greenville was so strange and foreign in comparison. Life there had become familiar, but only through practice and pretending I knew what was going on. This village was home. I could have walked from one house to another blindfolded. I knew all the best places in the river to wash clothes, to bathe. And yet. . . I second-guessed myself on the proper greeting for an elder, and I caught the hesitation in others' voices when they discerned which title to use for me: no one here knew what to think of a young woman who was tied to neither parents nor husband.

Once life in the village had been the only option I wanted to consider. But I had more choices now.

"We've missed you," said Kinci softly. Her smile was genuine, wobbly. "I felt like a bird with one wing, without you. I'm glad you're here." She laughed at herself and pulled the neck of her tunic up to mop her cheeks. Her fingers were so long, like Sarah May's; her nail beds were perfect ovals, but the nails themselves were dirty, jagged. She laughed again, at herself, at me for also crying. Then she leaned over to pat my face like she used to pat her little sisters. "*Nagaa xinnoo*," she told me. She patted me once more, then went back to stirring the soup.

I saw Maicaah the next morning, while Haadha Meti was washing clothes down at the river. I was supposed to be tending the enjera ovens, which wasn't really a job, when I heard the ibis call, the call that had haunted my dreams, the familiar call in the tone that could only be his. I ran to meet him at the base of the cape chestnut.

It was the flowering time of year for the tree. Big, spiky blossoms gave the foliage a purple haze.

And there was Maicaah, waiting at the base of it. Tall and thin and full of confidence—he was so. . . Maicaah. But as I got closer, I felt a shyness I had never felt before with him. A few feet away, I slowed and stopped.

There was a new difference in our respective heights—my eyes were now at the level of his chin, higher than they used to be. His hands were behind his back, and it made his chest puff out, broad and firm. But his presence was just like I remembered: sure, calming, tender.

He smiled, that small, secret smile that barely moved his

mouth but lit his eyes—as if he was as glad to see me as I was him. I put my hand on the trunk of the cape chestnut, leaning against it, a foot away from him.

"You've changed, Adelie."

That was his first comment? He had changed so little—the essence of him had changed so little. Had I really changed so much as to warrant it being his first comment to me? "I'm still me," I told him. "You still look like you."

He reached out with his fingertips to touch the short sleeve of my blouse. From there, he reached to touch a strand of my hair that had escaped from the pile I'd pinned up at the base of my neck. "You stand differently, too," he said.

"Those are just superficial things." I stumbled over the Oromiffa word for *superficial*. I hoped he didn't notice.

I wanted to ask if he had thought of me as constantly as I had thought of him. I wanted to tell him how I'd clung to the pomegranate seeds he'd given me. Would he even know what I was talking about? I turned slightly to trace a pattern in the rough, thick bark of the tree. "I heard rumors of you and a girl."

He scratched his head in frustration. "Did Kinci tell you? She's such a *hamma-ti*."

"Is it true?" My words came out very quietly.

He said nothing for several minutes. A couple of birds flew to the top of the cape chestnut, then loudly flew away again. "I haven't said anything to her yet," he said at last. "I waited for you, Adelie. Really. I wanted so badly for you to come home, but I wasn't sure whether you would, whether you'd be able to." I nodded, still tracing the bark. He continued. "I haven't promised her anything." He leaned toward me, and with his hand flat against my cheek, turned my face toward his. His eyes were so very dark brown, so serious. "Are you here for good now, Adelie?"

I remembered how, when I was maybe nine, every game we played was for the stakes of getting married. If he could beat me to the top of a tree, I would have to marry him. If he could swim to the other side of the stream and back, he would win the right to marry me. He had almost always won. "I . . . I don't know."

"What do you mean?" He chipped a piece of bark off the trunk of the tree and threw it toward the stream.

"I have the option of doing more school. I could go back and then come back here when I'm done."

The look he gave me sliced to the base of my sternum. "Do we mean nothing to you anymore?"

"You mean a lot to me," I said.

"Then don't go. You belong here." He ran his hand over his short, thickly crinkled hair. "You promised."

"It's not that simple!" I clutched the fabric of my blouse, pushed back the loose strands of my hair. My braid-free hair, my Western clothes. "I do belong here. But now there's a part of me that belongs there, too." With my parents and sisters. With Wendy and Emily Rose and Lion. With Grandmother and my aunts and cousins. Even with Aunt Be.

"You can't belong to two places," he said, punctuating his words with the side of his fist against the tree. "You can't be in two places at the same time."

"I know." He made it sound so simplistic, as if I could just make up my mind against it.

He softened his tone. "You promised," he said. "What about the life we always talked about having?"

I smiled at him. He remembered too. I reached toward his hand, ran my fingers slowly over the ridges of his knuckles, and opened up his fist. His skin was so rough when he pushed his fingers through mine. We clung to each other, palm to palm, and I never wanted to let go.

The village could be my home again. I could be with Maicaah, and I could belong in the village for real. I would never have to leave again.

I could learn to cook over a fire like Kinci's. Walk to the market every other week, same as I had done when I was younger. I could find a way to get through the long nights of worrying if my husband was going to move to the city because there wasn't enough work in the village. I could raise my children alongside Kinci's. We could wash clothes in the river together, send our boys to round up the goats together, pray together that childbirth would go smoothly. Maybe it would for us; maybe we would be the lucky ones.

Maicaah pulled on our hands to draw me in closer. He ran the fingers of his other hand up and down my arm. I shivered.

"Adelie," he said. All the years that we'd known each other, all the promises that we'd made, all the hopes we'd shared, were in his eyes. "Adelie," he said. "Stay with me. Stay and marry me."

The last time he had asked me for a promise, I had promised everything. I loved him still, still ached with the urgency to tell him yes and receive the permanency he offered.

But I also knew that this time I couldn't promise anything.

There was a long minute of silence. I stared at him, his newly angular face, the dark brown eyes I knew so well. There was a new scar on the side of his neck that I hadn't noticed before.

He didn't understand, and he never would. I was sure I would be in less pain if I could physically wrench my heart from my ribcage and hand it to him.

I looked away, at last, and watched the wind push through the tall grass in invisible currents. A feather—ostrich—fluttered a few feet away, just out of reach.

I felt too big for the village, somehow. Like I now knew too much or had seen too much to really belong here. I'd learned to drive a car and ride a bike. I'd learned about Shakespeare and Martin Luther King Jr, and how you shouldn't wear pearls and diamonds together. I'd gotten a job and earned my own money; I'd been to the beach. I'd seen the difference a few people can make when they set out to act according to their conscience— though I'd learned a drive-in theater isn't a good place for that. I'd been shown the privilege of my choice, and now that I'd seen it, I couldn't unsee that.

I did belong here in the village once, but I couldn't undo how I'd changed or who I'd become.

Now I had a choice, and it was up to me to decide.

I pulled out a small pouch from the pocket of my skirt and shook the five pale pomegranate seeds onto his palm. "I kept these," I told him.

Our fingers were still interlocked. He reached his other hand toward the seeds and fingered them wonderingly. Then I pulled my hand away from his and closed his fist around the seeds.

My hand already felt empty without him, my pocket empty without the seeds. And yet there was relief, too, like the emptiness of land cleared for new planting.

"Good bye, Adelie," said Maicaah. He smiled, slightly, gruesomely, painfully. His eyes were sad as he turned away, but he held his head high as he walked back to the cluster of houses that was the village. He was so tall, like the warrior he'd wanted to be when we were children.

When I left the village for the second time, there was no wedding day march to the market town. It was in the middle of harvest season, and everyone needed to stay close to the village to help.

I said good-bye to each person in their own doorway, before dawn. I kissed cheeks and gave long hugs. Haadha Meti tied a beaded bracelet around my wrist and gave me another one for each of my sisters.

"So they don't forget where they came from," she told me. Then she took my face between her palms. "Be good, Adelie," she said. "Live well and carefully so that you may come back to us someday."

I nodded like an obedient child. "I promise to behave myself," I told her. "God willing, I will be back someday."

Kinci bounced her toddler on her hip. She didn't look at me for a minute. When her eyes met mine, there were tears in them. "If my husband agrees," she whispered, finally, "and if this new baby is a girl, I'll give her your name. Then I'll always have an excuse to talk about you," she said.

"I'm honored." My voice broke. I kissed her cheek and her little boy's cheek, then the boy's hands. He had the same dimples that Kinci had when she was little.

"*Nagaa xinnoo simbirroo,*" she told me.

"Peace, my sister," I told her in return as I gave her one last hug.

I couldn't say anything to Maicaah, not here, not in public, not any more. He was eating a section of fig, nonchalantly, as if bored. I stopped in front of him anyway. He met my eyes, and I gave him a small, sad smile. I said good bye, in my mind, to him and to all my dreams of him.

Then I kissed his grandmother, next to him, with tears on my cheeks.

I was halfway to the bus when I felt the fresh fig in my pocket, the size of a toddler's fist and as smooth as a stone. Its skin was soft, a mottled deep purple. The flesh underneath was tender. I rubbed my thumb against the spot where the stem had been, against the small star at the base. I knew the fruit was ripe, even without opening it.

I had meant to get rid of my mementos of Maicaah by returning the pomegranate seeds. Instead, I had apparently traded them for a different fruit.

I closed my fingers around the fig and debated tossing it away, getting rid of it, pretending I'd never found it, pretending it had gotten in my pocket by accident and not intention.

I thought about how light and empty my pocket would feel, without being weighed down with worries of losing this new memento. Without something to clutch when I was worried or lonely. It would be good, probably, to not cling to something that was no longer part of my life. It had been my choice. I would have to learn to live with it.

I opened my fingers and looked at the fruit again. It sat there, ready to be eaten. If I threw it out now, birds would probably pick at the fruit and eat the seeds. Maybe the seeds would grow, eventually.

The fig and its seeds belonged here. They didn't belong with me. I would never see them grow, but that was just how things were.

And yet. . . My mother had made those Carolina sunflowers grow in the village. Pomegranates couldn't grow in Carolina, but could figs?

I thought of a place in Grandmother's back yard, near my porch roof, where I could maybe convince the seeds to grow. Maybe I could ask Aunt Be to advise me about the gardening process. It would be a nice Ethiopian tree in Greenville.

I dug my thumbnail into the skin and pulled open the fruit. The flesh was tender and pinkish-red, as it should be. I ate one section, savoring the sweet, slightly sticky pulp. I put another section, full of seeds, into my handkerchief. At least I could try to keep a piece of Ethiopia in Carolina.

And then I kept walking, eating the rest of the fig as I went.

ACKNOWLEDGMENTS

THEY SAY A WORK OF ART is an act of courage, and neither my art nor my courage would be possible without the help of many people.

First of all, I'd like to thank those who helped make this book a reality. I'm grateful to Zach Harris for a cover design that's so fantastic it made me cry. Thank you to Lindsey Bergsma for taking such fabulous author photos, despite my aversion to being on the record end of a camera. Thank you to Carolyn Barker for editing the manuscript with characteristic graciousness and precision. Thank you to Pat LaCosse for his generous help with the typesetting: it is a much more pleasant reading experience because of him! And thank you to my dad, the most thorough proofreader I know, for taking this book in hand despite a busy season in his actual job as an editor.

I'm grateful for the help of librarians Beverly Weinstein and especially Rulinda Price, who showed me archives of old newspapers and yearbooks in the South Carolina Room at the Greenville Library in August 2013.

I'm grateful for the kindness of the Johnson family: Daniel, Monika, Katja, Juliana, and Annelie, who served me peach cobbler and coffee as they shared details of their family's experience in Ethiopia. Thank you for taking this novel seriously before it even felt real to me!

I'm grateful for the support of Lindsey and Josh Evans, whose kindness and generosity as employers made the writing of this book possible. And thanks to Lila and Norah for being accommodating by taking long naps!

I am very grateful to the many writing teachers with whom I've had the privilege of working. In particular, thank you to Nicole Mazzarella for the guidance and wise input and for being such a model of graciousness. Thanks also to Pinckney Benedict, who gave me helpful feedback and encouragement on this manuscript.

I'm grateful to my writer friends, in particular my Chicago writers group, who read a very early draft of this book. Anne and Derek Boemler, Jake Norris, Zach Harris, Laura Crook, Sami and Chris Krueger, Alli Niebauer, and Hannah DeBoer: I miss seeing you all regularly! Thanks also to my Wheaton writers group— Carolyn Barker, Todd Kelsey, Dan O'Reagan, Subaas Gurung, Johannah Baltensperger, Debbie King, and Kit Curtin: I love getting to be creative alongside you!

I'm grateful for Redeemer Anglican Church in Chicago, my church home while I was writing this book. And thank you to the wonderful Church of the Savior in Wheaton: you show me God's love in so many ways.

I'm grateful to my Tyndale coworkers, from whom I have learned so much. In particular, thank you to the teammates who have most supported my double life as editor and writer: Dan Elliott, Charlie Woehr, Betsy Hinsch, Sam Michel, and Joseph Quiggle.

I'm grateful to my wonderful friends for putting up with me talking about this book for so long. In particular, Isabel Montoya Villegas, Sarah Moscicke, Juliana McMillan-Wilhoit, Anne Boemler, Abbi Rago, Carolyn Barker, and Lindsey Bergsma: I am grateful beyond words for such rich friendships.

I'm grateful to my brother, Jonathan Kindberg, who I have looked up to my entire life. I'm so glad we were able to grow beyond the fighting-in-the-backseat phase and the you-have-to-drive-me-to-school phase to actually become real friends who are moving through life together.

Finally, I'm grateful to my parents for all their love and support in big as well as many small ways. Thank you for believing in me and in my writing—and thank you for loving me regardless! Mom, thanks for being a tireless cheerleader: your enthusiasm for Adelaide's story kept me from losing faith in it. And thanks for being a research partner extraordinaire and sleuthing around Greenville with me! Dad, thank you for teaching me to love books by bribing me a penny for every page I read, and thank you for putting your time and energy into making this book so much better. I could never say thank you enough for all you two have given me.

Thanks for reading
The Means That Make Us Strangers!

*PLEASE TAKE A MINUTE TO
RATE AND REVIEW...*

Writing a few words
will go a long way
to help others discover this book!

For links to post your thoughts:
ChristineKindberg.com/your-review

CPSIA information can be obtained
at www.ICGtesting.com
Printed in the USA
LVHW032031251120
672678LV00006B/1345

9 781797 761350